The Star On The Grave

Linda Margolin Royal

16pt

9781038771322

Read How You Want
LARGE PRINT BOOKS, BRAILLE & DAISY

Copyright Page from the Original Book

First published by Affirm Press in 2024
Bunurong / Boon Wurrung Country
28 Thistlethwaite Street
South Melbourne VIC 3205
affirmpress.com.au

A catalogue record for this book is available from the National Library of Australia

Author photo © Sue Kupferman

TABLE OF CONTENTS

Linda Margolin Royal was born in Sydney, forever thankful her father and grandparents received life-saving transit visas from Chiune Sugihara in 1940, which enabled them to enter Japan and escape the Holocaust. This ultimately meant they could find a permanent, safe home in Australia in 1941. The remainder of her family, numbering in the hundreds, was murdered in concentration camps.

She trained as a graphic designer and then copywriter, and spent thirty years in the advertising industry both in Australia and the US, writing advertisement scripts for TV and radio, and general press advertising for multinational newspapers and billboards. Linda's creative bent extends to abstract painting and drawing from live models.

The Star on the Grave is her first novel.

For my late parents and all those who weren't saved
from the horror.
And especially to my grandmother Felka, my rock.

People say 'live for the future, don't live in the past'.
But I don't live in the past, the past lives in me.
Olga Horak, Holocaust survivor

KAUNAS TRAIN STATION, LITHUANIA SEPTEMBER 1940

Chiune Sugihara gazes through the train window at the stone-grey platform, crowded with groups of people and only just visible through the haze of train smoke and rain. Hardly anyone is sitting on the platform's benches of chipped wood with rusting wrought-iron legs; this is not a place to relax. He watches people bid farewell to their loved ones with swift, tight embraces that wrinkle jackets and dislodge hats – quickly readjusted by fastidious mothers. Everywhere, tears are lost among the drizzling raindrops.

As people board the train, Chiune thinks the scene could be an impressionist painting. The soupy mist and water smear the expressions of the people gathering at the train windows, continuing the farewell ritual with their loved ones and friends on the platform. Armed Soviet guards peer at faces as they patrol the station, eager to flex their authority after the USSR took over Lithuania some weeks back. The travellers are yearning for this town of Kaunas, even though they haven't left yet, remnants of fresh soil tended the day before still wedged under their fingernails. He closes his eyes, overwhelmed by the emotions on display, feeling out of place. Though he knows he stands out with his neat, crisp attire and his obvious Japanese heritage, what makes him feel other is the way he cannot imagine displaying such brazen, genuine, moving feelings.

'They're so grateful,' he says to his wife, Yukiko, as he looks back out the window. He sits down, bows his head, tries to breathe. To anyone else in the carriage, he would simply look to be deep in thought, but his wife correctly reads it as distress. She reaches out, laying her gloved hand over his. He allows himself to reach up and touch her face before composing himself.

Across from him, their three young sons chat excitedly, full of adventure and curiosity about their destination. He smiles at them and glances back through the window to see a boy staring at him from the platform. He is a teenager, perhaps fourteen, filled with innocence, beaming with hope: not yet a man, but on the verge. The boy pushes his thick, dark hair away from his eyes as the wind plays havoc with it, and suddenly Chiune recognises him. Michael Margolin. Michael accompanied his father to the Japanese embassy only days earlier. The father – Chiune doesn't remember the elder Margolin's name – scolded Michael several times for flicking his hair away from his eyes, just like that. The reprimand had no real heat, Chiune remembers; it was simply the exasperated affection of a parent, to which he could relate.

Chiune locks eyes with Michael, gives him a small smile through the window, willing Michael to understand: Yes, I remember you. Michael's face breaks into a smile of his own. He gestures at the window. Chiune opens it as the train begins to lumber away from the station.

'Thank you, Mr Sugihara!' Michael shouts, jogging alongside the carriage. A group of boys and girls begins to form, trotting behind. One teenage girl breaks from the others and catches Michael's hand as they run, her dark hair caught by the wind. They're all calling to Chiune. 'Goodbye!'

Unable to stop himself, Chiune leans out of the train window to wave, and sees the large emotional crowd of Jewish refugees back on the platform, waving and calling out their heartfelt, final farewells. Their words mingle through the rain and smoke, but he hears a young woman shouting, 'We will never forget you! We will never forget you!' Another is crying the words of a verse Chiune recognises from the Old Testament, and several call in a language he doesn't understand – Yiddish, he guesses.

As the train pulls away from the station entirely, Michael lets go of the girl's hand and jumps off the platform to run alongside the tracks. There's shouting in the crowd as two figures break away in pursuit: Soviet guards. Another man follows them – Michael's father – yelling something Chiune can't make out.

4

'Go back,' Chiune calls out to Michael, who can't hear him or his father over the train, and begins falling away as it picks up speed. Chiune anxiously leans out the window, trying to see through the fog, but the mist swallows them and makes them disappear.

Chiune braces himself on the window, sheets of rain sleeting into his face as he strains his ears. He can only hear the rhythmic chugging of the train; the shouts are muffled, steadily receding into the distance.

And then Chiune hears the gunshot, and the weather clears momentarily. His heart catches in his throat at what the evaporating mist has revealed.

Chapter 1

Sydney, Australia, July 1968

Rachel Margol pauses at the entrance to Hannah's hospital room. The old Polish woman is sitting in her bed, face turned towards the sun pouring through the window. She looks peaceful, and Rachel is sorry to disturb her as she knocks on the open door. Hannah beckons her in before turning back towards the light.

Rachel approaches her. Bathed in the golden glow, almost angelic, Hannah's face looks like porcelain. Her skin is fine and translucent, her veins duck-egg blue. Rachel thinks it's paper-thin, thinks she could see the blood surging through Hannah's veins if she leant in. The perfect light for painting her portrait – but even as Rachel wishes she had her paints at hand, her medical training kicks in. She commits the scene to memory. Hannah is only wearing a thin hospital gown over a light, long-sleeved blouse. Or rather, the gown is wearing her: it envelops her withered form. The old and frail are perpetually cold, Rachel knows.

'You shouldn't sit up without help, Mrs Radomsky,' she says gently.

'Blame my father,' replies Hannah, in a heavy accent. 'The stubbornness belongs to him. What is your name again, my dear?'

Rachel's told her many times, but she doesn't say so. 'Rachel.'

The old lady is delighted. 'Ruchalah! It's been so long.'

Rachel doesn't recognise this foreign pronunciation of her name. It's not Polish – her grandmother is Polish, and she's never referred to Rachel in that way. It's a puzzle she soon forgets, though, as she sets to preparing Hannah for her daily wash.

After she helps Hannah into the aqua-tiled bathroom, Rachel fills a plastic container with hot water from the porcelain sink's huge brass fittings and sets it in the shower recess. As she helps Hannah remove her gown, the old woman is confused. 'Where is the girl, the other girl?'

'I know it's normally another nurse's job, Hannah, but today it's been assigned to me,' she explains calmly. Even though Hannah has withered and shrunk in her old age, she still towers over Rachel's five-foot frame; Rachel is relieved when Hannah relaxes into the plastic seat. As she peels away Hannah's blouse, Rachel pauses. Numbers are etched into the old woman's left forearm, scarred into flesh with fading black ink.

'We were not names. Only numbers,' Hannah says, briefly catching Rachel's eye.

'What do you mean?' Rachel asks – she's sure she's heard or read about tattoos like this before, something to do with the war – but Hannah has already drifted off again, humming something, staring ahead with a tranquil smile.

Short attention spans aren't out of the ordinary in Rachel's work, so she continues on and removes the blouse entirely. She's turning on the taps in the shower, adjusting the temperature of the water, when Hannah suddenly begins trembling and moaning. Rachel glances up to see her staring stone-faced at the water pouring out of the shower nozzle.

'Hannah?' Rachel asks. 'What's the matter? Are you cold?'

Hannah clutches at Rachel's arm, fingernails digging hard into her skin. Her trembling turns to shaking, and she doesn't seem to hear Rachel trying to soothe her. The moaning has become a wail. Frightened, Rachel tries to free herself from Hannah's grip so she can fetch help when an orderly comes in. The orderly, a woman Rachel has seen around the hospital, immediately turns off the shower and wraps Hannah in a towel, ignoring Rachel entirely as she guides Hannah out of the bathroom and back to her bed.

Rachel is left in the bathroom, forearm already beginning to bruise. Her heart races in her chest – what did she do wrong? Moments later, the orderly returns and hisses, 'You can't ever put this patient in the shower.'

'I ... I was told to bathe her,' Rachel stammers. 'I don't usually wash the residents, they were short-staffed this morning – nobody said—'

The orderly sighs. 'You need to sit her in the chair and just attend to her with a cloth. Okay?'

'Okay.' Rachel swallows.

The orderly nods then storms out. Rachel takes a breath in, blinking back tears, and returns to coax Hannah back into the bathroom.

She carefully washes Hannah's back with a soapy washcloth, watching how the woman's wrinkled, soft skin moves with the pressure of the fabric, how her white hair, the consistency of fairy floss, almost melts into her neck as Rachel moves it away from the soap. Rachel rarely feels awkward when she helps the resident patients like this; they deserve compassion, care, respect. These are things Rachel can give them, and she often likes chatting with them about their lives as she does. But as she glances again at Hannah's tattoo, she finds she's too shaken to talk, let alone try asking more questions.

***

Rachel eyes the rows of cleaning supplies on the storeroom shelves, bottles lined up like soldiers awaiting inspection. An army waiting to attack and wipe out every germ in its path. She's preparing to wash bedpans. Not the greatest duty in her day-to-day responsibilities, but not the worst, either – though she knows her nursing friends, Kate and Susan, would disagree. She hefts a large container of bleach from the shelf and adds a glug to the sink she's filled with hot water, then gets to scrubbing the stack of bedpans she's wheeled over on a trolley. She doesn't mind cleaning them, really; it's meditative, and the storeroom is quiet and secluded. On days like today, she especially doesn't mind it. She's still shaken by the incident with Hannah. She berates herself; she should have asked about any special requirements. She should have done her due diligence.

After she finishes the last of the bedpans, she stacks them on a clean trolley and washes her hands, wincing at how dry they are. Her grandmother, Felka, tells her that if she doesn't take care of them, her hands will look like an octogenarian's by the time she hits thirty. Rachel smooths them with rich lotion from a small tube of hand cream she carries in her uniform pocket. Vanity. *You got that from me,* Felka said once, with more than a touch of pride and not a hint of judgement. Proud, loud and happy to be so. Rachel is nothing like her grandmother.

The storeroom door opens, and Rachel glances up. It's Thomas, one of the junior doctors. Rachel puts the hand cream away quickly.

'Hello, Rachel,' he says.

'Hello, doctor.'

He heads to the shelves, putting a row between himself and Rachel. 'You can call me Thomas when we're alone.'

If it were anyone else, Rachel might think this friendly and conversational, perhaps even flirtatious. She knows otherwise. Thomas, with his perfectly coiffed blond hair and irritatingly clipped private-school accent, has no interest in being friendly. As he lingers by one of the shelves, she wishes he would hurry up and leave. There simply isn't room here for Rachel, Thomas and Thomas's larger-than-life ego.

'Do you need something?' she says reluctantly, approaching the aisle he's in.

'Just these,' he replies, taking something off the shelf: an entire packet of latex gloves.

'Thomas, we bring them around if you need them.'

He edges back down the aisle to Rachel. 'Well, I need more than just a couple of pairs for once.'

'You don't need a whole box.'

'Don't be such a Jew.' He grins. 'Throwing piss bombs at the interns is a tradition.'

No, you're just trying pathetically hard to make it one, she'd love to say. Instead, she repeats herself. 'You don't need a whole box.'

Her contempt must come through, because he comes close to her then, towering over her. Rachel's short, but even then, he's tall – and he knows it, owns it.

'You're just a nurse,' he sneers. 'If you were studying medicine, you would understand. But that's never going to happen. So why don't you get back to scrubbing the bedpans, sweetheart?'

Rachel has so many responses jostling for space in her mind: that with her grades she could have studied medicine but *chose* to nurse. That nursing is a challenging and rewarding job deserving of respect. That he has no right to speak down to her. But rather than say any of this, she looks away, and he walks out.

***

Rachel is relieved later when Kate pulls her mid-walk from the hospital hallway into one of the hospital's ancient washrooms for a break. Susan's already inside, sitting on one of the benches. She watches as Kate compares her forearm to Rachel's to see who fared better over the weekend with tanning at Bondi Beach.

'You win again,' Kate says enviously to Rachel; her creamy arm contrasts starkly against Rachel's tanned one.

Susan snorts. 'That's a competition I won't be entering unless we're vying for who can burn and blister the fastest.'

As Susan and Kate swap tales of the day's painful patients, Rachel considers bringing up what happened with Hannah, and then with Thomas, but remains quiet. Next to towering Kate, with her bright dyed-auburn hair, and Susan, with her mass of bouncy curls, she feels inconsequential. When they're together, Rachel's voice is the quietest. Always.

She watches as Susan eases her way to the end of the room and attempts to crack a window open. The old wooden frame relents after a moment, unsticking and coming away, leaving a residue of chipping, bubbled paint on the ledge. Pleased, Susan lights a joint. Rachel hastily locks the door.

'Stop being such a scaredy-cat.' Susan grins.

Kate's peeling off her sensible stockings and swapping them for flimsy, alluring nylons. She pauses to say to Rachel, 'You're such a goody-two-shoes!'

'Blame a decade of Catholic school,' Rachel says, a little grumpily.

The bewildering, restrictive uniform; the strict, oblivious priests; the suspicious, sadistic nuns; the impenetrable verses. That school was more than enough to put her off getting in trouble; the last thing she wanted was another reason for her father to hate her.

Relenting, Susan comes over and gives her a squeeze. 'Oh, we love you anyhow.'

Kate pulls off her uniform. Her figure is slender, athletic, and Rachel looks away, fiddling with her crisply starched white apron. Susan catches her gaze, offering the joint. When Rachel shakes her head, Susan reaches out and jams it between her lips.

'Live a little,' Susan scolds. Rachel forces her mouth closed, raising her brows at Susan. She has no desire to reek of weed at work.

Susan sighs – 'Fine, fine!' – and plucks the joint from Rachel's mouth before returning to the window and taking a deep suck.

'Can one of you cover me for an hour?' Kate says after a moment. Rachel glances back at her; she's wearing a plaid mini skirt and a short-sleeved cashmere jumper with a plunging neckline. Slipping into black patent leather flats, she adds, 'I'm getting lunch with Owen.'

Lungs full, eyeballs popping, Susan shakes her head as she expels the smoky air in a bark of a laugh. 'Looks like he'll get dessert too,' she manages in between coughing her lungs out. Rachel grins, despite herself.

Kate rolls her eyes as she pulls an anti-war badge from her pocket and waves it at Rachel and Susan. 'You two coming tomorrow? Owen's making signs for Save Our Sons.'

'Sure,' Susan says, moving from the window to offer the joint to Kate. She takes it, passing both of them a badge.

Rachel turns it in the light. Cheap plastic wraps around the bold, colourful text – *NO JAIL FOR ANTI-NAZIS.* It's difficult to miss, and she's not sure that she could pull off wearing it. Kate, though, could make it look stylish.

'Owen's cousin ran away,' says Kate, gesturing with the joint. 'A deserter. I would have too. Why do we need to fight everyone else's bloody wars? What business do our lads have, risking their lives in Vietnam?'

Rachel puts the badge in her pocket and watches as Kate takes a drag. It smells earthy, and even as it makes her nose wrinkle, she finds herself taking a deep breath. Kate makes it look glamorous, somehow. Brash, alluring. She's taken her lush hair from the snug-fitting nurse's cap they all have to wear, and it falls just-so on her pale shoulders.

'Got a spare one of those, Suse?' Rachel asks before she can stop herself. Kate coughs.

Susan raises her brows. 'We'll corrupt you yet!'

Rachel smirks. 'Oh no, you won't. I pledged allegiance to Vinnies. Remember...' She becomes very serious as she repeats the mission statement drummed into them on entry into nursing school. 'We bring God's love to those in need through the healing ministry of Jesus. Compassion, justice, integrity and excellence!'

Susan prompts her, 'Integrity being ... come on, Rachel...'

Kate puts on a saintly expression as she jumps in: 'Ensuring our actions and decisions are grounded in our values, reflecting both honesty and authenticity.'

'Amen!' they all chant and cross their chests, then Kate shouts to the sky, 'Forgive us, heavenly Father.'

They crack up in unison. Rachel quickly pockets the fresh joint Susan passes her along with Kate's badge. She unlocks the door. 'Thanks, Suse. And I'll cover you, Kate – but I'm off. *Some* of us have to work.'

'Glad it's not me.' Kate grins, and Susan is laughing as Rachel closes the door behind her. Rachel has her own appointment to get to.

As Rachel walks down one of the long hospital hallways, she passes by one of the open common areas where patients can move about freely. Today they're gathered around a small television with a chipped wooden frame. Some of the patients are in light hospital gowns, attached to drips they wheel around on rickety metal stands; others are in their own night-clothes, covered up by floral or plaid dressing-gowns. They all gaze at the television with the same rapt attention as it blares with an ABC newsreader talking about the Tet Offensive and the student demonstrations against the Vietnam War in Melbourne.

Rachel isn't listening, though. As she walks past the nurse's station and smiles at the ladies behind the desk, busily inspecting files and discussing medication to be dispensed, she passes a window – and sees horrified young interns cowering in a courtyard as piss-filled gloves are pelted from the floors above.

＊

Rachel enjoys her and Dr Yanni Poulos's covert meetings, but today she really needs it, needs that sense of someone steadying her, wrapping around her. They meet in a hidden-away laundry room. The door is securely bolted shut, just in case anyone hears the noise of sex – rough, passionate – against the shelves.

Yanni finishes and falls away. He always does it so elegantly; it never feels seedy or cheap to Rachel. After a breath, he pulls up his trousers and Rachel dismounts the towel-filled washing cart. While he uses a clean handtowel to wipe himself, she pulls up her stockings and pats her hair back into place. She sneaks a glance at him, at his handsome, chiselled jawline, his smooth, dark, freshly shaven skin. She can smell his cologne and sweat on her, and it makes her chest ache with joy.

Yanni tosses the towel into the washing cart, and then grins at her. She grins back, and loops his stethoscope around his neck.

'Back to rounds,' she says affectionately.

'Right,' he says, adjusting his coat, and nods. 'Rounds.'

He watches her, eyes crinkling as she smooths his white shirt, then kisses her once more.

'See you at Maria's house tonight, then?' she asks.

He nods, already turning away to return to work. She wanted to ask him about Hannah, maybe even seek reassurance about Thomas, but she decides to bask in the afterglow; as she tidies the mess they've made, she's smiling to herself, heart full to bursting.

**

Felka Margol is enjoying a perfect morning cup of tea. Her tabletop is laid out just as she likes it: a lace doily to both decorate and shield the red-and-white Laminex surface from her favourite floral teapot, which is sitting there as it does every morning, as it has done for decades. She's already cleared away any remnants of her ritual breakfast, consisting of toast lavishly smeared with butter and cherry jam. Not a crumb in sight.

A pile of newly delivered mail also sits before her. She regards it as she lifts her teacup – pretty bone china, floral, matching the teapot. She sips carefully, but still leaves a smudge of her lipstick on the rim. Dark burgundy, it matches the various splashes of red throughout her home, from her perfectly manicured ruby nails to her crimson velvet bathrobe. Even Felka's mess, what little there is, is coordinated.

She sets the tea down, feeling quite relaxed, and begins sorting through the letters. The first envelope is a bill, which she sets aside; the second is a clothing catalogue, which she decides she will peruse during a bath that evening.

But the third envelope makes her pause. A telegram. Telegrams always mean news. Her heart thrums in her chest as she tears open the seal.

The sender's address is enough to make her diaphragm clench.

Joshua Nishri, Attaché to the Consul-General, Embassy of Israel, 3 Nibanchō, Chiyoda City, Tokyo, Japan.

Felka stops. She glances at the black porcelain vase she keeps on the deco cabinet, shot through with gold.

She turns back to the telegram and reads the contents. She puts it down. She sits at the kitchen table, motionless, staring into yesterday. Lost in the past, she's a young woman again, strolling with another, laughing, along a street dotted with rickshaws and Japanese street signs. By the time she remembers to breathe, she has to gasp for air. She begins coughing. Reaching out blindly for her tea, she knocks the cup over. It cracks, brown liquid spilling out and soaking the mail. The telegram's words blur. Stained, it looks antique.

Felka catches her breath, and is confronted with the mess before her. She sets the cup upright with shaking hands, cutting herself on the crack. The blood drips onto the telegram, mingling with the water. She cries out in frustration, sadness and fear, letting her guard down only because nobody is there to witness her doing so. She frantically mops at the telegram with a red napkin.

It's unacceptable: the broken teacup, the stained mail, the blood, the tears. Among everything in her home, so wonderfully ordered and pristine, she feels grotesque and out of place. And so, she spends an hour wiping down the table, detailing every groove and screw, until the shaking subsides.

***

The key clicks loudly and the front door to Rachel's house creaks open to a dark void. No matter how many times she has performed this lonely, silent ritual, it never becomes any easier. As she enters the empty house, her grandmother's voice echoes in her mind, as it always does. *Check every room. Under the beds, behind the curtains and doors. You never know where someone may be hiding. Promise me, darling.* Felka has always been paranoid.

She removes her shoes and treads softly from the entry hallway into the nearest room – her father's. Michael won't be home for hours. As she kneels to peer under the double bed with the plain bottle-green bedcover, she hears a loud *clang.* Her heart races as she jerks up. A whine sounds. It's just the cat next door.

She lets go of her breath and edges past the dressing table, left as her mother arranged it twelve years before. On it are a few silver picture frames, now dulled. One contains a wedding photo: Rachel's beaming mother, Shirley, next to an uncharacteristically cheerful Michael. Another is of Rachel as a baby being suffocated in a cuddle from her grandmother. A perfume bottle is still in its place. A bone-inlaid hairbrush. A small glass saucer where Shirley used to place her jewellery.

She tries the other two bedrooms. Nobody behind the doors, or in the closets, or under the beds. In the bathroom, Rachel swiftly pulls the shower curtain across. Ever since watching *Psycho* a few years earlier, she sighs with relief every time she finds it empty. The rest of the house is easy. Everything is in plain view, and all clear.

She enters the neat kitchen and peers in the fridge. As usual, there's a pre-cooked meal of meatloaf and limp vegetables with a note from Felka, but Yanni has warned her there will be a mountain of food at the engagement party. She decides instead on a banana.

It's 5.30pm and she's not due at the party until 7pm, so she wanders back to her bedroom. Opening the door is like detonating an explosion of colour in the dark, dim house. The room is large, but the bed and wardrobe have been crowded into a corner by a large desk sitting under the window and dozens of canvases featuring rich blues, reds, yellows and greens. A bookshelf beside the desk is full of sketchbooks, novels and art history titles, and the desk itself is littered with loose sketches, pencils and an old pickle jar filled with worn paintbrushes. The smells of linseed oil and turps mingle in the air.

Rachel picks her way between the stacks of canvases and sits at her desk. She retrieves one of the works from a pile beside her chair and sighs. Not her best. When she first sketched the scene she was excited to try something new – a view through Felka's window into the kitchen, Felka leaning into the frame from the left as though demanding to be seen. But the perspective has come out all wrong, which often seems to happen when she's trying to translate a three-dimensional scene into the simplified, flattened style she prefers. The reds have turned out more muddied than pure, too. It can't be salvaged.

She will reuse it. She ruthlessly brushes white paint over the whole thing then grabs her hairdryer and waves it gently over the canvas until it's just dry, the old painting barely showing through. When it's ready, she selects the least shabby of her well-used brushes from the old pickle jar and squeezes the remnants from a near-empty paint tube onto her palette. She curses when it is barely enough. She is in dire need of new equipment, but art supplies are so expensive, and she's trying to save as much as possible of her nursing wage. Michael could help, but he has never seen the point of spending so much money on a hobby. Instead, he fills her wardrobe with expensive clothes she never asks for: his attempt to express affection, she supposes.

She tries to recall the scene from the morning, of Hannah bathed in sunlight. The initial sketch comes easily: Hannah's limbs drawn round and loose as she leans in her chair, face to the sun, the figure evoking the work of Matisse, Rachel's idol. She begins to fill in the base colours: large, flat patches of blue for the hospital gown against a yellow wall. When she finally pauses to check the time, relaxed and a little weary, it's past seven. *Oh God.* She jumps from her chair and races out to call for a taxi, then quickly gets dressed.

As the taxi driver beeps his horn outside, she dashes back to her desk and collects a wrapped vase and a small hand-painted card – a bunch of bright cherry blossoms in a vase. Perfect.

Just before she leaves, she pauses one more time to look at the half-finished portrait of Hannah. It's good, she thinks. She'll finish it on the weekend.

Chapter 2

In the well-manicured backyard, a young, beaming couple stands before a priest as he intones solemnly in Greek before an enormous crowd. Rachel watches, awkwardly standing by herself; she arrived mid-ceremony and can't see anyone she knows. At least she's warm in her long dress and cardigan. She's hoping the conservative outfit will garner some approval from Yanni's parents, though the red beret she impulsively added – a nod to Felka – might ruin the effect a little.

As the ceremony continues, Rachel quietly sets her gift on the table among the others and is relieved when one of Yanni's friends, Ella, appears from the crowd.

'Hi,' Rachel whispers.

'Yanni's over here,' Ella replies, leading her through the huddle of bodies. She's just caught sight of Yanni when the guests shout in unison:

'*Syncharitiria!*'

'Thanks, Ella,' Rachel says before crossing to Yanni. She buries her head in his chest, content and warm.

'Nice of you to join us,' Yanni teases.

'Sorry,' Rachel says. She doesn't know how to explain to him how she got so lost in her painting. She gestures at the crowd. 'What did that mean?'

'Congratulations,' Yanni says. Rachel jumps as a dinner plate smashes against the terracotta tiled path. Then another. Purposefully thrown. Yanni laughs. 'Part of the ritual.'

The crowd applauds and ouzo flows from bottles into shot glasses, swiftly passed around and spilled down throats in celebration. Rachel takes one and hesitantly throws it back; it burns on the way down, and she struggles to keep her smile.

The engagement party is for a close friend of Yanni's, Maria, and her fiancée, Paul. Their home is beautiful, Rachel thinks, looking around as Yanni chats to his friends. Carefully tended rose bushes in full bloom are interspersed with fragrant jasmine trees, and the garden has been perfectly lit with strings of warm fairy lights.

'Gorgeous house,' Rachel says to Yanni when he comes back with drinks.

He shrugs. 'Typical upper class, suburban home. The mark of the educated immigrant. Except for the lemon trees,' he adds, gesturing to the rear wall. 'Very Greek.'

One of his friends, Nico, chimes in. 'Not all of us can have vegetable gardens.'

She asks them about the ceremony; perhaps flattered by her interest, they tell her about the three blessings of the rings, the significance of wearing them on the right hand in biblical history. Yanni easily throws in facts about Greek history and religious lore.

Rachel loves this, loves that it's such an integral part of who he is. She can't think of any ritual her own family unit performs. Her Catholic schooling seemed perfunctory, a nod to the majority; they've never gone to church or said grace at dinner. There's no strong feeling of togetherness or tradition like she's seeing here. No sense of connection to something significant. She feels distinctly separate from the other guests. But once she is Yanni's, she will fit right in.

The evening is a blur of joyous traditional dance, Greek delicacies (including bougatsa, Rachel's favourite since Yanni brought her some a few months ago) and lots and lots of drinking.

After making her way through greeting after greeting, Maria approaches to thank them both for coming. Beaming, she thrusts the glittering diamond on her right finger into Rachel's face.

'We've already found a house and Paul's grandparents are helping with the deposit,' she shouts over the noise of the guests. 'And we're going to honeymoon in the Greek Islands, after we visit the family in Athens, of course.'

Rachel can't help but return her enthusiasm. 'The ring is so beautiful! Did you choose it?'

Maria laughs. 'Of course! Paul wouldn't know the first thing about jewellery!' Her expression turns sly. 'So, when are you going to have a ring of your own?'

Rachel doesn't know what to say, and looks to Yanni, who is looking equally uncomfortable. She's been wondering that herself. They've been dating a year already, and he's finished his specialisation study.

Seeing his wide eyes, Maria cackles. 'Come on, what are you waiting for?'

Yanni laughs nervously, and is visibly relieved when Maria is pulled away by a friend. Rachel knows it was unfair of Maria, but still – surrounded by his family and friends and culture, she can't help but feel deflated.

So when he says, a little shyly, almost as a throwaway, 'Well, we could, I guess,' she stares at him.

'Really?'

'Yeah,' he says, stronger this time. 'How about it?'

'Do you mean that? You're not just saying it?'

He looks at her very seriously. 'Marry me, Rachel Margol.'

Rachel throws her arms around him, laughing as she squeezes the life out of him.

He laughs, hugging her back. 'If you think you've seen Greek rituals tonight, wait until you see what's to come for us!'

As he releases her, Yanni's mother, Sophia, approaches.

Yanni whispers, 'Don't mention anything yet. I'll break the news to them later.'

Understandable, Rachel thinks – she doesn't want to take away from Maria's night.

'Rachel,' Sophia says warmly. She's a tall, elegant woman, with pale blue eyes in a gently lined face. Her accent, usually quite faint, seems stronger tonight, as though her past is being drawn out of her.

'Hi, Mrs Poulos.'

'You look lovely, dear. Why don't you come meet some of the women?'

Yanni winks at Rachel, and she lets Sophia lead her into the house. The kitchen is crammed with women and food. The chatter echoes off the polished wood cabinetry and bright lemon-and-lime-coloured wall tiles. It's so colourful and inviting that Rachel almost forgets she doesn't know how to cook. And this crowd of women – a mix of ages, all regarding her with interest or suspicion – must have had recipes passed down to them and been taught how to prepare the sumptuous dishes spread across the countertops. The thought is intimidating. Yanni may have proposed, but she's not one of them yet. She knows what they're thinking as she enters: she looks Greek, but they don't know her. And Rachel knows that everyone who is Greek knows everyone else who is Greek.

Sophia introduces her: 'This is Yanni's friend, Rachel.'

One lady turns to another. 'Rachel? That's not Greek!'

'What is your surname?' asks another.

'Margol,' Rachel answers.

'Where is that from? Where were your parents born?'

Rachel spins to answer. 'Poland. Polish.'

They grimace.

Another: 'Because you look Greek. Or Italian.'

'Yes, I get that a lot.'

An elderly woman, presumably Maria's grandmother, chips in. 'You like Greek food? What can you cook? My Maria can cook a banquet!'

They all wait in silence as Rachel fumbles for an answer, embarrassed. She settles for honesty. 'My mother died when I was nine. I didn't really learn much from her, so...'

The embarrassment is now on them, she sees with some relief, but she's uncomfortable with the clear change in mood: *This poor girl. Motherless. Unthinkable.*

Another asks softly, 'You have sisters, yes, aunties?'

Rachel bites her lip, shakes her head.

'Just you?'

'And my grandmother,' Rachel replies, and then adds, 'and my father.'

Rachel watches Sophia. She can see the wheels turning in the woman's brain. *Who is this girl? Not Greek. No family. Other.*

But rather than say something to redeem her to the group, Sophia breaks the silence with a change of subject. 'Come! Let's go find Yanni.'

Sophia leads her back outside; no words are spoken, and Rachel is relieved when she sees Yanni and can excuse herself.

'What happened?' he asks. 'You look spooked.'

'An inquisition,' she mumbles. 'I don't think your family like me very much.'

Frowning, he goes to say something but is interrupted as a few young men approach and greet him. He introduces them to Rachel.

'These are my first cousins on my mum's side, Theo and Alexis.' Rachel smiles and nods dutifully. 'And this is George, the son of my dad's uncle Hector.' Four more relatives approach and Yanni continues: 'And these are my first cousins on my dad's side, Eleni and Apollo, and Jason and Helen.' Again, Rachel greets them, feeling overwhelmed as they chatter away. The night goes on, and dread begins to settle in the pit of her stomach. She has no family to introduce Yanni to, aside from her father and grandmother.

Not a single soul.

***

The next day, Rachel strolls down a sun-drenched lane in the affluent suburb of Double Bay. It's dotted with tall, shady trees, thick with foliage, sheltering weathered awnings of long-established businesses. She knows this route well – she's walked it hundreds of times. The end destination is 21 Espresso, her grandmother's favourite cafe. She comes to a stop in front of it just as a neatly dressed waiter drapes a clean red-and-white chequered tablecloth over the top of a recently vacated table.

The waiter sees her, smiles widely, and welcomes her. Two elderly women eye her from a nearby table. They're dressed flamboyantly in clothing perhaps a little too young for them, and they're dripping with heavy gold jewellery.

'Felka's granddaughter,' she hears one of them say to the other. She glances over, and they give her a smile and a nod as she takes a seat at the freshly cleaned table. She takes a book – *To Kill a Mockingbird* – from her bag. For days she's been engrossed in its beautiful writing and characters, but the cafe isn't conducive to reading. She tries to concentrate but finds herself too distracted by the people walking past.

Eventually she gives up. She relaxes into the sunny day and the crisp breeze and observes. What books do these women recommend to their daughters? What do they teach them? Anything other than fashion and make-up tips? What would her own mother have taught Rachel, if she'd had the chance?

The restaurant is full of Europeans: Polish, German, Hungarian. Varying languages are spat out at varying volumes. Some patrons seem to be in stiff competition for airtime, shouting over one another. Rachel quietly takes it all in. With the speakers all gesturing wildly, almost like conductors, it makes for an amusing, if somewhat shrieky, continental orchestra that spills out onto the footpath.

The thought is halted by a screeching of tyres. Felka has arrived. Rachel looks over to see her grandmother's Monaro slow next to an empty parking spot across the road. Bright red, of course. The biggest, boldest statement. Rachel sighs, grinning a little despite herself, as she watches her grandmother reverse parallel park – one wheel slapping the kerb, the bumper almost hitting the car behind her. The same women who smiled at Rachel tut and murmur disapprovingly in what Rachel recognises as Polish.

Felka strides across the road, wrapping her thick burgundy coat around herself as she sweeps up to the cafe. She stops to greet the two women, all ritualistic air kisses and more loud Polish, before she turns to Rachel.

'My beautiful girl!' she says in delighted, thickly accented English. 'Come over here, let me introduce you!'

Reluctantly, Rachel wanders over. Felka hugs her, then kisses her many times on the cheek, leaving a thick smudge of ruby-red lipstick behind. Felka tries to rub it off with a chubby finger, but only succeeds in smudging it further. She abandons it, and turns to the two women.

'Rachel, this is Mrs Dombrovsky. Say hello! Don't be so bashful!'

'Hi,' Rachel says, wishing she had a napkin for her cheek. 'Nice to meet you.'

'What a darling girl, Felutkah!'

'She's a nurse,' Felka exclaims proudly. 'But she could have done medicine, too, my beautiful genius!'

They are clearly impressed and respond with wide-eyed smiles, eyebrows raised.

'Also she is a talented artist!' Felka continues. 'So even at her little hobbies she excels!'

This stings, but Rachel keeps smiling.

'And this is Mrs Dunn. Rachel is a beauty, yes?'

'Like her grandmother,' Mrs Dunn answers, and turns to Rachel. 'Look at your grandmother's skin. Doesn't look a day over forty!'

'I'm starving!' Felka announces to all, and begins ushering Rachel back to her table. 'Come, Rachel. Let's eat.'

The waiter approaches just as Rachel is about to reach for a napkin, and Felka beams up at him. 'Klem, how are you, darling! Do you see this beauty? But she is taken. You had your chance, Klem!'

'My loss.' Klem winks at Rachel, who is cripplingly conscious of the lipstick still smeared on her cheek. He offers them menus.

'You didn't order?' Felka asks Rachel.

'No,' she mumbles, finally reaching for a napkin.

'You should have ordered! I will order.'

Rachel watches, wiping her cheek, as Felka flicks through the menu and orders in Polish. Rachel doesn't understand, but she still knows it's far more food than the two of them could possibly eat. Klem, clearly used to Felka's shenanigans, obediently writes on his pad and hurries off to the kitchen.

With that done, Felka turns all of her attention to Rachel. Any lingering embarrassment or annoyance dissipates when her grandmother looks at her like this; Cyclone Felka will always appreciate what is most important, and what is most important is family.

'You are my millions,' she says solemnly to Rachel, reaching across to grasp her hands. She goes to say something else, but starts coughing. It's a nasty cough, one that has Rachel frowning.

'Are you okay, Grandma? Where's your inhaler?'

'I am magnificent,' she declares, clearing her throat. 'How are you?'

'I'm fine.' Rachel pauses, her mind leaping to Hannah.

'What's wrong? Something is wrong.'

'Nothing's wrong,' Rachel answers. 'But something odd happened at work yesterday.'

'Something odd?'

'It's ... I'm not entirely sure. I was helping a patient to wash, and she panicked.'

Felka is confused. 'You hurt her? She fell? Panicked. What do you mean, panicked?'

'It was really strange. She was fine until I turned on the shower. She completely froze up, started to shake, cry out in fear. She was fixated on the shower head. It was just all so bizarre.'

She glances at Felka, who looks uncharacteristically serious. Rachel continues. 'Anyway – an orderly came in and told me off, took care of it. The handover from the other nurses didn't say anything about it, but apparently we're never to turn on a shower near her.'

There's a long pause. Rachel thinks Felka might say something, but instead she breaks into an easy smile and shrugs. 'Okay, so it's all fixed. You don't do it again. No harm done. Not your fault. Did you tell them it's not your fault?'

Rachel shifts in her chair. 'Well...'

Felka raises her voice. 'Darling, you must speak up when it isn't your fault! You can't let people walk all over you! Okay? Deal?'

'Yes,' Rachel says. 'Deal.'

Felka doesn't know, then, Rachel supposes. A shame. She'd really like to figure out what happened to Hannah.

Felka clearly has other things on her mind. She slaps the table: 'I want to go on a trip!'

'A trip?' Rachel says, confused, but Felka breaks into another coughing fit. Klem comes back just in time with water and cutlery, and Felka gratefully watches as he fills up her glass, gulping it down to soothe her throat.

Rachel realises she doesn't have a fork just as he leaves. 'Excuse me, my fork—'

She's too quiet, though, amid the noise of the other patrons, and she sighs, turns back to Felka. 'What trip, Grandma?'

Felka is already shouting for Klem, gesturing for a fork. She looks at Rachel. 'You don't keep going when things aren't right, you fix them. It's not a favour, it's a fork. You need a fork.'

Rachel sighs. 'It's fine, he didn't hear me.'

'He didn't hear you because you speak like a mouse,' Felka tuts, and starts coughing again.

'Grandma,' Rachel says, worried, filling her grandmother's water glass again. Klem places a new fork on Rachel's table, but she's too busy looking at Felka to thank him.

Once Felka settles, she continues. 'Speaking up is important, especially for us women. When you're a man, you talk – they listen. When you're a woman you must talk loud.'

'Are you sure you're alright, Grandma?'

Felka waves her question away. 'I'm fine. I'm great!'

Rachel knows nagging her will do nothing, so she tries to steer the conversation back. 'A trip where?'

'To meet friends. For a reunion!'

'Reunion?'

'Old friends. Because I am turning sixty and you, my beautiful *pupelle,* are going to be twenty-one. Twenty-one! You know what *pupelle* is?'

'A doll.'

Felka doesn't hear her as usual.

'A doll.'

'Actually, Grandma, it's *poupée. Poupée* is a doll.'

'Yes! What I said. Pupelle. A doll. You will be an old married woman and you will still be my pupelle! What a wonderful age! Born on the same day. You were my birthday present. The best present! And we must celebrate life!'

Felka is always celebrating life. Every detail, every minute event. Rachel is constantly in awe of it. She is one-third her grandmother's age and most mornings she must drag herself out of bed.

The food arrives: a large, heavily-fried veal schnitzel with sides of cucumber salad, creamed spinach and a mountain-sized portion of mashed potato for Felka. For Rachel, fried chicken livers with onion on rice.

'Grandma, you know I hate chicken livers.'

'Nonsense,' Felka says briskly. 'You look tired. You need some iron! Now, tell me, my darling. How is work? How is Yanni? What have you been doing? Dancing? Singing? Celebrating? Tell me! Tell me everything!'

There it is. The familiar barrage of questions. 'Work is okay, I guess.'

'You guess? You must *know.* You must love what you do. Otherwise, you won't want to jump out of bed and do it every day.'

Rachel thinks she would enjoy it more if Thomas weren't there and if she had more power over how the patients are treated, but is weary just at the idea of bringing it up. 'Okay. It's good.'

'Good. Okay. Good is a start. Great is the goal, ha! You are smart! You just don't have the belief in yourself. You put yourself down. I never understood why! Don't ever be scared to try!'

Rachel smiles tightly, nods.

'And your beau? Yanni?'

Rachel feels her smile loosen, become a little silly. She can't wait to see Felka's expression when she tells her. 'We're engaged. As of last night.'

But Felka stills. 'Engaged?'

Ah, Rachel realises. She's overwhelmed. It happens even to Felka, sometimes. Rachel can already see the gears turning: where the wedding will be held, what the bridal party will wear, what will be served at the reception. She's been planning for this day since Rachel was born.

Rachel decides to head her off at the pass in case she's about to suggest the wedding dress be red to match the bouquet. 'We really don't want a big fuss.

Just something low-key. Besides, he wants his parents to meet you and Dad first.'

'Are you sure?'

'Yes, nothing big.'

'No,' Felka says, shakes her head. 'About this boy. You haven't been seeing him long. And you are still so young...'

Rachel is taken aback at this response. 'I – yes, yeah. I'm sure.'

Felka holds her gaze for a moment, looking at her intensely, and then seems to relax. 'Well, I was going to suggest you come with me on my trip. But now you will be busy organising.'

'I could come,' Rachel protests. 'I could get time off. Besides, it's not like we're getting married tomorrow. But where ... where is this reunion?'

'No, you have a lot to do. Your father can come with me.'

Rachel snorts. 'You know that's never going to happen.'

'You have a word on his ear, yes?'

Rachel grins. 'A word *in* his ear.'

Felka waves her hand. 'Yes, yes, in, on, what does it matter? What's important is you get to the planning.'

'There isn't much to plan.' Rachel shrugs. 'We already know where we'll get married – Yanni's church in Surry Hills, seeing as I don't belong to one.'

Felka, in the middle of a bite of schnitzel, chokes.

***

After lunch with Rachel and a visit to the doctor, Felka rushes to Michael's factory in Surry Hills. She lifts herself out of the deep bucket seat, huffing and puffing. She pauses after, to catch her breath, trying to stop herself from coughing. She's more flustered than she likes, thanks first to Rachel's news and then to the appointment. The doctor had been late, and the chairs had been so uncomfortable, and, of course, there was the news.

I'm so sorry, the doctor said. A very young man, almost too young. She will be fine. She has to be fine, at least for a while longer. She has already lived through things that should have been the death of her, and she sees no reason to give up the fight now. She's certainly not going to cancel her trip, despite the doctor's advice.

As she enjoys the crisp air and lets her lungs settle, she watches the garment-and-fashion district, alive and buzzing as usual. Vans pull up side by side and deliver racks of almost identical garments to nearby establishments, all run by industrious, ambitious refugees – most of whom she knows – trying to make good in their new home as she and Michael did. They are in fierce competition with one another, all except Michael, who Felka can proudly boast has a monopoly on the latest fashion trend.

Satisfied her chest is fine, she crosses the road to the factory entrance. The sign above the door reads *Margol – Australian Denim with New York, Paris, London Flair.*

Inside, the constant mess makes her purse her lips; the factory floor, laid with original wooden floorboards, needs new varnishing, and the large windows are covered in long-ignored layers of dust that only allow a few biblical shafts of sunlight in. How many times must she tell him he needs to clean?

Passing the workers puts a smile on her face, though. Their ages range from early thirties to late sixties, a fairly even spread of men and women, and they're sewing garments of all kinds, all in denim. It fills her with pride to hear their Polish, Austrian, Hungarian, Australian and French accents mingling. A gathering of kindred folk whom she and Michael have helped, many having escaped their respective homelands in search of a better life. Workers greet her as she passes; she responds to some by name. 'Fritz. How are you? Mary, Anya – how's your daughter's asthma?'

'Much better, thank you for asking!'

'Henri! When are you bringing in some more of those croissants your wife makes?'

A thumbs-up from Henri.

Felka is sincere, but strategic. She knows it's vital to keep their employees happy. One big family. From their expressions, she's doing it well. There is not a hint of jealousy that her son owns the business – no animosity, just support and camaraderie.

Felka throws open the door to Michael's office. The iceberg glass trembles in its wooden frame.

Michael is on the phone, and he holds up a hand, glancing at her in warning. Felka graciously gives him a moment to wrap up the conversation, and takes the opportunity to examine her son. He's looking a little too lean for her liking. At forty-two, his slimness could be mistaken for athleticism, but Felka knows it's thanks to cigarettes and working into the night rather than any sporting habits. His dark hair is slicked back with Brylcreem, showing his lovely olive complexion, and he's wearing the well-fitted white business shirt and tan woollen slacks she bought him for Christmas last year. They're paired with a narrow, navy tie, though, which irks her. When will he add a bit of colour to his wardrobe?

At least a minute has passed, and there's no indication he's finishing up.

'Michael!' she says sternly.

He frowns at her, and she walks to his large, old-fashioned desk. She drops her handbag into the chair opposite it, but remains standing.

Michael holds his finger up, gesturing impatiently, emphatically. She relents a little. But not entirely. More quietly now: 'Michael.'

Michael speaks into the phone receiver: 'Sorry, Jack, can you hold a moment?'

Oh, it's only Jack! Felka reaches across the desk and plucks the phone from Michael's hand, ignoring his exasperated huff.

'Jack, darling! It's Felka!' she exclaims. 'How are you? I need to speak with Michael, do you mind?'

'*Of course not,*' Jack says. He has a soft spot for her, she knows.

'Wonderful, I'll get him to call you back. Send my love to Marjorie!'

She puts the phone back in its cradle and looks at Michael. 'He's happy for you to call him back.'

'Mum, you can't just – for Christ's sake, I—'

She cuts across his affronted stuttering. 'The floor needs redoing. The windows are dusty.' He rolls his eyes. She pretends not to see it, and continues. 'But that's not why I came. I have news. Rachel and Yanni are engaged.'

Michael stops. Finally, she has his attention. He slowly takes a cigarette from the pack on his desk, lights it and takes a deep, long inhale.

'Well?' she demands.

He exhales; the smoke plumes around them, and she can feel her throat tighten in protest as he taps the ashes into the chunky red glass ashtray. Another of her gifts. Usually, seeing him using it would please her. Instead, she waves the smoke away, impatient.

He exhales again, loudly. With intent. Then, he says curtly, 'Okay.'

'Did you hear what I just said? Your only daughter is engaged.'

'Well,' he says again. 'It was to be expected.'

Felka doesn't expect any gushing from Michael, but this disappoints her.

'She has to be told.' She pauses, then adds, 'Everything.'

'I don't need the workers knowing our private life,' he snaps, too loudly; Felka's sure it's echoed through the door. He lowers his voice, hissing, 'I'm not going to drag up the past. It's done, it's gone. Telling Rachel about it won't do her any good. Besides, she's gone to Catholic schools her whole life – it's not that big a jump to Greek Orthodox.'

This stops her. He's right, of course, and she hates it; she remembers once hearing Rachel, only eight or nine, saying prayers before bed.

Heavenly Father, her darling granddaughter had said, words from this strange religion put in her mouth.

Forgive me for I have sinned. If you just let my mum live, I promise I will be good forever.

She should never have gone along with Michael's plans.

'Rachel is crying out for love and attention!' Felka says. 'You don't know how to parent!'

'I learned from the best.'

That hurts. 'I had to be mother and father to you. In difficult circumstances. Don't you ever forget that.'

'And I don't know the life of a single parent? Really?' he says.

'But you had me filling in for you. Being a mother to her. Picking up the pieces. I had nobody.' She glares at him. 'And I had to go along with *your* instructions on how to raise her.'

They stare at each other. For a moment, she thinks Michael is moved, but then he shakes his head, picks up the phone. 'I need to speak to Jack, Mum.'

'Fine,' Felka says, and turns to walk out. But then she spins back around to add, 'But we are telling her, whether you like it or not.'

And then she leaves and doesn't close the door behind her, taking great satisfaction in how his office is filled with the sounds of others at work.

***

After Felka leaves, Michael watches his cigarette smoulder, lost in thought, in another place and time. Ordinarily, he chooses to block it all out, but his mother's parting words have allowed a memory to make its way through a tiny fissure in the wall.

He looks up, and in his mind a pretty young woman smiles at him as she beckons, a flirtatious glint in her eye. *Come.*

'You will come!' The ethereal Shirley says, smiling as she departs through his office door. It's dark in the factory, and she turns back, gesturing for him to follow. He remains seated, buying into this familiar game of foreplay.

'I might, I might not,' he retorts, teasing.

She skips along the factory floor. She calls back. 'You will. You always do. You can't resist me.'

He gives chase and catches her, pushing her onto a large pile of fabric offcuts. As they lie there, he kisses her passionately.

Emerging from his abyss, Michael vigorously stubs out the burning cigarette, continuing to stub long after its glow has expired.

Chapter 3

Rachel watches as a spoon of dripping, sticky honey is thrust at the face of her unsuspecting grandmother, and another towards Michael. This is how Sophia greets them at the door of her stately home in Vaucluse, followed by a hearty 'Welcome!'

Yanni laughs, and his father Dimitri explains as Felka looks to Rachel for help. 'This is the ritual greeting for an intended bride and her family. Please accept the honey as a symbol of the sweetness of married life that is to follow.'

Felka cautiously accepts, as does Michael, albeit with much less drama.

'Nice on a pancake,' Felka comments. 'Or a crumpet. With banana. And some ice cream. On its own – very sweet!'

Rachel winces, but keeps a wide smile as she glances at her future parents-in-law. They don't appear too perturbed, but she is always on tenterhooks when introducing her family to others. Embarrassment mixed with caution. Her father, the closed book, presents well enough. Felka, though, never fails to make an impression one way or another.

They are welcomed into the vast parlour and invited to sit down at a table laid with fine bone china. ('Noritake,' Felka says approvingly, lifting a plate to check the maker's mark.) Silverware polished to eye-squinting perfection is set atop a white lace-adorned tablecloth. As Dimitri, Sophia, Yanni and Michael politely chat, Felka leans over to Rachel.

'Not very Greek, is it,' Felka says in what is probably meant to be a whisper. Thankfully, the others don't seem to hear it. Rachel knows what she means, though: save for an assortment of Greek magazines and newspapers on the ornate gold and marble coffee table, and an array of family photos in elaborate frames featuring elderly people from the Old Country, nothing about the decor seems especially Greek. Yanni's parents live, for all the world, much the same as any other upper-middle-class family in Australia.

After a few minutes, a tiny, hunched figure dressed in black appears from the kitchen, laboriously carrying a tray laden with icing sugar-dusted biscuits and sweets.

'My mother, Athena,' Dimitri says. Athena looks Rachel up and down and then whispers to her son. His soft reply is apparently upsetting; she exclaims something loudly, and Dimitri hushes her.

Rachel nudges Yanni. Yanni whispers, 'She wants to know if you're from our ancestors' village. When Dad said no she said, "What will people say?!"'

He laughs, and Rachel tries to smile but feels like she's back in Maria's kitchen, being measured and found wanting.

Perhaps Yanni sees this; he wraps an arm around her. 'It's her go-to when I bring someone home, don't worry.'

She summons some levity, mock-gasping and bringing a hand to her chest. 'And how many have you brought home?'

'Does it matter? You're the last,' he teases, squeezing her.

They quickly get to formalities. When Yanni asks Michael for Rachel's hand, her father accepts without any fuss. They shake hands. Done, dusted, over in a flash, and tea is served.

As they eat, the doorbell rings again. Dimitri gets up to answer it, and when he comes back, a priest is with him.

'This is Father George, our priest. Father, this is Rachel, the bride-to-be, and this is her father, Michael.'

Michael stands to greet him, and Rachel sees how Felka is staring pointedly at Dimitri, who ignores her.

She loudly introduces herself: 'And I am the grandmother!'

Amused, the priest acknowledges her. Rachel feels a flush creep up her cheeks as Dimitri explains the reasons for the visit.

'We now need the priest to bless your union for the ritual to be complete. Of course,' he adds, 'we'll do it officially at the engagement party, rings and all. Father George is here to talk with you about the ceremony and what to expect.'

Rachel is proud that she knows about the rings, and eager to learn more. She may not be from Yanni's village, but she'll do him proud; at the next engagement party, she'll walk into the kitchen and know who's who. She'll be the one tutting at the newcomer.

As Father George talks to Yanni about his part, though, Rachel finds her gaze drifting to Felka, who sits quietly, watching her with sad eyes.

Rachel doesn't understand – where's her loud, brash, joyous grandmother gone?

∗∗∗

Sometimes, after long evening shifts, Rachel stays the night at Felka's. It's close to the hospital, and her grandmother always makes sure there's food in the fridge. Tonight is one such night, and Rachel quietly enters the house and curls up on the lush, ridiculously large couch, instantly relaxing. She smiles to herself at the sound of Felka's snores echoing from the bedroom. This place feels like home.

Felka has volunteered her house for the first proper dinner with Yanni's family tomorrow night, which makes Rachel both grateful and nervous. Felka's house is certainly more welcoming than Rachel and Michael's, but it's also where Felka is most comfortable, and a comfortable Felka is unpredictable. If she's being honest, Rachel is a little worried about her grandmother in general: the cough, the strange, solemn reaction to Rachel's engagement – she resolves to try to speak with her properly soon, but not before the dinner. Everything must go smoothly at the dinner.

A single lamp is on, lending a warm drowsiness to the room that Rachel finds quite comfortable. On the deco cabinet sits one of Felka's most treasured possessions, a simple black vase with gold lines cracked along its body. The light catches these veins, almost making them glow. Something about the scene tweaks a fragment of a memory, long forgotten. It reminds her of the gold clock in her own home, burnished to a shine, and how it chimed so loudly on the hour, it almost concealed—

The sound of her mother sobbing behind a closed door. *You don't understand! I never wanted this. I'm not like you, I can't just give it all up.*

Her father's voice, too muffled to understand. Her mother's response is clear, though.

I'm not, I – You can't tell me who to speak to. Loretta is all I have.

Rachel blinks dozily. *Loretta.* An unfamiliar name. Who was she? She doesn't remember very much about her

52

mother, can't remember any of her friends. Just who was Loretta? The thought stays with her until she drifts off.

***

Rachel's shift the next day flies past in a rush of nerves as she tries to focus on her work. She arrives at Felka's house to find her grandmother in a whirl of activity, and by the time Yanni and his family are due to arrive, Rachel wishes she could just shut herself in the bedroom and wait in silence until they all leave. Then she remembers Kate's joint, sitting in her coat pocket for weeks now, forgotten. She sneaks into the bathroom.

She feels guilty, but frankly, she needs something to take the edge off. Thomas was an arsehole again today, snapping at her for not asking his permission before adjusting a dosage he'd mistakenly prescribed, as if she hadn't saved the patient several hours of pain and nausea. Adding this dinner into the mix has sweat gathering on the nape of her neck.

Maybe, secretly, some part of her likes that she has the nerve to pull the joint from her pocket. It's the sort of thing Kate and Susan tell her about, the sort of thing she usually laughs admiringly at. Besides, she knows that from a medical standpoint she'll be fine as long as she doesn't overdo it.

So, Rachel turns on the extractor fan, slides the window up and takes out a lighter she's stolen from

Felka's drawers, lighting up. As the muffled sounds of the guests arriving echo outside the door, she takes a cautious puff, and when her lungs don't seize up, she takes another. She likes the light-headed feeling it gives her, but decides not to push it, sticking her head out the window to exhale.

'Rachel?' she hears Felka call.

'In the bathroom,' Rachel calls, flushing the joint and waving the smoke out the window.

'What?'

'In the bathroom!' she shouts, and then blushes. Everyone in the house will have heard that. She takes an extra second to scrub a toothpaste-covered finger across her teeth and fan out the last bit of smoke with a *Women's Weekly* magazine.

'Did you drink a fountain?' Felka exclaims when she finally emerges. 'Heaven forbid we start before my granddaughter finishes pissing.'

'Mum,' Michael says disapprovingly, but when Rachel looks at him in surprise at the show of support, he's not looking at her, but at Dimitri. Of course. He's worried about his reputation. The joint smooths her annoyance into acceptance, and she turns to Yanni.

Yanni at least looks as amused as he does embarrassed, smiling at Rachel. Athena murmurs something that makes it clear she's unimpressed, but

Yanni takes no heed. Rachel is filled with affection for him. So long as he accepts her, it will all be okay.

'Come help me serve,' Felka commands, and Rachel obediently follows her into the kitchen, which is full of large dishes overflowing with enough food to feed twenty people. Roast lamb, crispy potatoes, perfectly seasoned peas, salads, the works. Rachel helps her carry it out and lay it on the table, which fairly groans under the weight.

'My goodness,' Sophia says approvingly.

'You are my guests,' Felka says as she begins serving everyone. 'We are lucky to have whatever we like these days. Enjoy. You can never have enough!'

If there are ten for dinner, Felka will cater for fifty. Rachel once asked her years ago why she always does this. *I will never take food for granted again.* It was always the same answer. During the war years, there were shortages. In Australia they had ration cards for everything.

Dimitri stands, clinks his fork on his crystal wine glass and beckons them to lift their glasses. 'A toast! To Rachel and Yanni! Welcome to the family, Rachel!' He takes a big drink of wine.

The guests respond in unison: 'To Rachel and Yanni!'

Relieved to have made it this far, Rachel takes Yanni's hand under the table. He leans in to kiss her on the cheek, then pauses, sniffing. 'Is that—?'

She grins a little. 'I was feeling a bit stressed.'

'You shouldn't need a crutch to get through dinner,' he whispers.

'Stop being such a doctor,' she mutters. He takes a long breath, but she can see him bouncing his knee until it hits something. They both glance under the table: an unused packet of spaghetti on the floor. They both look at each other, and the tension thaws out.

'My grandmother,' she explains. 'Her little habit thanks to food shortages in the war. She hides food around the house in case we might need it. What can I say?'

'Huh,' Yanni says. He clearly wants to know more, but Rachel is glad when he doesn't ask. Instead, he nods at the Japanese prints on the wall. 'Your grandmother really has a thing for oriental art.'

'Japanese,' Rachel corrects him. 'She's had them as long as I can remember.'

'Reminds me of your paintings,' Yanni comments, and Rachel beams. It's true; she's heavily influenced by the beauty and simplicity of Japanese woodblock prints, as well as Miró and her hero, Matisse. 'They look like the flowers you painted on Maria's card.'

Rachel goes to talk about the different techniques she uses, but Felka interrupts.

'Yanni! You want to specialise, yes?'

'Yes, I was looking at—'

'Cardiacagist,' Felka supplies triumphantly. Yanni smiles, not unkindly.

Rachel responds: 'Cardiologist, Grandma.'

'Yes, yes. That's what I said. And you can take time for a honeymoon. A honeymoon is very important.'

'Yes, uh, I hope so.'

'He will be able to get away at some point, yes, Grandma.'

'And Sophia, Dimitri,' Felka continues, turning to them. 'You must be so proud.'

Dimitri looks up from his roast potatoes. 'Yes, of course. Though there was never any doubt Yanni would follow me into medicine,' he boasts.

Finally, Michael says something. 'So you had to retrain to practise in Australia?'

'Yes. A bit of an inconvenience but well worth it to live here.'

Sophia adds, 'Yanni was always a bright boy. Always a top student. We want our children to do well. Especially in a new country. I'm sure you feel the same way, Felka.'

Yanni interjects: 'Mother, please.'

Felka takes the reins. 'Why "please"? It's a pleasure, it's a miracle, to watch a son excel! Sophia, you are right. So hard in a new country. Everything for the children. Only the best. Such a joy. What you live for.'

Sophia and Dimitri nod in agreement. There's a brief lull, in which Athena – who Rachel had forgotten was even there – gets a translation of the conversation from Sophia. Dimitri and Yanni begin talking about footy, the Roosters. Rachel has never seen her father express any interest in football, but he seems to be holding his own. Michael always knows how to blend into a room. Rachel wonders if the others can see how clearly he doesn't want to be here. She hopes not.

She can feel herself beginning to relax a little, and she tucks into the food. Hearty, warm, sustaining fare. It's going better than she expected. A thought that comes too soon, as Felka speaks up again.

'And Dimitri – you are a gastric?'

'A gastroenterologist,' Yanni corrects Felka. Rachel can see how Sophia is trying not to laugh, and flushes with embarrassment.

'Yes. What I said. A gas ... Yes.' Felka pauses, grins. 'This is looking up the back passage all day. You need a strong constitution! You would want your patients to have washed, ha!'

Rachel closes her eyes. Silence. A very long, awkward silence.

'My Rachel,' Felka continues. 'She could have been whatever she liked. She chose nursing. She is an excellent nurse, but I'm sure she could be an excellent gastriodoligist!'

'Grandma,' Rachel hisses. The comforting warmth of the joint is fading fast.

'Why not say it! You should be proud!'

'It is something to be proud of,' Sophia says. 'But it's not really a profession for a young lady, is it? Not when you must think about bringing up babies. Cooking for a large family, washing, ironing.'

Felka is not so impressed with this remark. 'Yes, well, this I agree. But there is room for a career.'

Yanni, blessedly, steps in. 'Anyhow, I can tell you she's a great nurse.'

Rachel smiles at him.

'A wife's duty should be to her home first,' Dimitri says defensively, patting Sophia's hand. Rachel frowns, but Yanni squeezes her hand – whether in support or warning, she can't tell.

'I think this way of thinking is a little old-fashioned, dear. If the woman has a brain, the woman should use the brain!' Felka retorts, and for once, Rachel is glad her grandmother doesn't know when to stop talking. 'She can combine home and work, yes? Never rely on a man completely.'

Dimitri, credit to him, realises he is not going to win on Felka's home turf. He concedes his position, and changes the topic. 'So Felka, you came here ... when?'

Felka graciously goes with it. '1936.'

Sophia takes over. 'That was lucky. We were in Thessaloniki until 1947. It was tough to live through the war in Europe. Much suffering. It was lucky we all got out. My parents, my three sisters, my two brothers. Dimitri's five brothers and mother. And of course, the uncles and aunts. We are a big family.' She laughs. 'Do you have any siblings?'

Silence. Rachel is surprised when neither Felka nor Michael responds in the negative: *No, none.*

'Uh, no,' Rachel says after a moment. 'No, we're a very small family.'

Sophia clears her throat. 'Rachel mentioned you're turning sixty, Felka. Do you have anything special planned? A trip?'

Felka and Michael answer at the same time.

Felka: 'Yes.'

Michael: 'No.'

Sophia laughs, and Rachel is incredibly grateful when the others do, too. *See?* Rachel wills Sophia and

Dimitri (and Athena, she supposes) to understand. *We aren't that bad.*

Felka smiles and points her fork at Michael. 'I am going to Japan. If your father was here, he'd go too. He loved to travel. You should come. Get out of the office.'

Rachel blinks. Japan? She assumed Felka would be going somewhere warm, sunny – the Gold Coast, perhaps. But now she thinks about it, Felka never answered when she pushed her on a location...

Michael grunts, and Dimitri changes tack, asking about life in Poland. Quickly, Felka shifts to showing off one of her greatest skills: weaving a good story.

***

After they bid Yanni and his family goodbye, Michael sits and has a late-night glass of whiskey in an attempt to wind down. His head is swimming from small talk and trying to bear his mother's disregard for social niceties.

Exhausting. It's exhausting, how Felka can be. He pinches the bridge of his nose. She spent most of the dinner swapping stories about the Old Country with Sophia and Dimitri, glancing at him every now and then as if he had anything to add. How can she not understand? He *can't* go back. And even if he could, he wouldn't. Not in his mind, not in his body. Why must she idealise everything? Sugar-coat it? Even the vase that sits on her cabinet, the black porcelain – when it broke all those years ago, she was determined to keep it as a token of the past, patching it back together and making its faults golden, unmissable. Kintsugi, she told him the method was called. The art of fixing the broken. She thinks it's beautiful; he thinks it's a glaring display of her faults. Leave what's broken alone.

'Where would you rather be?' he hears Felka ask Rachel. He can hear them cleaning up in the kitchen, the sound of water splashing, plates clinking together. 'A party?'

His daughter laughs. It sounds just like her mother's. 'Nowhere else.'

'Liar,' Felka gasps, but he can hear her smiling. 'I think you took so long in the bathroom earlier because you were embarrassed.'

'Well – you can be very enthusiastic. Maybe a bit too much.'

'I am what I am! I won't change me for anyone. And Greeks aren't meant to be enthusiastic?'

'I guess.' Rachel's voice is both exasperated and affectionate. There's a lull, when all that can be heard is the sound of washing dishes. After a moment, Rachel speaks again. 'Will we still go, even if Dad refuses? Japan?'

Michael closes his eyes, holds the glass of whiskey to his forehead. Cool, soothing.

Felka responds quickly. 'I will go. On my trip.'

Rhetorical question, really. Rachel should know better. For all their disagreement, Michael agrees with Felka on one thing: Rachel is so young. She has her whole life to work, to marry. She should be making the most of all the opportunities that come her way. He just wishes this weren't one of them.

'If your grandfather was here, he wouldn't be on his arse drinking whiskey, not when there's washing up to do,' Felka continues. Michael rolls his eyes. 'He was a doer. And men, women, he didn't see the difference, God rest him. He got in and rolled up his sleeves! Anything to help me have a break, no matter how tired. I made mistakes, I didn't appreciate him. That's a real man. You make sure Yanni is a real man for you, do you hear me?'

'Yanni takes good care of me,' Rachel protests.

'We will see, with a father like that Dimitri. "A wife's duty is to her home." Bah! You are not going to end up a Greek washerwoman! I don't know if this boy – if this family – is right for us. For you. You are so young, still. You need to find things that fill you with passion!'

'Like your collection of everything red?'

'Exactly!'

Rachel sighs. 'Why are you trying to find fault with Yanni and his family? They're good people.'

Felka says something non-committal, lost in the splashing water. She can't very well say it's because they're Greek, of course.

Rachel suddenly asks, 'Where are the rest of your family? Are there any left in Poland? Why didn't they come out?'

Michael holds still, strains his ears. He hasn't had a chance to talk Felka out of revealing the truth to Rachel yet.

'I don't remember,' Felka says casually. 'So long ago. There were some. Few. We weren't close. They were old, didn't want to travel, to make a big change. But that's not important. What's important is your wedding, and my trip.'

'Dad hasn't said he's going. I don't think there's any way you can get him to go.'

'Don't worry about it,' Felka says. She never seems to worry about anything: social norms, manners, getting her words right.

It is the bane of his existence.

***

When Michael and Rachel get home, he disappears into the yard. Even after she cleans up for bed, he's still out there, smacking the odd spider off the walls. Australians and their venomous spiders.

She gathers her courage, then opens the flyscreen door and peers out at him. 'Dad?'

He glances back, as close to an invitation as she's likely to get.

She walks to the swings and sits down facing him. The swings are old, erected in honour of Rachel's childhood, made of steel. They could probably hold a horse. Nothing but the best for Felka's only grandchild. These are the swings her mother pushed her on, that Michael pushed her on. The seat is a little small for her now, but she can squeeze into it. Her legs drag on the ground, stopping her from swinging freely. She lifts them up and out, straight in front of her, the momentum carrying her gently back and forth.

Rachel looks at her father. He's a shadow, hidden by the dim light from the house, but she can tell he's looking at her. The smoke from his cigar swirls into the wind.

She remembers how he used to turn her around while she sat like this, tightly twisting the chain so that when he let it go, she would spin, yelling with excitement.

'I've got some new samples at work, if you'd like them,' he says after a moment. A white flag, perhaps. As if a new pair of jeans, another gift offering, will make up for a decade of emotional distance. She wants to say *How about a new set of paintbrushes?* She wants to change the topic and say *You should go with Grandma.* But he's made it clear what he thinks of the trip. She can't understand it. He should go, if only because Felka is his mother. Rachel would do anything to go on a trip with her mother.

In a small voice, she says, 'Mum would tell you to go.'

Michael exhales, slowly. He doesn't say anything, but stubs out his cigar. Stands. Walks towards her. She stops swinging.

Closer. Still a silhouette. Closer. He covers the windows. Refracted light spills onto his face, but she can't read his expression as he stops in front of her.

'Your mother—' He stops, tries again. 'Your mother...'

For a moment, a single moment, Rachel thinks he might be angry, or sad, or some terrible combination of both.

He exhales. 'Your mother isn't here.'

It's a cool night, but his words are colder. She clenches her jaw. Being Michael's daughter is a winter like no other, with no spring in sight.

He taps the swing with his hand, straightens and walks back to the house, into the glare of the doorway.

Desperate for a reaction, some sort of emotion, Rachel calls out before he can step inside.

'Who was Loretta?'

He stops. She continues, studying his expression. 'I remember Mum talking about her once or twice. Long ago.'

'Nothing to concern yourself about. Nobody.'

And he disappears inside.

Chapter 4

At the nurses' station in Oncology, Rachel sorts through paperwork while Kate assesses medication charts close by, chatting about her courtship with Owen.

'I don't know where this is heading,' Kate's saying. 'He's pushing, but I don't know. How do you know when someone's "the one"? Really, how do you know?'

Rachel isn't sure how to answer.

'Ladies,' Thomas says. Rachel ignores him. 'Can you please advise if you've commenced the MOMP protocol for cancer on the old Jew, Hannah Radomsky?'

Kate busies herself, and Rachel continues reading through her paperwork.

Thomas huffs. 'Ladies!'

'Doctor,' Kate replies coolly. Rachel's told Kate about his recent rudeness, and she's pleased her friend has her back.

Thomas looks at Rachel. 'This would be an example of when you'd call me "doctor",' he says.

She ignores him. His voice turns cold. 'Nurse.'

She relents, then. 'Yes, doctor, we've commenced the protocol.'

'Good. Know your place in the pecking order, *Rachel*.'

He walks away, and Kate raises a brow at Rachel, who shrugs. Thomas's problem with her is a mystery. Her crankiness is replaced with cheer as Yanni passes by, carrying a stack of patient files. He stops and leans in towards Rachel.

'Happy Monday,' he smiles, drumming the desk with his fingers before he continues walking.

'Happy Monday,' Rachel echoes, biting the inside of her cheek so she doesn't grin. She knows that code.

Kate knows it too, and has no such reservations, elbowing Rachel. 'Go, go. I'll cover for you.'

The storeroom. Rachel loves the secrecy, the risk. Besides, there's little privacy for them anywhere at his house or hers – though her father works late, so does Yanni. And the car is ... restrictive. Rachel is usually one to follow the rules, but, as with the joint, she can't help but enjoy an outlet here and there.

***

Afterwards, as Yanni zips his fly, he turns to Rachel. 'Do you mind if you take those files with you back to Oncology?'

'Sure,' she says, gathering them in a pile. Seeing Hannah's file, she pauses. 'Yanni – Hannah Radomsky, do you know her story? She has breast cancer.'

'Oh, you mean the old Jewish patient? No idea. She has dementia, so it's hard to get anything out of her. Why?'

The way he says 'Jewish' is casual, neutral, unlike how Thomas sneers 'Jew'. But still, Rachel is confused by the relevance of Hannah's religion. She doesn't want to ask about it, though. For all that dinner didn't go as poorly as she feared, she worries that she isn't as welcome in Yanni's family as he makes her feel. She doesn't want to give him a reason, any reason, to doubt her.

'Just had a strange experience with her the other day,' she says instead, and smiles at him. 'Never mind.'

***

The denim factory is silent when Rachel arrives after a long bus ride. She can see most of the lights are off, save for two: one in Michael's office, and one in Henri's. Henri, the office manager, has always had a soft spot for her. He almost feels like part of the family. She sticks her head through the open doorway as she walks past, and Henri's shiny, bald head pops up from his desk.

'Sweetheart! Haven't seen you in ages!' He stops what he's doing and rushes over to her, embracing her warmly. Like Felka, his ease with affection astonishes and mortifies her. 'Have you seen the new range from New York?'

'Yeah, Dad told me I could come by to grab a pair. Again...'

He retrieves a pair of jeans from a box, and hands them to her. 'These should fit. Take them home. Anything for my Rachel.'

'Thank you – um, actually, do you have them in size ten and twelve as well?'

He smiles at her knowingly; it's not the first time she's picked up extras for Kate and Susan. But he finds a pair in each size and hands them to her without remark, waving her off as she walks towards her father's office.

As Rachel reaches the doorway, she hears a female voice. Her father is seated at his well-used wooden desk, piled high with fabric swatches, ledgers and invoices. He has his head down doing paperwork as a woman leans over him, murmuring something into his ear. Rachel eyes the woman, wondering how long she's been in Michael's life. Seeing her, the woman swiftly removes her arm from around his neck, and he finally looks up.

'Good,' he says. 'Henri gave you some samples. I'll see you later.'

Rachel doesn't leave the doorway, ignoring the dismissal. 'I wanted to talk to you.' She glances at the woman. 'I'm Rachel. His daughter.'

The woman smiles, but it looks a little awkward. 'Nice to meet you. I'm Betty.'

Before Rachel can respond, Michael turns to Betty. 'I'll see you out front in twenty minutes,' he says to her. She takes her leave, edging politely past Rachel. Once she's gone, he leans back from his paperwork and puts down his pen. Rachel commences.

'You're never home and we need to discuss some things. Like the wedding. And Grandma's trip.' She approaches his desk. 'You work and work, even when it's something important.'

'She can go if she wants to, but I won't,' he says crisply. 'She's perfectly capable of gallivanting around without my being there.'

'Dad—'

'No. I don't have time for indulgence, for your grandmother's ridiculous romantic ideas. You wouldn't have what you have, either of you, without my attitude towards work.'

She bursts. 'I never asked you to work all day! I'd much rather us be poor and you actually give a damn about us than have a few extra pairs of jeans in my wardrobe. You won't talk about my wedding, you won't talk about a holiday with Grandma. I barely see you at home. Why have a family at all?'

For once, the careful neutrality of his face gives way to surprise, anger.

'What do we have, really, Dad?' she asks. 'A house, some food. That's it. No more than what I had after Mum died and you spent every night for a year in this goddamned office!'

Unable to bear the sight of him, she turns to walk out. She's halfway there when Michael, striding towards her, grabs her, forcing her to look at him. His fingers are painful around her upper arms; she'll probably bruise, she thinks, stunned. Even as they lock eyes, she sees he regrets it. He releases her immediately.

He's never, ever laid hands on her before. But now he has, and she knows he doesn't have the capacity to apologise even when she most needs it. She wishes she knew why. It might make it easy for her to forgive him. Instead, she retreats, her lips quivering. He doesn't care. What she did have, when she was nine years old and her father didn't come home for days at a time, was Felka.

She turns and walks out in tears. Henri sees her rush past, asks after her with great concern, but she keeps going. It's not his comfort she needs.

She almost goes to Felka's, but she doesn't have the energy to deal with what will no doubt be an overwhelming feast of comfort and chocolate. Instead, defeated, she just goes home and climbs into bed.

Loretta, Rachel thinks dully, casting about for a distraction. Who was Loretta? Her mother was on the phone a lot, she remembers. Which is odd, now she thinks about it. The calls were only ever when her father was away, or asleep. She cried, sometimes.

A memory: Rachel peers through a crack in the closed door to see her mother in tears, cradling the phone to her ear. *I love you,* she says. *I miss you.* But her father wasn't in a different city.

He was asleep in front of the television.

***

It's already dark when Michael and Betty emerge from a small cafe near the factory. Betty says she wants to walk off dinner. Michael agrees, restless, and they stroll in the city streets arm in arm. He doesn't want to go home and see Rachel there.

He needs to do … something. God knows what. Betty steers him into a jewellery store. They're about to close, but the middle-aged, balding shop assistant seems more than happy to have a well-dressed businessman come in.

'How can I help you?'

Michael doesn't know how to answer that. Betty does, but she refrains from saying anything.

'We're just looking,' Michael says shortly.

Betty meanders around happily as Michael's bored gaze rests on a set of trinkets in the cabinet.

'Shall I take the tray out for you?' the assistant asks him.

'Please,' Betty interjects. She tries some on and comments on their beauty, but she soon senses she is unlikely to win a prize tonight. Back they go into the display cabinet. Deflated at not having made a sale, the assistant swiftly ushers them out and closes up after them.

Michael walks Betty home, explaining he has to return to the office. She looks at him shrewdly but doesn't comment as she retreats into her warm apartment.

He continues to walk until he finds himself opposite the park on Elizabeth Street, in front of the Great Synagogue. It stands out from the other buildings, lit up with a yellow glow, its large wrought-iron gate open, welcoming in congregants for the Sabbath prayers.

He knows that after, they'll retire to their respective homes to partake in warm family reunions, gathering together for the ritual of the Friday night Shabbat meal.

Michael pauses outside momentarily, drawn in by the soulful melody wafting through the doors. It envelops him, like stepping into a hearth-warmed room.

A man entering the building pauses to tip his hat at Michael, who nods automatically. He watches as the man disappears into that warmth, and then keeps walking.

Soon, he passes a different jewellery store in another part of the city. It is still open. He walks in and picks out a diamond and ruby heart-shaped charm. The young female shop assistant suggests a chain to match it.

'A lovely choice, sir,' she says, flirtatiously. 'Is it for your wife?'

A stone-cold Michael answers emphatically. 'No.'

There is a pause and then, more formally: 'Shall I gift-wrap it?'

Michael answers, 'Please.'

***

'How are you, young lady? Let me look at you.'

Kate's father greets Rachel at the front door. She realises it's been ages since she last saw him – at least a year. He welcomes her warmly with a hug, which she accepts with gratitude.

Rachel smiles after he lets her go. 'I'm good, thanks, Mr Miller.'

'Still a little girl,' he continues. 'Up to my kneecaps. Not like lanky lass over here! I don't know where she came from. A giraffe, maybe!' He gives his daughter an affectionate wink, and Rachel laughs.

Kate gives him a one-arm squeeze, rolling her eyes. 'Well, certainly not from you, Mr Hippo.'

Mr Miller chuckles. After the last couple of days, Rachel's so jealous of them that it sits heavy in her throat, a rough stone.

'I'm ready to go,' Kate says, holding up the placards that Rachel painted last week as they lay in the sun and listened to records. Rachel takes one, examining her handiwork, pleased by how the paint has dried.

'They look excellent, girls,' Mr Miller comments.

'All thanks to Rachel,' Kate says, and the stone in Rachel's throat smooths out a little. 'Look how precise the lettering is!'

'Very easy to read,' he approves. 'Good on you both, giving it a go. I'm not convinced the pollies will listen to us, but still. I wouldn't want to be sending a son off to fight over there. My time in the war was rough. I wouldn't wish it on anyone.'

Rachel wants to ask about this – Felka and Michael rarely talk about it – but Kate's already walking out the door. 'Susan's meeting us at the bus stop down the road in a minute, we'd better go.'

'Excuse me!' her father says, and taps his cheek. Kate dutifully gives him a peck on the cheek, and then they head off. Rachel tries to swallow her bitterness, relieved when they reach Susan just in time for them all to get on the bus.

They're all wearing the sample jeans Rachel got from the factory, matching. Like a uniform, a symbol –

they're in it together. It's a nice touch, one that fortifies Rachel when they get off the bus at one of Sydney's downtown parks, the Domain. It's swarming with people, crowds of university-aged youths who march as one, body against body, arm in arm. There's no room in between them as they thrust roughly painted peace signs attached to wooden sticks in the air, chanting loudly. Brightly coloured paisley flares, miniskirts, hotpants and minimal footwear are on display despite the fact it's winter. Unspoken camaraderie is as thick as the pot smoke that hangs in the air.

Rachel feels silly all of a sudden, with her artistically painted signs and her perfect new jeans. She tries to make light of it. 'A lot of ripped denim. Maybe I should take to my dad's inventory with some scissors?'

'We're all here for the same reason,' Kate says with a confidence that Rachel envies. 'We'll fit right in.'

'Is Yanni coming?' Susan asks, as they each take a placard and hold them up high.

Rachel shrugs. 'When I asked him a couple of weeks ago, he wasn't too interested. He says he's too old to be carrying a placard and chanting anti-war sentiments with a bunch of hippies.'

'He might feel differently if he were in danger of being drafted,' Kate mutters, and Rachel blushes.

'He supports the cause,' she says quickly.

'He had better,' Susan says, as they watch mounted police in clean navy uniforms and caps try to keep the peace as the crowd boos and jeers at them. Rachel's sign, hoisted from a lower viewpoint, is head-height to the girls. They laugh. 'Got your stilts handy? You'll be crushed, Rach!' Susan giggles, then turns serious. 'Our blokes going over – still kids, really – forced into battle in the prime of their lives. Can you imagine the stuff they're seeing? It's hard enough seeing the things we see as nurses.

'Imagine being a villager over there,' she continues. 'Knowing nothing about the ridiculous conflict going on around you. Farmers. Working in rice paddies minding their own business. Then whoosh! In swoops a bomber and blasts the living daylights out of your little community, maiming your kids, killing your parents, blowing your livestock to smithereens.'

Kate nods. 'How do you live knowing you've murdered innocent people? How do you just slot back into society like nothing has happened? Dad fought in New Guinea. It was twenty-five years ago now and he still has nightmares.'

Susan turns to Rachel. 'Wouldn't your folks have seen things before they came to Australia? They would have been pretty close to the German invasion if they were in Poland.'

'They didn't really see much of it, I think,' Rachel says. 'They left before it got really bad.'

But it sparks a thought, bolstered by the mystery of Loretta: maybe they did see something. Something that scarred her father, her grandmother. Something that would explain her father's coldness, her grandmother's obsession with cleanliness and fear of people lurking behind and under furniture.

They join in on the chants as the march winds its way down the streets. The angry excitement keeps feeding into itself, and by the time an hour has passed, one of the protesters near them becomes a little too exuberant and begins shouting at the police. Others join in and the police on foot push back. A young guy throws a punch which doesn't land, and the intended victim, a cop, grabs the offender's arm and wrestles him to the ground to handcuff him. The cop is set upon by the angry crowd. Rachel tries to draw back as the throng of bodies presses ever tighter, but Kate has the opposite idea: she rushes over in support, whacking the officer with her placard.

'Kate!' Susan yells as another officer pushes their friend to the ground and restrains her. The mounted police are fighting their way through, trying to break up the crowd. Rachel is terrified; she didn't think it would be like this, a writhing mass of careless, angry limbs. Susan grabs her by the hand.

'Come on,' she shouts over the crowd, trying to shield the smaller Rachel while dragging her over to help Kate get free. The police restraining Kate are already being set on by the crowd, and it doesn't take much more than pulling Kate's hands to get her out. The cops have more on their mind than a young woman; a man with an iron bar is bashing another cop in the head, splattering blood on the ground.

'Get him!' Kate howls in glee as Rachel tries to drag them away.

'Come on,' Susan says, hauling her after them. They fight their way out of the angry mob as police sirens howl from down the street, and once they're free of the crush, they run several blocks over until they come to a quiet park.

'Jesus,' Rachel gasps, hands on her knees.

'You alright, Kate?' Susan asks, grinning.

Kate laughs as she sits down heavily on the grass. There's a cut on her cheek and the palms of her hands are scraped, but, for the most part, she seems fine.

'I can't believe you did that,' Rachel says, admonishment and admiration all in one. 'That was terrifying.'

'I'd do it again,' Kate declares.

'Give us some warning next time, please,' Susan says drily.

'I reckon we should steer clear of downtown for a bit,' Rachel says. 'I don't really want to get arrested.'

'Oh?' Kate teases. 'Big plans?'

'Well, actually, I'm kind of engaged?'

Kate screeches. 'You're what? When?!'

'Well!' Susan grins. 'This calls for a celebration!'

***

Agreeing that perhaps the clubs aren't the safest place to be tonight, they decide to head to a party at the house of one of Susan's friends. When they get there, Rachel loves the ambience: it's dim yet colourful, lit by red lava lamps and green and yellow rays emanating from light globes wrapped haphazardly in coloured plastic sheeting. Chocolate-brown velour bean bags – the new trend, apparently – are scattered around the dingy room. The only downside is that it smells of stale bong water, though this is partially masked by sandalwood incense burning in cheap, rickety holders on a mantlepiece. They toast Rachel's engagement with cheap cans of beer, smiling widely, before mingling with the rest of the crowd.

Still feeling shaken by the protest, Rachel accepts a joint from a guy sprawled out on a tattered armchair, taking it all in as the weed kicks in. Music pounds out, unfamiliar strings and dreamy melodies. Kate is talking to someone about the war as Susan joins a bunch of people grooving in the kitchen. Despite the smoke she's inhaling, Rachel awkwardly listens in on several conversations until one of the guests shouts to the host.

'Oi! Tom! Aren't you a painter?' He jerks his head at one of the living room walls, huge and blank with peeling plaster in desperate need of a paint.

'It's a big job.' Tom shrugs.

The man gestures at the crowded room. 'Well, mate – now's as good a time as any. Plenty of hands on deck!'

'Paint party, paint party!' someone yells dopily, the rest of the guests joining in. Tom grins. He pulls out a well-used, stained drop sheet and sets out tins of paint across it. Some of the men push the threadbare couch out of the way, and the guests grab brushes from a pile and begin to open tins and slap on colour.

Relieved to be given something to do, something she likes, Rachel joins in, taking a bit of space in the corner. She isn't thinking too hard as she goes, feeling more and more relaxed; Japanese-style flowers take shape, weaving in between a bold peace symbol.

'Are you a painter?'

It takes a moment to realise the question is directed at her. She turns around; a woman with thick, wavy blonde hair is just behind Rachel, looking at her painting.

'Oh,' Rachel says. 'Um, no. I'm just a nurse.'

The woman takes a long drag from a joint and shakes her head. 'You're a painter,' she says, very seriously. Rachel finds herself feeling trapped by her gaze. The woman's eyes are thickly lashed, framed with freckles. Perhaps it's the weed, but she can't look away.

'How long have you been painting?' the woman asks.

'Since I was a kid.'

'They look like Japanese woodblock prints,' she says. When Rachel looks surprised, the woman smiles at her. 'I'm an art major.'

An art major. Rachel is almost envious. At least she can paint whenever she likes. 'That's really cool,' she breathes. The woman's smile turns into something else – something Rachel doesn't really know how to describe.

'Do you have a favourite painter?' the woman asks, moving in a little closer; between the music and the chattering painters, it's a bit hard to hear. Moving closer means that Rachel can see the finer details of her: the curve of her collarbone, the way her teeth press into her bottom lip. She feels terribly embarrassed, and is almost thankful when there's a crashing noise. The room turns as one to the source.

A young man lies on the floor in a pool of vomit, begins to convulse. Rachel's moving before she realises it.

'I'm a nurse,' she yells, pushing through the gathering people. 'I'm a nurse, move!'

She isn't sure where Kate and Susan are, but it doesn't matter. She turns the man onto his side, strength and adrenaline rushing through her veins, looking for someone who knows him.

'What happened?' she says to the dulled faces in front of her. She's still not quite sober; their faces smear together. 'What did he take?'

'I think he's just drunk,' someone says uneasily.

'If he's this drunk, there's a problem,' Rachel says, slapping him lightly on the face, trying to get him to wake up. No response.

'Rachel?'

Rachel looks up to see Kate peering over the crowd. 'Kate! Call an ambulance, quickly!'

Kate nods, rushes to find a phone. Rachel checks his pulse, for obstructions in his throat, and then starts administering CPR.

By some miracle, the paramedics burst into the house only a few minutes later, though it feels like an eternity. She briefs them as they lift him onto a stretcher and load him into the ambulance.

'Likely alcohol poisoning, but can't rule out an overdose of marijuana or LSD,' she tells them. 'CPR was performed for three minutes.'

'Well done,' one of them says, and the impressed tone of voice warms her. 'We'll take it from here.' Then he adds: 'Med student?'

'Nurse,' comes the answer. He seems surprised and Rachel is quietly pleased.

And then the ambulance is screeching off. The adrenaline begins petering out, and she starts trembling. St Vincent's Casualty is just around the corner; she's pretty sure the man will be fine.

'You okay?' Kate asks from behind her.

'We should follow them in.'

Kate nods. 'Yeah, of course. Let me find Susan, and we'll head right over.'

***

Rachel's seen death and injuries and the like before, but it feels different being there in the moment, when she's not in uniform and part of a team of professionals. There's a more immediate concern, and fear, for the person being wheeled into the hospital.

The last time she was on the other side of it was the night her mother passed away. The worst night of her life. Watching her mother be wheeled out of an ambulance on a trolley, covered in a blanket. Her father whispering to the emergency staff. A nurse taking Rachel's hand. Her father sitting in stony silence with her at Shirley's bedside.

She remembers leaning her head on her mother's stomach after the doctor told them she had passed. Shirley was still warm, and remained so for another few hours; Rachel didn't move until her father eased her away.

'Is that the doctor?' Susan asks, and Rachel is pulled back to the present.

An older man in scrubs has entered the waiting room. He speaks to the nurse at the station, who points at Rachel and her friends. Approaching, he's smiling at them; Rachel relaxes.

'He's pulled through, thanks to you,' he says to Rachel. 'Do you know him?'

'No, we were just at a party,' Rachel says. 'No clue who his next of kin is, of course.'

'Well, we'll track someone down for him. Well done again – you could be a doctor, you know!'

Kate pipes up proudly. 'We're all St Vinnies nurses, actually.'

He smiles with a nod of acceptance: they're all on the same team. If only Thomas had that attitude.

Rachel swells with pride as Kate and Susan clap her on the back. After how scared and little she felt at the protest, this buoys her. In a crisis, when it was within her realm of ability, she came to the fore. She's so used to being the nurse, the assistant. She *would* make a good doctor, no matter what Thomas or Dimitri think.

***

Susan, who hasn't been drinking, drops Rachel to Felka's, which is closer than home. Felka is long asleep, but even after Rachel tries to unwind with a cup of tea, she doesn't feel drowsy. She's turning the evening over in her head again and again; the flush of victory she felt when it turned out that young man was going to be fine thanks to her. She's never hated being a nurse, but now the idea of her next shift, of having to answer to the doctors, to Thomas, feels distinctly underwhelming.

Rachel needs a distraction. Thinking of the blonde art major, she decides to pop up into the attic to see if Felka has any more woodblock prints or paintings, and carefully, quietly climbs up the tiny ladder leading to the attic concealed in the roof.

It's filled to capacity with old suitcases and trunks. And, oddly, there's a thick layer of dust on everything. It smells musty, like it hasn't been aired out for a while. It must be the only dirty room in the house – it's not like Felka to let her home get this bad.

There's a shelf behind a tower of boxes that looks promising, though, with large folders and the cardboard tubes used to send posters by mail. She sidles through to it and starts searching the shelves. But there's no art; instead, it's filled with various certificates and paperwork. Immigration, she thinks, but she can't read any of the languages. A dog-eared pocket translator from German to Japanese, which makes her frown, and empty envelopes addressed out of Warsaw to Japan. Why would Felka have any of this?

Downstairs, the toilet flushes; Felka's midnight ablutions. Rachel suddenly feels like she shouldn't be up here, and creeps out of the attic after she thinks Felka has gone back to bed.

She has so many questions. And she has so few answers.

Chapter 5

The sun streams through the open door of Saint Sophia Cathedral in Paddington. It looks almost fake in its perfection, how it hits the shiny glass teardrops of the large crystal chandelier suspended from the high ceiling.

Rachel stands below it, turning in a circle as she takes it all in, this place in which she is to be married to her fiancé. She observes the gilt-edged, intricate, brightly coloured paintings of saints and Madonnas, the ruby-red carpet that has seen many a glowing bride teeter down its well-worn pile, the dark wood pulpits and the simple olive-green leather seats.

It's a lot; she slips her arm through Yanni's, rests her head on his shoulder. There's a knot in her chest that she doesn't understand. Yanni isn't going anywhere, she reassures herself.

'What a building!'

She turns to see Felka standing at the entrance. Her grandmother, who has never moved tentatively in her life, takes a small, shuffling step through the front doorway. She peers around the interior, assessing every inch, running her fingers along ledges as if inspecting for dust, removing her spectacles to get a closer peek at the finer details in the brushstrokes on the artwork. Analysing, regarding. Criticising.

Rachel greets her and kisses her on the cheek. 'Isn't it gorgeous,' she says, less of a question than a statement. A request, even. *Please be nice.* She points out the key locations: 'This is where we will stand, and you and the bridal party will be here, and we need to organise floral arrangements to go there and there.'

She turns back to see Felka staring at the icon of Christ on the cross. Felka peers into the eyes of Jesus and he peers back.

'Felka?' Yanni says, glancing at Rachel, who shrugs.

Felka shakes her head. She's trembling, Rachel realises.

'Grandma,' Rachel says, crossing to her. 'Here, sit down.'

Rachel and Yanni guide her to a pew, which she all but falls into, still staring at the icon.

'Grandma? Yanni, can you get her some water—'

Felka exhales. 'I need to get out.'

She climbs to her feet, and starts stumbling down the aisle, almost running.

'Grandma!' Rachel calls, running after her. 'Are you okay?'

Yanni catches up and they steer her to a bench outside. She closes her eyes, breathing. Rachel's worried she's going to start coughing, but her breaths are even, deep.

'I think we should take you home,' Rachel says after a moment. 'I'm worried about you, Grandma.'

'I'm fine, I'm fine. Emotional.'

'Grandma,' Rachel says, a little more sternly than she means to. 'You are *not* fine.'

Felka cracks an eyelid to peer at her. 'Did you just raise your voice at me, pupelle?'

'I – sorry.'

'No, no.' Felka smiles. 'I wish you would more often. But not too much. I am your grandmother after all.'

'Do you want me to get your car, Felka?' Yanni asks.

'No, no. I can drive.'

'I'll come home with you,' Rachel says. 'No buts. I'm worried about your blood pressure.'

Felka exhales. 'I think that's a good idea, pupelle. Let's go home.'

***

Rachel drives, insisting Felka try to relax. As she stares across at her beautiful granddaughter, the light of her life, Felka knows it can't be put off any longer. She knew the moment she stood in that enormous church, staring at Christ, that it was time. The moment Rachel closes the door behind her, Felka hands her the telegram.

Rachel, bemused, looks at the sender's address – *Joshua Nishri.* A name she has never heard. She reads it aloud.

'*On behalf of Jewish refugees saved by Chiune Sugihara at the Consul-General of Japan in Lithuania in 1940 ... he's finally been located alive and well ... you are cordially invited to attend a reunion in Kobe...*'

She looks up. 'Japan? What is this? Who is Sooji – Sahji—'

Felka finishes the word. 'Sugihara.'

'Who is he?'

'I – we – Come here, pupelle.' She leads an unresisting Rachel to the couch. 'It's time you knew.'

'Knew what?'

Felka can see she's put the cart before the horse. These creases can't be ironed out. But where to begin? Back to the start, she supposes. Time to drag up the heavy burden of the past. But slowly, slowly, not all at once.

Rachel, though, is impatient. 'What is it? This Sugihara is Japanese, right? But who is Joshua Nishri, and why did he send the telegram? Are you going to support these Jewish refugees? Is this your trip you keep talking about?'

Felka shifts on the sofa, tweaks the edge of her skirt. She needs a glass of water. She swallows, coughs. 'Wait a second. Wait. Let me explain.'

A moment, just another moment, before she reveals her and Michael's great betrayal. She takes Rachel's face in: the smooth, sun-kissed skin, the wonderful way her nose curves ever so slightly, her wide, brown eyes. Her beautiful granddaughter.

'I will tell you some things now,' she says, putting a hand on Rachel's. 'Pupelle, yes, I'm going to Japan.'

Rachel frowns. 'But why?'

'When we left Europe, we got visas to transit through Japan. August, 1940. It was the only place we could go.' She stretches over to the cushion next to her and retrieves a large document. She hands it to Rachel. Rachel glances at it but it's mostly in Japanese and some other languages she can't identify. There is only one line in English: *TRANSIT VISA seen for the journey through Japan (to Suriname, Curacao and other Netherlands colonies) 1.8.1940.*

'The only place?' Rachel asks, looking up from the visa. 'What do you mean? And didn't you emigrate in 1936? Suriname? Curacao? What?'

Felka holds up a hand. 'Michael and I came to Australia in July, 1941. We were let in on a six-month visa, and we ended up staying Michael was only young, but he was so serious, even then. He'd spent every day with little Shirley Schagrin from the second we landed in Kobe and he was heartbroken when he realised he might not see her again. Your mother's parents loved Japan. They wanted to stay. They were sent to Shanghai for a time, while the war went on, but when it ended, the whole family, including Shirley, returned to Japan for good. Michael loved her, couldn't move on. They were childhood friends who became sweethearts on the journey. You share an experience at such a young age, you grow close, even at fifteen, you know what I'm saying, pupelle? She felt the same. They wrote constantly, they sent photos.

'Once we had a home in Australia, and I had a job, Michael became determined to bring her here. He worked many jobs to save what he could, and I gave him the rest. In 1946, he went back to Japan and asked Shirley to marry him and move to Australia. Shirley's parents never forgave Michael for it. They stayed in Japan till they died.'

'Japan?' Rachel is still utterly confused. 'Why didn't you tell me – wait. You haven't answered my question. Why have you been invited to support these Jewish refugees? Was my grandfather a diplomat? Is that how you know this Sugihara? How you got the visas to Japan?'

Here it comes.

'No. Not going to support them.' A huge breath that threatens to turn into a cough, and she clears her throat. 'We are them.'

'Them what?'

'Those Jewish refugees.'

Rachel stares at her. 'We're ... Jewish.'

'Yes.'

'So I'm – I can't be – *Jewish?*'

'Pupelle,' Felka says, aghast, trying keep her voice level. She can't bear to hear this from her own granddaughter. 'What is so terrible about that? To be *Jewish?* Is it so unthinkable?'

'No. It's just—' Rachel is surprised at her own response. 'It's just a shock. I mean, I went to Catholic school. I'm Christian. At least, I guess I am? I know I don't go to church, but ... you never did anything to make me think otherwise ... what does this make me?'

Rachel is rambling. It's unlike her. Felka decides this needs to be addressed immediately, with great finality.

'You are Jewish. A Jewess. If your mother is Jewish, you are a Jew.'

'Am I?' Rachel snaps. 'No! Then why don't I know anything about being Jewish? How come we've never gone to synagogues? Why did you hide it from me all these years? Why aren't you living as a Jew. Jewess. Why?'

Felka looks to the floor. She can feel Rachel looking at her for an answer. It's easier to talk if she doesn't look up.

'We wanted you to grow up free. Without fear. Without ever having to run for your life and hide.'

'Fear of what?' Rachel still doesn't understand. How can she?

'Fear of being singled out as a Jew. Of being hated and persecuted because of what we were born into. People judge us, darling,' Felka tries to explain. 'People hate us without reason. It is just how it is. How it has always been.' She picks up the visa in Rachel's lap and gently turns it over. Two black-and-white portraits: Felka and Michael, Felka's details written beside them in Polish.

Rachel frowns, reading aloud. '*Margolin* ... not Margol?'

'Your father thought it would be better, once he started the business. So easy. Cut off two letters and *fft,*' she slices the air with a hand. 'We are not Jews. Nobody knows.'

She risks a glance at Rachel, who is staring into nothing. 'You went to Japan to escape the Nazis,' she says slowly. 'Not just Poles. Polish Jews. We're Polish Jews. I'm also trying to understand ... Hitler murdered all our family. Is that right? Because otherwise – where are they all?'

Felka can't respond to this. She can't. She doesn't have it in her. Rachel continues.

'So you were saved, came here to start a new life, changed your name.'

'We had to protect you,' Felka says. Begs.

Rachel looks at her. 'Protect me from what? *The truth?* That I'm *Jewish?*'

'Pupelle, please. I couldn't let you get married and convert without knowing. Don't get mad at an old woman.'

'Don't get *mad?*' Rachel repeats. Felka's never seen this expression on Rachel before. She may have her mother's face, but in this moment, she looks just like Michael.

Rachel stands up, walks to the front door and grabs her bag and coat.

Felka calls after her. 'Wait, Rachel—'

'I can't be here right now,' Rachel says, and walks out the door.

***

Rachel pounds the pavement. She's not sure where to go, where to turn. She's on a late shift today. She has the morning to digest all of this, alone. Yanni is at work, she can't call him. Yanni – how will he even take this news?

As she walks, she finds herself gazing at strangers. Do any of these people really know who they are? Do other people have secret lives hidden from them? Is she alone in this experience? She sees a couple sitting on a bench, kissing. Do they have secrets the other doesn't know? Other family hidden away? Rachel remembers a doctor who used to work at the hospital – a big, gruff man with a thick moustache – and how surprised she had been to learn from Susan that he was gay. The things that people hide. A middle-aged businessman strides towards her, crisp suit and trilby hat, official-looking, serious, professional. For all she knows, he might be a spy in his spare time.

It's all too much to take in. She heads for the centre of Kings Cross and waits at a bus stop. Maybe she'll go home and paint. Her go-to diversional therapy. But when the bus pulls up, she can't bring herself to get on; it leaves without her, and she stands on a congested street surrounded by people, yet so totally alone.

She was right, about there being some big trauma that she didn't know about. She tries to remember what she learned about World War II at school. What largely comes to mind is the Nazis, and a vague idea that many, many people were killed, Jewish people chief among them. But it mainly focused on military movements, key moments marking the rise and fall of Hitler.

What happened to Felka and Michael, before this Sugihara saved them? What did they see? If she knew, if she understood, maybe she'd understand why Michael is the way he is. Maybe, maybe, maybe.

And really, this is the problem – the sense that Rachel's not being told the full story. Even if she can be overbearing, Felka only ever wants what's best for her. How far would Felka go to make sure Rachel is happy and safe? What would she hide? The thought has Rachel furious and sad and frustrated all at once. She has a right to know. And it's this determination to get to the heart of her family's story that spurs her to return.

When she rings the doorbell, two hours after she left, Felka answers immediately. The house stinks of bleach, and she's wearing the apron she puts on whenever she cleans. Rachel glances at her grandmother's hands; they're red from scrubbing.

'Pupelle,' Felka cries, and wraps Rachel in her arms.

***

Felka swamps Rachel with old photo albums retrieved from the attic. Pages and pages of sepia photos from another era: photos of men in black coats and large hats from what must be the early 20th century; photos from Japan with Michael as a young teen; photos of him with Shirley. Photos concealed from her for over twenty years.

Felka tries to help her by going back over the history that she already knows. 'Remember, I told you things. A long time ago. Poland was a good place for us. We made it what it was. Warsaw was a city of intellectuals, of culture, music and theatre.'

Rachel has heard this all before, but nods. 'My daddy – your great grandfather – had a successful business selling furs. Not the coats, the hides. We lived in a beautiful apartment. We had a cook, a nanny, a gardener. I had a dog – a German shepherd – King. I loved him.'

'I didn't know you liked dogs.'

'Of course,' Felka says, and smiles ruefully. 'There is a lot you don't know about your old grandma.'

An understatement.

'King walked with me to school, and then he waited in the window for me to come home from school, every day,' Felka says. 'He was a good boy. A good dog. But back to the story: when I was seventeen, I fell in love with your grandfather. My parents said I was too young, but I wouldn't look at any other man. I couldn't wait any more. We got married when I was just eighteen – 1926. Your father was born nine months later.'

Rachel knows this, but she hasn't heard the story of her grandmother's great love for many years. As an adult, hearing it brings up questions. 'But I thought you went to university?'

'Oh, I went,' Felka sighs. 'In 1925. I studied law. But life got in the way; Jews were not permitted there. That's why I never want you to give up your work for family. I always wished I could have finished my degree.'

Felka had always said she stopped studying because she fell pregnant. 'Jews weren't allowed? But this was ages before the war.'

'Hating us is a European tradition,' Felka says simply. 'Anyhow. September, 1939 – Hitler invades Warsaw. And my daddy said, "Right. You all get out. Get out now." Your grandfather was in the army, he was on the Lithuanian border. I couldn't wait for him.

'But I am lucky. One day, a Gestapo officer arrives on my front door. He gets out of a nice big, black, shiny staff car. And I think to myself, I'm going to get a ride in that staff car to the border.' Felka grins, but it's hollow. She continues.

'He's come to talk to me about our house. The Nazis want it for an office. He says to me, "Madam, this property, we are going to use it. You can live in the room in the back, but the rest is ours." He thinks I am just a Pole, but I am fluent in German. I use it, and tell him, "I am a Berliner. We have been here for five years. This is our home, our place of work." He is very surprised. "I am sorry, *fräulein,* I did not know you were a fellow countrywoman. I apologise. I will give you a document that will state that this property belongs to you, but we will take all the contents, and at the conclusion of this war you can present it to our offices in Berlin and your property will be returned."'

'They could just do that?' Rachel says, aghast. 'Take your home?'

'And worse,' Felka says. She's settling into her story now. 'So, I say to him, "What if I make this little transaction more worth your while, sir? How about I give you access to some American dollars? Cash, of course." His eyes lit up! I know I have him now, and say, "Of course, I'd love if you could give me a little help. My son and I need to get to the Lithuanian border. I have business there, and I like the look of your car." I show a bit of leg, just enough. He looks down. He looks up. He says, "Certainly." And then he says, "But, *fräulein,* how do you know once I've taken your money I will keep my part of the bargain?"'

Despite the sense of anger and betrayal still lumped in her chest, Rachel is on the edge of her seat. She loves her grandmother's stories, always has. Felka has a way of creating drama, suspense.

Felka continues. 'So I say, "I knew you were going to say that. Once I am safely in the car and away, I will tell your driver where I have left the money for you." And he agrees with a wink but then says he wants fifty per cent up front, and I agree. I had no choice, really, I was already trying my luck. So, it was up to me to take Michael. He was just thirteen. I packed a suitcase for me, and a little rucksack for

Michael. At three in the morning I get a sleepy Michael out of bed and by four we are ready to go. I kiss my parents goodbye, the staff car pulls up as promised and we get in.'

'So they dropped you at the border?'

Felka huffs. 'Of course not, the filthy, lying krauts. They drop us in the middle of nowhere, because they're worried about their precious car and its stupid wheels! Minus twenty degrees, snowing in the middle of December, and they dump us like we're just around the corner from a hotel! And I still had to tell him where the rest of the money was because I was scared for my parents.

'But what can I do? So we wander, and by some miracle we come across a hut. We go in, the coffee in the mugs on the table is still warm. I am a little scared the Germans are going to return, but our fingers are about to fall off. So we lie down and fall asleep. But then there is a commotion, and we are woken by shouting. The Germans have returned. And—' Felka falls silent.

Rachel nudges her. 'And?'

Felka shakes her head. Her face is pinched, as if in pain. There's something of Hannah there, and Rachel reaches out, takes her grandmother's hand.

'So, you eventually got to Lithuania,' Rachel prompts.

Felka gives her a small, grateful smile. She pauses, then continues. 'Yes. We wandered in the forest, met up with other fleeing refugees. Then a German patrol found us. They ordered us to strip naked and line up. They were about to shoot us when their drunk captain stumbled up and told them not to waste expensive bullets on filthy Jews. Instead, they loaded us into a rowboat on the nearby river, and pushed us off the bank so we would float over to the other side so the Russians could deal with us. Thousands fled across the border hoping to find an exit route. There was none. But we got lucky. We found a way.'

'And my mother's family?'

'They found the same route.'

'What happened to everyone else in our family? Your parents?'

'We never saw or heard from any of them' – she cracks – 'again.' Felka breaks and bursts into tears. She holds Rachel's hand to her forehead, pressing the knuckles close. Rachel is not prepared. Not for this. It's the first time she's seen her grandmother cry, let alone this deep, primordial sobbing and wailing, like the grief is wrenching the breath from her lungs. She feels awful for how callously she talked about Hitler killing them before, as if they were of no consequence.

'It wasn't a good time in history,' Felka manages after several minutes and many tissues. 'No need to burden you about the war. It was a time to forget. Many people, many nations suffered. But thanks to Sugihara, and to Jan Zwartendijk – he was the Dutch consul – many of us were saved.'

'Tell me about them.'

'There was a couple, in Lithuania. They couldn't go back, it was too dangerous. The woman, Pesla, had a sister in America. Pesla Sternheim. Her name. And the man Izaak Lewin. Everybody heard of them. They started the visa craze. They couldn't get to America, but they could get close – a Dutch colony, Curacao, near Venezuela. If they could get there, perhaps they could eventually get to America. There was a Dutch consulate in Lithuania, so they went to Jan Zwartendijk and asked him for permission to travel there. He gave it. Word got out, of course, among us, the refugees. In a cafe, in a food market, at the synagogue. Everyone who heard went to Zwartendijk. He was wonderful. He didn't refuse anybody, even though none of us were Dutch citizens. Such a dangerous thing to do at that time, so brave. But there was one problem: to get to Curacao, you needed to transit through Japan. So everyone went to the Japanese consulate and waited. Waited to see Sugihara, the Japanese diplomat.'

Felka sighs. 'You can't imagine the desperation. Hundreds of people, day and night, waiting outside this tiny building. There must have been thousands, because thousands managed to get to Kobe.'

'Thousands?' Rachel gapes. 'These men saved thousands of complete strangers?'

'Yes,' Felka nods. 'Sugihara and Zwartendijk. It is a debt that we will never, ever be able to repay. They both went who knows where after the war – the havoc, you have no idea, pupelle. It was common for people to vanish. People died, they took different names to hide and never came back. Zwartendijk could be anywhere, but Sugihara has finally been found. That is why the telegram.' She takes Rachel's hand. 'That is why I must go to Japan.'

NORTHERN MANCHURIA, 1934

Chiune Sugihara peers out of the car window at Baroque and Byzantine facades that could have been picked off the streets of St Petersburg. This is Harbin, the Japanese Empire's latest conquest. How strange to be Deputy Foreign Minister here, to have such command and power in this odd city, built by Russia on Chinese land to service the Chinese Eastern Railway. It's a fishing village turned international city in less than a generation. A place where empires collide.

When he first came here, Harbin was still under Russian control. He remembers teaching Russian to his countrymen at the Harbin Gakuin, many years ago, when his reach extended only to his classroom doorway. Back then, his students listened to him. Witnessing the scene before him now, Chiune is not certain he could command the same respect.

A group of Japanese soldiers, teenagers, all of them, jeer at a Chinese beggar curled up on the street corner, trying to escape the snow. Chiune cannot hear what they say through the car window, but he can see the condescension on their faces. He knows the words they use. It makes his heart clench; it tears at his conscience. Only last week, he saw a Japanese soldier dragging a Chinese woman down the street. She had been limp in his grasp, non-responsive. And only days before that, the herding of Chinese men, like cattle. Chiune has heard the League of Nations is building an inquiry into Japan's conquering of Manchuria, that it is stirring great anger in his fellow leaders and government men, but Chiune finds himself secretly aligned with this action. What is being done here is not what he expected of his countrymen.

The car moves on, and he loses sight of the beggar, passing on through the streets. He should be celebrating, joyous: not even half an hour ago, he mediated the reversion of the Chinese Eastern Railway to Manchukuo ownership. It is the greatest achievement of his career to date, the result of years and years of hard work. But as he gazes out at what his country has done to Manchuria, at the crumbled rubble and struggling locals, Chiune feels hypocritical.

He feels conflicted.

The weeks pass, and the thoughts linger. Chiune's colleagues and underlings regard him with new respect after his successful mediation, but he can appreciate none of it. There is word of revolution among the Chinese, a rumour repeated with sneers.

The newspapers back in Japan, which he occasionally manages to have sent to him, vary in sentiment. Some are simply reporting the war movements; some are fanatical. Even the poet Akiko Yosano, Japan's most famous pacifist, declares the purity of dying for the Emperor in battle. Words written by fools. Chiune cannot look upon the streets of Harbin and liken them to a battle. He did not leave his home for this, did not miss his adored mother's passing for this.

Harbin Gakuin's code consists of three aims: Do not be a burden to others. Take care of others. Do not expect rewards for your goodness. Chiune cannot say in good faith that the Japanese forces here uphold any of them.

Less than a year after the Manchuko claims the Chinese Eastern Railway, he resigns from his post.

He packs his belongings in a bitterly cold and empty apartment. His friends express their surprise and disappointment at his decision. He will miss his baseball and ice hockey matches with them, the late-night games of Go. But they know it is not reason enough to stay.

He is not willing to compromise his integrity to be a part of the horrors his country is inflicting.

Chapter 6

Rachel goes about her work the next day with her mind firmly planted in Felka's living room, in the photo albums, in her grandmother's tears, in the visa – a piece of paper that has come to represent life. Being distracted doesn't mix well with a role requiring utmost attention.

'Rachel!'

Rachel looks up blankly at Kate, whose brows are raised at the four pills in her hand.

'Shouldn't that be two?' Kate prompts.

'Oh, my God!' Rachel gasps. 'Thanks, Kate.'

'You okay?' Kate asks as Rachel returns two of the pills.

'Yes. No. I think I need a break.'

'You can talk to us, you know,' Kate says gently.

'Just not feeling too well,' Rachel says evasively. She appreciates the sentiment, but how can Kate possibly understand what she's going through?

***

After Rachel tells the matron she has cramps and is given permission to take a break, she heads to the nearby park with her lunch and sits on a bench in the winter sun. She's too lost in thought to eat, and most of her sandwich goes to the hungry pigeons. She's spent the last twenty-four hours trying desperately to make sense of her hidden identity and a lifetime of secrets. She needs more information. More maybe than Felka, or certainly Michael, can give her. She searches her memory for anyone she knows who might be Jewish. The odd acquaintance, at most. Some of the regulars at 21 Espresso? A couple of the doctors at the hospital? And even then, how could she know who of them has endured what Rachel's family did? Who can she consult with?

The thought is like a lightning bolt: Hannah.

When she returns to the ward and begins her rounds, she goes to Hannah first. As Rachel feeds her, one small spoon of puree at a time, Rachel struggles with how to broach the topic. Whether she even should. Hannah has dementia and is barely lucid at the best of times. Indeed, feeding her is itself an exercise in patience; it takes nearly twenty minutes, with light strokes of her arm to soothe her, like a newborn chick being tended to by its mother. After the feeding ritual, Rachel brushes her wispy, white hair as Hannah stares into oblivion.

What is she seeing? What decade is she in? Rachel wishes so, so desperately that her mother was alive.

Rachel attempts to break the silence. 'Hannah?'

Hannah looks at her blankly, then smiles, gently.

Rachel tries again, very softly. 'Hannah? What was it like? Being Jewish?'

Hannah's eyes suddenly come into focus. 'Mireleh! It's nearly dark. Don't wander too far ... we can pick blueberries tomorrow, when it's safer...' She trails off.

Rachel attempts to bring her back. 'There were blueberry bushes where you lived? Mireleh is your daughter?'

'Lublin,' Hannah whispers.

'Lublin,' repeats Rachel. 'What is that, Hannah? A name?'

'Quick! Inside! Before they see! Quick! Under the floor.'

Rachel tries one last time. 'Can you tell me about the war? If you can ... would that be alright? My family was there. But they don't want to talk about it.'

Hannah's gaze slides to Rachel. 'Your family?'

'My father. My grandmother. They're from Warsaw.'

Hannah suddenly becomes clear, focused. A rare moment of lucidity grips her, but only a moment. 'Warsaw. Beautiful. A beautiful city. Far from Lublin.'

Ah, so Lublin is a town. She takes Rachel's hand, kisses it, and keeps holding it, nestled within her own. Rachel has never seen her expression so clear. 'My child, you do not want to know.'

Rachel softly strokes the tattoo. Asks the unaskable: 'What happened to you, Hannah?'

Hannah peers down at the numbers. 'Like cattle. One after the other.'

Rachel pushes. 'Where, Hannah?'

'There were no trees. There was no sun. Only darkness...'

Hannah begins to weep softly, curling up on her bed. Rachel feels sick with guilt, and covers her tenderly with her blanket before leaving her. She is beginning to glean some understanding of her family's wish to protect her. Just how horrible was it there, wherever Hannah was in that darkness, that she cannot speak of it?

But still, Rachel needs to know more.

***

'Jacek, darling! More dumplings!' Felka shouts across the small room with no compunction, no awareness. Michael winces. The friendly, middle-aged waiter obeys, bypassing the kitchen and hurrying over with a plate of steaming treats. They share a joke in Polish, laughing together. Michael understands it – Felka is playfully chastising the waiter for being overdressed in this tiny, shabby restaurant in a basement of a pre-war building near the city centre. Michael often speaks to Felka in Polish, his mother tongue. It's handy when they want to talk about things Rachel shouldn't hear.

As the waiter leaves, Felka shouts to him in English, 'You know we love your food – our favourite cuisine served at the only authentic European eatery in Sydney!'

Everyone in the restaurant – admittedly, fewer than twenty people, but still – turns to look.

'Are they paying you to be a walking, talking advertisement?' Michael mutters.

They are already mid-way through their meal. Felka continues to demolish a hefty serving of boiled beef with a thick dill sauce and the extra serving of fluffy dumplings to mop up the remnants. Michael has a plate of the sweet version of the dumplings, filled with fresh apricots and dusted with sugar.

They resume their conversation. Felka speaks, matter-of-factly, mouth half full. It always is. She loves her food. He is settling back into his meal when she says, as casually as if she were commenting on the weather, 'I told Rachel.'

'You *what?*' Michael snaps. Now it is him everyone turns to look at, but he's too angry to notice.

'She had to be told. Everything. It's gone too far. We made a mistake. We must fix it. Quickly.'

'Why would you do that? Why now?'

'Because. So I told her about Warsaw, about our escape. I showed her the visa.'

'Why?'

'Because.'

'Stop saying because! Why *now?*'

A game of word ping-pong.

She pauses, and then says briskly, 'I can't see her married there – in that *church.* With the creepy staring Jesus. *Oy vey!* An insult to the memory of my beloved parents. And she would find out anyhow, probably when it's too late.'

She shoves a dumpling into her mouth. Michael sits, so angry he can't speak. Felka continues with a full mouth. 'It was your idea. Not mine. Not Shirley's. Not Shirley's parents. I went along, I had no choice. What was I going to do? Lose you? Lose contact with my granddaughter?'

'Don't give me that guilt trip,' he manages. 'You know why we did it. You saw how bad it got for us in Europe.'

'It was a mistake. One we must fix. So we must start by going to Japan.'

Felka dabs her mouth with the napkin. Michael rubs his eyes. 'Japan again? Mum, what the hell are you talking about?'

'I got a letter. Sugihara has been found alive. That's why I want to take my trip. A reunion is taking place. And you *could* come. You should come.'

Michael can't say a word. Not only is he speechless, but his body feels numb.

'Maybe Rachel should come too,' Felka adds thoughtfully. 'Get her away from Yanni. Change her mind about marrying. About converting.'

Finally, he finds his voice. 'Why would you go back there? For what?'

Felka levels her gaze at him. It's formidable. As she speaks, she punctuates each word with a jab of her finger. 'We owe him our lives, Michael! Or have you forgotten?'

***

Rachel pushes the imposing iron gate forward. Its rusty hinges creak, in need of oil. It's morning at the local synagogue, a place she's passed many times before without a second thought. At this time of the day, it's quiet, deserted. A foreign place. It's strange to think that Rachel has never been inside one before, a realisation that sits oddly given how many times she's been inside a church.

She walks up the stone steps and into the lobby. Ahead of her are two sets of glass doors, with large brass handles. To the left and right are stairs, with a wooden sign at the bottom of each: *Ladies' section upstairs.*

Rachel climbs the left staircase, opens the door at the top. Rows of seats fill the balcony, which is a 'U' shape overlooking the level below. All the seats downstairs face the front of the synagogue, where a handsome wooden lectern stands in front of a small structure, concealed by a curtain embroidered with foreign lettering. It must be Hebrew, Rachel deduces, and feels a twinge in her chest that she can't read it. Above the curtain flickers an electric light, mimicking a candle's flame.

She sits on one of the plush red velour seats, gazing out over the room, taking it in. She's overcome by a welcome sense of peace. It's not just that the room is empty, nor how it seems to swallow sound, swaddling her. It's this sense of history, calmness, spirituality that seeps from the walls. This synagogue may be new, compared to those in Europe, but its history is old. Rachel is but one of many who has come through its doors, seeking answers to age-old questions.

It occurs to Rachel that Felka and Michael must have passed this synagogue, and others like it, many times without entering. Or have they snuck in? Rachel's never felt a connection to religion, but she thinks if Felka hasn't been here, it must have hurt her terribly, looking through the doors and never coming in.

Rachel retreats downstairs, searching for the rabbi. She finds an office off to the left of the entrance and asks the secretary sitting inside if she can speak with the rabbi.

'Are you a member of the congregation?'

'No,' Rachel replies quietly.

'Good morning, young lady,' a man says, before the secretary can respond. 'I'm Rabbi Brasch. I'm in training here. How can I help?'

He doesn't look the way Rachel thought he would. Stereotypical images of Orthodox Jews with heavy black coats and hats, and curls of hair, give way to an ordinary-looking youngish man in a dark suit, sporting a simple round cap on the crown of his head.

'My name is Rachel,' she says awkwardly. 'Rachel Margol—Margol*in*. I'm Jewish. I guess. I only just found out.'

She can feel the secretary's eyes burning into her.

'You'd like to reconnect with your faith?' the rabbi says carefully.

'Yes. No.' Rachel sighs. 'I'd like to learn more about what happened to my family in the Holocaust. What it means to be Jewish.'

Rabbi Brasch ushers her into an office and closes the door. He beckons for her to take a seat in front of his desk, littered with books both in English and Hebrew.

He sits opposite her, leaning forward attentively. 'Start by telling me about them. Your family.'

Where to begin? 'I wasn't brought up Jewish, and I went to Catholic school. But I wasn't brought up to believe in anything in particular. My mother died when I was nine, and my dad's—' she pauses. 'I never really got a chance to ask questions about much.'

'I am very sorry,' he says gently. 'That's a tragic loss.'

'I just wish my parents had told me. Even if we didn't practise, or anything. I know they were worried about what people might say, but still,' she says, around the lump in her throat. 'I don't know who I am.'

The rabbi sighs. 'Some families believed that concealing their faith was the way to move forward and heal, so as never to be singled out again and to endure what we endured as a people. People did whatever they could to save themselves and their loved ones. Some even converted, gave their children to Christian families.'

'I feel betrayed,' she confesses. 'They've been lying to me my entire life.'

'Where exactly were they from? Do you know who they lost?'

'Warsaw. They left their families in 1939 and never saw them again.'

'That's very sad to hear. Do you know how their families died?'

Rachel shakes her head. 'My grandmother won't speak about it.'

The rabbi rolls up his sleeve, shows her the inside of his forearm. A tattoo, several numbers. Just like Hannah's. 'Do you know what this is?'

Rachel is surprised. 'I think so. It's to do with the Holocaust, isn't it? I'm a nurse – one of my patients has one. But she has dementia, I haven't been able to really ask her about it. I tried, but ... well...'

'Even if she was able to explain it, I'd be surprised if she did. This is a mark of someone who has endured and witnessed the unspeakable. I did too. I was quite young, so maybe I find it easier to talk about it. Do you know what a concentration camp is?'

'I've heard the expression. They mentioned them at school, but didn't really go into detail.'

He exhales. 'Jews from all over Europe were herded together into large labour camps. These tattoos were how they kept track of us and stripped away our identity. Numbers for identification, like cattle. They were very organised, the Germans. They needed to be. There were millions of us to exterminate, after all.'

He speaks lightly, clinically. Rachel dares ask. 'How did they ... do it?'

He doesn't respond immediately, and Rachel knows that, as with Hannah, she's pushed too far. He says eventually, 'If you'd like to learn more, I can suggest some books.'

'Thanks,' says Rachel. 'That would be great. Um, I have another question – do you know about a man named Sugihara? He was a Japanese diplomat in the embassy in Lithuania at the time. He and a Dutch consul issued thousands of visas to Jews so they could flee to Japan and on to Curacao.'

The rabbi looks shocked. 'No, I haven't – Sugihara, you say?'

'Yes. He disappeared after the war, but someone, a survivor, tracked him down. My grandmother wants to go to Japan and thank him.'

'Lithuania was a terrible, terrible place for the Jewish population. It is a brave thing to do. To face the past again.' He holds her gaze. 'If you want to learn more about your heritage, your family, you should consider going with her.'

'I'll think about it,' Rachel says, and means it.

The rabbi adds, 'May I ask how you came to find out about your heritage?'

'I'm engaged to a Greek man. A non-Jew. I was going to convert for him. My grandmother said she couldn't let me do it without knowing the truth.'

'Rachel,' he says carefully. 'There is much fear among Jews of assimilation. Your family may have chosen this path, but it sounds like your grandmother is now understanding the ramifications of it. Once you marry out of the faith, you are gone to them. Neither you or your children will ever be accepted by them as part of the family again.'

'Oh,' Rachel says in a small voice.

The rabbi nods. 'It's a very big decision. One you shouldn't make without consideration. It sounds to me like you need to go to Japan.'

Chapter 7

The Roma Theatre on George Street, Sydney's downtown area. It's Rachel's favourite cinema: lovely, intimate, with an impressive Art Deco interior. She and Yanni have come to watch *2001: A Space Odyssey.* Rachel would have preferred *Funny Girl,* or *The Party* with Peter Sellers, but she doesn't mind; she doubts she would have been able to pay attention to it anyway. As they line up for tickets, Rachel is bursting to tell Yanni about everything. She manages to keep it in until he compliments her dress.

'You look like a little Greek goddess.' Yanni smiles.

She can't contain herself. In the foyer, surrounded by people, in a rapid, quiet voice that he has to lean in to hear, she tells him.

'Grandma told me she and Dad are only alive because this Japanese man illegally issued my grandparents transit visas to Japan. This was in Lithuania, in 1940, after they fled Poland. They didn't come here in 1936 like I thought – bizarre, right? Anyway, apparently, there were hundreds of them waiting outside the Japanese embassy each day, they were so desperate to get out of Europe.' She pauses. She has his attention, and she can tell from his furrowed brow that he's reading into the subtext. She ploughs ahead. There can't be any confusion. 'The entire extended family left behind were murdered. In concentration camps. Do you know what I mean? But my family made it to Japan. They survived.'

He often wears an excellent poker face at work, a neutral look of warmth that reassures patients without giving them the wrong impression. He's wearing it now as he nods.

'I've lived my whole life not knowing any of this,' she tells him. 'Not knowing that I'm Jewish. They've kept this all from me.'

Yanni exhales. 'That's a lot to take in.'

'Yes,' she says, and finds herself smiling, lightened by her confession. But later, as they settle into the plush velvet cinema seats, she reaches for his hand, and he doesn't take it, letting his hand stay limp. She glances out of the corner of her eye. He's staring ahead, deep in thought. Her heart sinks.

After the film has finished, they order coffee and sorbet at an intimate cafe on Bayswater Road. It's a quirky little hole-in-the-wall, comprising only four tables with rickety, mismatched chairs. The walls are plastered with dated movie posters. It's the sort of place that lovers go and giggle together over their orders. But Yanni's responses to anything she throws at him are monosyllabic, curt.

'We should start looking at venues and choose a date soon,' she tries. 'Spring is a busy time for weddings.'

'Sure.'

'Yanni, what's going on? If you're having problems, I want to help you solve them. Isn't that what a marriage is all about?'

He smiles faintly – the most affection she's got all night – and pats her hand. 'It's okay. Thank you. I just have a lot on my mind.'

'Is this about me being Jewish? Is it a problem?'

Yanni takes too long to answer, and her chest clenches. 'From my perspective, not so much. But I think we need to talk to my family.'

***

Sophia and Dimitri are surprised to see them, but invite them both into the living room to talk. Where she once felt warmth, excited to be joining the family and all its stories, now she feels claustrophobic. She notices the abstract painting, the fashionable coloured vase, a shag pile rug. Quality items strategically placed to complement an interior: *We have made it in our new homeland, and we have assimilated.*

'Rachel has some news,' Yanni says as they sit down. Sophia and Dimitri turn to her, perhaps expecting something like *I'm pregnant,* or *I'm deathly ill.* Rachel has the sense that these situations might be preferable. She clears her throat.

'I'm Jewish,' she says. 'I just found out a few days ago.'

Sophia and Dimitri stare: first at Rachel, then at each other. Rachel shifts, wishing desperately that Yanni would say something, even reach out to her. He doesn't.

'You realise, Rachel,' Dimitri says eventually, 'This is very ... confronting news. Two vastly different faiths and histories coming together.'

Rachel nods, but something about the phrasing irks her. Why is it confronting that two long, storied faiths should come together?

'Marriage is difficult,' Sophia adds. 'You are a lovely girl, but these differences bring new...' She pauses. Rachel can sense she is grappling for an inoffensive way to phrase it, whatever 'it' is. 'New ... challenges. How would your children be brought up, for instance?'

This isn't going to work, Rachel realises, as Yanni refuses to meet her gaze. The thought brings tears to her eyes.

Dimitri clears his throat. 'Conversion is still an option, if you are both serious about this union.'

Sophia puts a hand on Dimitri's shoulder. 'We will make some tea. Maybe you two should talk for a bit, yes?'

After they've left the room, Rachel looks to Yanni, who is leaning forward, head in his hands. *Conversion?* There is, of course, no question that it would be

Rachel converting, which Yanni confirms as he finally addresses her.

'Rachel, this is serious. No one in my family has ever married a ... *would* you consider it? Converting?'

Rachel swallows. Yanni's parents are in the kitchen, speaking in low voices. In Greek, she guesses. Even if she could hear them, she wouldn't understand. Behind the sick feeling in her gut, the fear of a suddenly uncertain future, there's anger. Why are they punishing her for something totally beyond her control?

Yanni is looking at her. She licks her lips. 'I know nothing about being Jewish. I don't know if I *want* to be a Jew. I've always considered myself Christian, if only because it's what I know from school, from friends. I don't know. I guess if I had to convert, for us. Maybe I *would* rather be Greek Orthodox...' she trails off, and there's a second when Yanni looks hopeful. A second when she has an option to take another path. But she keeps going. 'But the one thing I know for certain is that I can't make the decision right now. I have no idea what I'd be deciding *between!* And if I prefer the Jewish faith, then what? Would *you* consider converting ... for me?'

Yanni's face falls. Sophia returns with some tea, followed by Dimitri. As they sit, Sophia sees Yanni's expression, and sighs, turning to face Rachel.

'Rachel, dear, there are many differences between your family and ours. If we all agree to this union, you would need to entirely embrace our way of life for it to work. Is that what you want?'

She pauses. Rachel can't answer that. How could she? She finds herself tearing up.

'Dimitri and I think you need to consider your options very carefully,' Sophia continues, looking at her with great compassion. 'You need to work out whether you want to follow your own traditions or take up ours. You are very young, and have so much still to learn and explore. This is a big decision, one that could cause everyone involved much heartache either way, yes?'

Rachel can't ignore the truth to her words, and nods. It hurts, though, that Yanni says nothing. That he doesn't make some statement about overcoming differences. She looks at him, and he looks almost like a little boy: curled in on himself as his mother speaks for him. The idea that she may be about to lose him – his big strong arms and smile, how he wraps himself around her – makes her feel sick.

Felka once made a joke about Yanni being a decade her senior: *A father figure. I understand, my darling. But it's not always a good idea. You will end up being a nurse in your personal life. Is that what you want? To be feeding mushy pumpkin to a toothless, drooling old man in a nappy while you still have life in you?* But she doesn't understand how starved Rachel is for it, the certainty he offered. Rachel can still remember how her mother had less and less energy as the cancer sapped her life. Rachel would quietly open her door and tiptoe in, climb into bed and cuddle her, attempt to read a passage from her latest book, but Shirley would doze off in the process. Rachel would talk to her about her day and, even though her eyes were closed, Shirley would always nod.

An unwavering devotion. Something she thought she and Yanni had.

He meets her gaze, and her hurt is somewhat soothed by how clearly torn he is. It would be horrible if she were the only one confused and hurting.

There is little left to say. Sophia and Dimitri give Rachel warm, sorrowful embraces before Yanni drives her to Felka's house. The ride is excruciating. Quiet, leaden. When he pulls up to the kerb in front of her house, neither of them gets out immediately.

'I think I need to go to Japan with my grandmother,' she says eventually. He finally takes her hand then, and she tears up. 'I need to figure out who I am before I decide. Before *you* can decide.'

'I understand,' he says roughly. 'I'll wait for you.'

She nods, and leans over to kiss him – but not on the mouth, taking in the unfamiliar feel of his skin. And it occurs to her – till then she hadn't even known the feel of his rough cheek against her lips. It is so impersonal that she shudders. From lover to acquaintance in an hour.

And then she leaves.

***

Felka is in the middle of some late-night cooking when Rachel comes in. Her hands are wrist-deep in minced meat mixed with egg, parsley, salt and pepper. She's trying to get out a bit of egg shell that's made it into the mix. Her fingers – chubby, ageing, heading towards arthritic – are not what they used to be.

Extra crunch, Felka decides after chasing through the slippery mixture. She gives up and raises her head to see Rachel standing there. Her face is tear-stained, distant.

'What is it, darling?' Felka asks immediately.

'The engagement is off.'

Felka's first response is pure relief, but she reins it in. 'Just a second, pupelle. Then we can talk.'

Felka tips the mince out into a baking dish, pats it into a log and shoves it into the hot oven. A quick wash of the hands, and she's ready; she beckons for Rachel to come and sit on the couch. Rachel sits down slowly, gazing at the photos on display around the lounge room, all from after they came to Australia. Now that the truth is out, Felka wonders if it's time to bring out those photos she treasures, from her childhood, from Michael's childhood, from their time in Japan.

'I'm sorry to hear this, Rachel,' she says seriously. Her relief has come at the cost of her granddaughter's heartbreak after all. 'These people, Greeks, they don't understand. They are not foreign like we are foreign. You don't fit in. They see that. They don't really want Jews.'

'Yanni isn't like that,' she argues. 'Neither are his parents. You can't generalise.'

Felka keeps her voice level. 'I can. I lived it. I lost everyone. You lose trust when you lose so much. You can't understand. I can't expect you to.'

'Well, you're no better – you don't want Greeks either!'

'Rachel...'

'What's the point of being saved, what was the point of Sugihara doing what he did, if you're too scared to be who you are? You were saved, but you're still running!'

'Jews run because we learn anyone can become a Jew-hater.' She touches Rachel's beautiful thick mane of hair. She lets the locks fall through the gaps in her fingers, then she lifts Rachel's chin up, so they meet each other, eye to eye. 'Pupelle, you do not understand anti-Semitism. The hatred at the level we knew. No one stood up for us as we went from being considered people to pests. Not our neighbours, not our friends, not our co-workers. Many even participated in our persecution! Do you know what a betrayal that is? Gentiles all have the capacity to turn. Sophia and Dimitri and Yanni – now you are not only not Greek, but also a Jew. I'm not saying they hate Jews. But you are different. People are scared of different.'

'If I don't convert,' Rachel says. 'It will be over. And I doubt he'd convert for me. Don't you want me to be happy?'

'Rachel,' Felka says, trying not to be exasperated. Trying to remember what it was like when she was that young. 'Of course I want you to be happy. But you are so young to be getting married, let alone converting! You love Yanni, I know. But if you marry him without exploring all the other parts of your life, he *will* be your entire life. There will be no room for who you could be!'

'I thought you wanted me to get married,' Rachel mutters.

'I do, so long as he is the right man for you! Yanni is a nice man, but if you want to be Jewish – God willing, I hope you do! – it is a part of you he will never be able to accept.'

Rachel tears up, and Felka rubs her back. She waits patiently as her granddaughter struggles to find the words. 'Why did you have to tell me now, Grandma?' The words are a wail. Felka feels like she's a decade younger once more, comforting a young Rachel over her mother's death. The sort of grief and confusion that unhinges things.

'When you face certain things at my age, certain ... truths, you think about making things right. The church was the straw that broke the legs of the camel. You know this saying?'

Rachel manages a smile. 'The camel's back, Grandma.'

'That's what I said,' Felka says confidently, and Rachel gives a watery chuckle.

'You make it sound like you're dying. All that's happened is I got engaged.'

Felka relents. It's time. 'I am.'

'You're what?'

'Dying. I'm dying. So I must fix everything before I go.'

Rachel is staring at her, tears forgotten. 'It's not asthma, is it.'

'Cancer, the doctor said. So that's it.'

Rachel gasps. 'How long, Grandma? What stage? Did they say a number?'

'Stage, schmage. You think I listened? He says be careful, that I can't travel, that if I go I won't come back. I can't drink, I can't do this, I can't do that. I said, I'll die when I die. I'll die living, thank you very much! *Finita la commedia!*'

Rachel shakes her head and tears up again. Felka does as well, despite her bravado. So much to fix, so little time. She pulls Rachel to her, wrapping her arms around her and holding her granddaughter's head to her chest.

'You are a deep thinker,' she tells Rachel. 'You are a smart girl. My parents, God rest their souls, would be turning in their graves to know that they died in vain. They would say what you just said: "Felutkah, look what you have done! Your granddaughter would have chosen faith, strength, been courageous. She is a Margolin. Margolin women are survivors."' She shakes her head, holds Rachel tighter, desperate to make her understand. 'I didn't want to, Shirley didn't want to. Michael forced us. To hide it. He was so worried you would get hurt. But now, look what it's done! Yanni's parents are right. Marriage or not, you have to be educated.'

'I'm coming to Japan with you,' Rachel mumbles into her chest.

'You're what?'

Rachel breaks the hug, looking Felka in the eye. 'I'm coming with you. We can thank Sugihara together.'

'*Oy vey,*' Felka says, chest swelling. Rachel doesn't think she's heard Felka use this term before, but it seems oddly natural now. 'You know what? Lovely. Yes. We will go to Japan. I hoped you would. I was not sure I had the courage! But with you, I think I will.'

'Good. And you can accept whatever I decide. Because you're going to dance at my wedding even if it is to Yanni. You're all I have. From the time I was born, you promised me you'd dance at my wedding. You didn't make any provisos that included a Jewish groom.'

'I will try,' Felka says, if only because she doubts she'll live long enough. Rachel's brow furrows: not good enough, for either of them.

But before she can say anything, Michael says from the door, 'What's going on?'

'Michael?' Felka says in surprise.

'I wanted to talk to you,' he says gruffly. 'What is it?'

Rachel looks at Felka, who breaks the news. 'Rachel and Yanni are postponing the engagement. She wants to go away and think about what she wants. Because we're Jewish.'

'Grandma tried to explain things,' Rachel adds quickly. 'To help me understand why you hid it.'

Now, if ever, is the time for Michael to show some compassion. Felka gazes at him, begging him to give his daughter some hint of reassurance. But his stare is blank.

'Well ... now you know,' he says eventually. 'And now that it's out, you'll see who your allies are. And it won't be your friends, or Yanni. No gentile wants a Jew.'

'You're just as bad as Grandma,' Rachel snaps, and Felka winces. 'You're bigots, the both of you!'

Michael snorts. 'So you've never heard anyone say anything bad to a Jew? Or even about them?'

Felka explodes at him in Polish. 'You can't comfort your only child after she breaks off her engagement?!' Rachel looks to her for a translation that doesn't come.

Michael snaps back in his mother tongue. 'It wouldn't have happened if you had kept your mouth shut for once in your life!' He brings his hand down on the mantlepiece, knocking a frame, which in turn bumps Felka's kintsugi vase, sending it flying onto the floor.

Rachel gasps next to her. Michael flinches, mouth opening. The oven timer goes off. The meatloaf, Felka thinks distantly, staring down at the vase's pieces. It was her mother's, and broken on the boat to Japan. A kind craftsman in Kobe had repaired it for her, laying the gold leaf on with such care that Felka had felt it in her heart. And here it is, shattered again.

She looks up at her son, eyes dry. She has failed him. She will not fail Rachel.

'I am going to Japan,' she says in English now. 'And Rachel is coming with me.'

Michael doesn't apologise. She didn't expect him to. 'Rachel doesn't need to go with you,' he says, also in English.

'I'm a nurse,' Rachel snaps. 'I can take care of her. And I want to. I want to meet Sugihara.'

'What does being a nurse have to do with it?' Michael says, bewildered.

'You didn't tell him?' Rachel says to Felka, who can't bring herself to meet either of their eyes. 'What is with this family and keeping secrets? She's dying, Dad. Terminal cancer.'

Michael is astounded. An unexpected chill grips him. Rachel continues. 'Hiding in your office. Do you even have the faintest idea what's going on in your family? Do you ever ask? It's not healthy, Dad! You never talk about the war, you never talk about Mum. You've never once asked me how I feel, if I miss her, if I'm doing okay!'

Michael can only stare at the two of them. Felka is astonished, and she can't help but be proud of how loud Rachel is being. Of the space she's taking up, swelling to fill the room.

'I don't know who I am, I don't know what I am, but I do know one thing: if you don't confront what happened to you, our family will never heal. At least

Grandma's trying, by going to Japan. You'd be stupid not to come with us.'

'We can't all just get up and go wherever we want, whenever we want,' Michael says. 'I have a business to run.'

'Your mother is *dying,*' Rachel howls at him, shaking, 'and all you can think about is your *fucking denim factory?*'

The ensuing silence is profound. Rachel and Michael stare at each other. Rachel's chest is heaving, tears of rage dripping down her face. Michael stands so still that he could be hewn from stone.

He opens his mouth, closes it. *Come on, son,* Felka urges him. But he can't. He just doesn't have it in him.

'Do what you want, both of you,' he says finally. 'I don't care anymore. Just leave me out of your nonsense. I tried to protect you your whole life. We got lucky here. This country's been good to us. And now that's down the drain. Your neighbours, your friends, they'll turn on you. Don't think they can't. Ours did.' He turns to Felka and adds in Polish: 'And I hope you're ready for what she'll find in Japan.'

'Will you stop trying to hide what you're saying, *please?*' Rachel says, her frustration barely under control.

Michael's words have instilled fear in Felka. She hadn't thought of who they might see in Japan. But does it really matter? She only has so much time left. And if Rachel finds out the whole truth, then ... well. Whatever happens will happen. She tilts her chin up defiantly, and he shakes his head, then walks out.

Rachel immediately begins picking up the vase's pieces. 'I can't believe him,' she mutters. 'I can't believe I thought he could change.'

Felka joins her, collecting the shards. The damage isn't as bad as it looks; the porcelain largely broke along the original fault lines.

It can be fixed.

She glances up at Rachel. Her eyes are tear-swollen and her cheeks are flushed.

'You swore,' she says reprovingly, delightedly. When Rachel looks up, clearly about to apologise, Felka shakes her head. 'You were magnificent.' She beams. 'Such vim and vigour! You are no longer my little pupelle, I think. Truly, you are a Margolin!'

'Don't you mean a Margol?' Rachel says – snide, but with the hint of a smile.

'No, a proud, Jewish Margolin.'

'He deserved it,' Rachel says, tiredly, but she's smiling. It turns to a frown when she starts sniffing. Felka can smell it too.

'*Oy vey!*' she gasps. 'The meatloaf!'

***

It goes without saying, of course, that Rachel stays the night at Felka's. For all her throat-shredding anger earlier, she doesn't think she could possibly face her father right now.

You've never heard anyone say anything bad to a Jew? Or even about them?

She was about to say *no* when she remembered Thomas: *Don't be such a Jew.* Her heart caught in her throat.

Rachel lies on the couch, covered in one of Felka's furry blankets as she thinks about this. She can't navigate the world as she did only a few days ago. Felka and Michael seem to think anti-Semitism is as pervasive as it is inevitable. But she's sure the other Jews she's met don't think like that. Or is that just the front they present to the world?

Rachel sighs and turns over. Being Jewish was never something she had to even consider, and now it's suddenly the most important aspect of her life. It defines her, apparently. Whether she wants it to or not. So who was she before this big reveal, this life-changing event? Was she devoid of personality, identity? Was she simply a blank wall, ready to be painted, like the one at that party?

Just a nurse. That's how she had described herself to the woman who complimented her art. Is she still 'just' anything?

And what of this new facet that being Jewish brings? She thinks it's like a battered suitcase, bulging, packed full and bursting with a heritage of persecution, suffering and loss. A heavy piece of luggage to have to drag around her whole life. There's a part of her that wishes she had never picked it up, or that she could lug it to a train station, swap it for someone else's bag before boarding the train into the bold unknown.

She didn't ask for this legacy, and it wasn't something that was slowly, gently, osmotically transferred to her – through her mother's milk, through regular ritual, through bedtime stories or anecdotes from uncles and aunts at family gatherings. Like Yanni's clearly was. It was brutally thrust upon her, chained to her in perpetuity.

Rachel closes her eyes, takes a breath. She'll learn how to drag it along with all her other baggage, because she has to.

Because, she thinks, she wants to.

Chapter 8

The next day is blessedly uneventful, until Rachel comes into Hannah's room to see the woman on the floor, unconscious and contorted. She's cut her head open, perhaps on the bedframe. There's a gash in her forehead, blood dripping down her neck. Rachel kicks into emergency mode and rushes to her side. She's still breathing, eyes open.

'Hannah?'

No response. She stares vacantly at Rachel.

'Hannah. It's Rachel. Ruchalah, remember?' Rachel tries.

Hannah focuses on her. 'Ruchalah.'

Thank God. 'Yes, it's me. Are you okay? Did you fall?'

'Tripped on the rug,' she says. There's no rug in the room. Rachel's heart sinks. It's never good when dementia patients have their first big fall. It's possible it's more, too; something about her face doesn't look quite right.

'Silly rug,' Rachel says, plastering a smile on. 'Let's get you cleaned up and off the floor, shall we? I'll be right back.'

She goes to the nearest nurse station and lets them know what's happened as she collects a cloth and some bandages.

'Second time this week,' the nurse says grimly to Rachel. 'Poor thing.'

Very likely more than a fall, Rachel concludes as she cleans the last little bit of Hannah's wound. She's considering whether she should get someone to help lift her up when a doctor comes in. For a moment, she thinks it might be Yanni, and isn't sure how to react. But when she looks up properly, it's Thomas. Of course it is.

He says nothing as she struggles to help Hannah up. The moment the woman is sitting back in her bed, he pushes his way in front of Rachel before she even has a chance to step back. She watches as he takes Hannah's pulse and brings his stethoscope to her chest.

'Doctor,' she says. He doesn't look at her. 'This has happened twice this week. I'm thinking she's having transient ischaemic attacks.'

Thomas glances at her then. He raises an eyebrow but says nothing.

If she can yell at her father she can handle Thomas. 'Transient ischaemic attacks. Mini-strokes. That would be my guess, given the dementia. She doesn't suffer from low blood pressure or vertigo, and her balance is usually good. I see it in a lot of our elderly patients. It's possible she's heading for a significant event. She should be put on a blood thinner.'

Thomas rolls his eyes. 'Thank you, doctor. Excuse me – *nurse.* I disagree. She's just a little dehydrated. Give her an IV bag, would you?'

He swans out. Daringly, Rachel gives the finger to his back, and surprisingly, Hannah giggles. Rachel smiles widely.

'Let's get you comfortable,' Rachel says to her, checking the bandage is holding after helping her sit back. When she goes to organise the IV bag, she tells another nurse what she thinks and what Thomas says. The nurse shrugs.

'We have to do what he says' is her only response, and Rachel resists the urge to throw something.

***

The next morning, Rachel makes a detour from her normal rounds to pop into the Oncology department and check on Hannah, but she's not in her bed or the bathroom.

Rachel instinctively goes cold. She sees her colourful painting of the old woman leaning up against the window ledge. She was so proud of how it turned out, how well she'd caught the light on Hannah's face. She had brought it in to cheer her patient up, and some of the nurses had complimented it, even asked for commissions. But seeing it now, sitting there without its subject nearby, it issues a sense of foreboding. Like museum portraits of departed souls. She walks over to the nurses station. Sally's on today; Rachel's seen her around, and even if they don't know each other very well, Sally's usually on top of everything.

'Sally, I just came to see how Hannah is today. She fell yesterday.'

Sally shakes her head. 'She had a major stroke overnight, poor thing. She was taken to the ICU. I'm not sure how she went.'

She shouldn't, but Rachel races over to the other side of the building, into the ICU, and gets Hannah's room number. When she arrives, family members are huddled around a bed, weeping quietly. A rabbi consoles them softly. Rachel stands just outside the doorway, staring. There's an overwhelming sense of relief for this poor, traumatised woman, who has seen so much suffering and endured the worst humanity can unleash. She's at least finally free from the memories that taunted her. Rachel stands there a moment, watching them. Is this what it will be like for Felka? The thought is too much, and she turns away. The sadness turns to fury. If Thomas had just listened to her – if he wasn't such an *arsehole* —

When she finds him, he's sitting in the break room with several other doctors, all listening to the radio. She walks straight past them and stands in front of Thomas.

'Can I help you?' he drawls, crossing his arms.

'She's dead because of you,' Rachel tells him.

'What are you talking about?'

'Hannah. *The old Jew?* She had a massive stroke overnight. She's dead. You should have listened to me.'

He frowns, shakes his head. 'Doesn't mean you were right. The two incidents were likely completely unrelated.'

Rachel is aghast. 'Are you serious?'

'Yes, I am,' he says, and stands up. He towers over her, but she's too angry to feel small. 'And if you were actually a doctor, you'd understand that. Besides, what makes her so different to the other patients you've seen die? Is it *because* she's a Jew?'

'Thomas,' one of the other doctors says warningly.

Rachel jabs a finger into Thomas's chest, hard. He flinches, steps back, knocks into his chair. She advances. 'I don't know. Did you let her die *because* she's a Jew, Thomas? Or purely because you're an arrogant wanker?' she says. 'A shit doctor. That woman is dead, all because you wouldn't listen to me. Was it because I'm a nurse? Or is it because *I'm* a Jew?'

Thomas blinks, flushes.

'Yes, Thomas. I'm a Jew. Do you have a problem with that? Does anyone else?' she casts a glance around. None of them meet her gaze. Thomas's ears are dark red. 'That's what I thought,' she says, satisfied, and marches out. She's only shaking a little. In the past she'd have been a wreck. She wishes Felka could have seen her.

Maybe if everything with Hannah had happened earlier, or a few weeks later, when the truth had time to settle – but now? She's had enough. She's sick of other people ignoring her opinions and expertise and feelings.

She sits down at the station, scrawls on a piece of paper, and takes it down to Mrs Hutchings, the hospital matron. She's had some dealings with Mrs Hutchings before; she's harsh but fair. And indeed she is, when Rachel hands Mrs Hutchings her resignation letter, and explains to her what she didn't want to put in writing.

The woman's firm demeanour gives way to compassion as she learns of Rachel's grandmother's tragic past and terminal diagnosis; Rachel's unusual and compelling reason to want to accompany her on this significant journey; the situation with Yanni's family; Thomas's offensive behaviour and gross negligence as a physician.

'So' – she looks at Rachel with new eyes but, Rachel is pleased to see, no less respect – 'you're Jewish.'

'Yes,' replies Rachel, fatigued by the fact that every person she reveals her heritage to will react to the news in some way. 'Well, recently, at least.'

'This is quite a story,' Mrs Hutchings says. 'This Sugihara must be a very brave man. Alright. Well, good luck on your mission, Rachel. And all the best for your grandmother. Take good care of her, and of yourself, my dear.'

'Thank you, Matron. I will.'

The woman's eyes narrow. 'And I can assure you I will be having a word with the doctor concerned.'

The thought of Thomas being lambasted by Mrs Hutchings, ideally in a very public place, is immensely satisfying. It's just what she needs after the last few days, and she all but floats down to Susan's unit, just off Oxford Street in Darlinghurst, in walking distance of the hospital. It's Susan and Kate's shared day off, and the two of them often spend it lazing in Susan's garden. Indeed, as Rachel rounds the corner, the two of them are sitting on an old velvet lounge suite Susan rescued from the side of the road last year. The rear window of one of the units is cracked open and through it wafts a song Rachel recognises from the Doors' new album, *Waiting for the Sun.*

Her friends turn, smiling, as she approaches. Rachel gets down to brass tacks.

Rachel doesn't anticipate any of this fuss from Michael. They've barely exchanged any words since she yelled at him for his callousness. Indeed, he hasn't said a thing since he checked that Rachel had packed her passport and tickets before he drove her and Felka to the airport.

An announcement comes over the intercom: the flight to Japan will soon board and they must now head to customs.

Kate and Susan, at least, make her feel like she's going to be missed. They wrap her up in a huge hug that gets everyone teary.

'We want postcards, okay?' Susan tells her.

'Rachel?'

She turns. Yanni stands before her, handsome and lovely.

'We'll leave you to it,' Kate murmurs, glancing at him before giving her a final hug.

Susan does the same – 'Take care of yourself, please!' – and they head towards the exit.

'How did you...?' she asks as Yanni approaches her.

'Your dad,' he says simply. Rachel looks at Michael, who is watching them from his seat next to Felka, face neutral, arms crossed. 'How long do you think you'll be gone?'

'At least a few weeks. Maybe more. Felka and I might do a bit of travelling after.'

He nods. 'I heard about Thomas.'

'Oh,' Rachel says.

'And that you quit.' His eyes are questioning. Rachel doesn't know what to say. 'He's been put on suspension while they look into everything.'

'Good,' Rachel says, with a ferocity that surprises her. 'He's a dickhead.'

Yanni blinks. 'Yeah. I've heard him say some pretty awful stuff before.'

Rachel wants to ask, *so why didn't you say anything?* But Yanni keeps talking.

'What are you going to do when you get back? Job-wise, I mean.'

He sounds hopeful. She shakes her head gently. 'I don't know.'

'Okay,' he says after a moment. 'Promise me you'll call while you're over there?'

'Of course,' she says, and he wraps her in his arms. She closes her eyes, takes in his familiar cologne and the feeling of his chest. Her heart thumps painfully, and he leans in for a goodbye kiss. She offers her cheek, but he moves her face and their lips meet. It's soft, chaste. She can feel tears running down her cheeks. Not yet acquaintances. Still very much lovers.

'Take care of yourself,' he says gruffly, and she watches as he walks away. When he turns to look back, she waves, sees how he smiles and rubs at his eyes before continuing on.

Rachel walks towards Michael and Felka, who elbows Michael. He scowls at her, and then, unexpectedly, gives Rachel a hug. It's over before she even realises what's happening, the briefest squeeze.

Not meeting her eyes, he reaches into his suit pocket and pulls out a small box. He hands it to her. 'For your birthday.'

Rachel takes the gift. 'Thanks,' she says, utterly bemused. He nods at her, gives Felka a similarly awkward embrace, and then abruptly departs.

'Men,' Felka says. Rachel laughs; if she doesn't, she thinks she might cry.

Once they're sitting in their seats on the plane, Rachel opens his gift. A heart-shaped charm inlaid with rubies and diamonds; it must have been incredibly expensive, she thinks distantly.

'Very pretty,' Felka says, peering over, and helps Rachel put it on. She can see it sparkle in the reflection of her window. This tiny, bejewelled object represents a lifetime of love. There's no denying it is beautiful. There's no denying it is an out-reach of sorts.

But she cannot hug a necklace.

Chapter 9

A railway attendant pushes Felka firmly into a carriage crammed with bodies. She sees how Rachel is affronted when the attendant gives her the same treatment, and taps her granddaughter on the shoulder, pointing. Rachel deflates when she sees the other railway attendants doing the same for other commuters. As the doors close, through the glass panels, Felka can see the mass of the crowd moving like a colony of ants, each one efficiently going about their business – orderly, with clear intent. The Haneda Airport train station is clean, neat and sparse, save for the masses of bodies. Though it's busy, far busier than Felka remembers, it lacks the organised chaos of the stations back in Australia. And everyone seems to blend together. Nobody calls attention to themselves. In Sydney, there would be the odd drunk leaning against a wall, a paper bag concealing his poison in one hand, the other hand a crutch to prop him up; there'd be a busker or two in hippie gear belting out a Beatles favourite with a blanket spread out for a bedraggled dog; a rowdy group of office workers would be stumbling in heels and cackling their way to the platform.

Felka is immediately offered a seat, which she accepts happily. She grins up at Rachel, who is standing with their bags, trying to accustom herself to the mass of bodies pushing against hers.

When they get off at Tokyo Station, Felka takes the lead as they wander in search of a sign to their destination – the bullet train to Shin-Kobe Station. The bullet train is so new that it's not in the guidebook Felka bought when she booked the trip, and everything is in Japanese, of course. Felka can speak enough to get around, but reading it was never her strength.

She taps a passer-by, a respectable-looking middle-aged man. 'Konnichiwa.' She smiles. 'Bullet train wa doko desu ka?'

'Bullet train?' the man repeats, confused. Felka shrugs to indicate they are lost, and gestures at a nearby train and then makes a motion of speed.

'Ah, shinkansen.' The gentleman smiles. He points at a sign with a specific Japanese character, one Felka doesn't recognise. 'Ano kanji ni tadoru, shinkansen ni kimasu ne.'

'Wakarimashita.' Felka smiles as Rachel looks on in astonishment. 'Arigatou gozaimasu!'

'You can speak Japanese?' Rachel asks her as they follow the signs.

'Not as much as I used to be able to,' Felka replies, but is pleased by how Rachel looks at her in awe.

They arrive with plenty of time before the bullet train leaves. It looks strange, snub-nosed and flat, longer than most trains Felka has seen and far more futuristic. She gawps at it as they hand their luggage off to the guard, who carefully stows it.

The train astounds Felka. All those years ago, as Japan was beaten into submission, she would never have thought the country would produce such a marvel. She can't stop trying to take it in as they climb up, Felka with a few coughs, a few pauses, and a little help from Rachel. They find their seats easily and sit in the wide, comfortable chairs.

As they wait for the train to depart, Felka stares out the window at all the people passing by on the platform, wondering how much Kobe has changed since she and Michael left. Is the greengrocer she liked still on the corner near her old house? How about the hole-in-the-wall restaurant that did the most fantastic miso noodle soup? How many of her friends stayed behind? How many are still alive? She doesn't know Joshua Nishri, the man who sent the telegram, but she's glad he went to the effort of tracking her and everyone else down to pass on the news about Sugihara.

They begin to move. The train is too fast to make sense of the landscape, but Felka remembers the traditional houses, the rice paddies, the farmers, the different types of trees, the rickshaw drivers. Rachel has been quiet since they left Sydney, no doubt worn out physically now as well as emotionally. When Felka begins sharing memories of Japan with her, though, she is pleased to see how Rachel leans in, wanting to hear more. She worries terribly about what will happen to Rachel. Her granddaughter deserves so much more than Michael and Yanni. But when she remembers how Rachel stood up for herself with Michael, and with this Thomas character, Felka finds herself relaxing a little. Rachel may be hurting now, longing for Yanni, but Felka can see the excitement swelling in her granddaughter.

In the middle of describing the texture of mochi, Felka sees how Rachel's eyes are glazing over. She takes Rachel's hand.

'Oh, you must be exhausted,' Felka says.

'I'm fine,' Rachel protests, but her eyelids are drooping. 'Keep going.'

Felka covers Rachel's hand. 'Sleep, pupelle. I'll wake you when we arrive.'

Rachel dozes off even as Felka says this. It reminds her of how she used to fight to stay awake when she was a child, as if she would be chastised if she fell asleep. All it took was permission in the form of a story, and she'd be out. Michael was the same. Felka keeps hold of Rachel's hand, gazing out the window as the landscape whips by. Her throat feels tight, and she coughs into a handkerchief she stowed in her purse. When she removes it from her mouth, it's speckled with blood. She quickly scrunches it up, conceals it in her pocket. This trip must be perfect, Felka thinks, praying that other secrets will stay away.

***

Kobe is a bustling city, so Rachel is surprised by how their hotel sits amid a landscape of beautiful Japanese trees and gardens. The hotel exterior itself isn't particularly stunning; it's simple but understated, modernist.

'We will see plenty of lovely old buildings,' Felka says to Rachel as they walk inside. 'Besides, traditional hotels only offer mats! I deserve a little luxury at my age, I think.'

Inside, the counter is unattended. Felka slaps the bell several times. Seconds later, a young man in uniform comes out of the back office and, in broken but comprehensible English, enquires, 'May I help?'

Felka swaps to Japanese, and the man, pleasantly surprised, responds in kind. Rachel takes the hotel in while he and Felka back-and-forth on the check-in process. It's as elegantly nondescript on the inside as it is on the outside, but clearly of a high quality. It's largely empty at this time of day, guests having long since left to enjoy the city. Rachel's gaze passes over the cleaners going about their duties and several foreign businessmen conversing in the corner, and lands on a Japanese woman in a chic baby-blue dress and, despite the heat, stockings. She sits on one of the lounges near the entrance. Her thick hair is perfectly cut into a bob that sits at the curve of her jaw, framing a pretty heart-shaped face with big dark eyes. She catches Rachel's eye and smiles; it lights up her face. Rachel finds herself smiling back.

'That's the group's tour guide,' Felka says to her. 'Mizumi, I think her name is.'

The woman stands up as the male attendant waves her over. She walks so gracefully that Rachel feels clumsy just looking at her.

'I am Mizumi,' she says, and bows. Felka bows back and elbows Rachel, who hastily does the same. Mizumi smiles at her again. 'Welcome to Japan. To Kobe. My city.'

'Lovely to meet you, Mizumi,' Felka says. 'I'm Felka Margolin, and this is Rachel, also Margolin. My granddaughter.' Rachel likes hearing her new, old name. 'She's twenty-one – you can't be too much older than her, so I'm hoping you two will be great friends!'

'As do I,' Mizumi says. Up close, Rachel thinks she might be in her mid to late twenties at most. 'Are you tired from your journey? Australia is a long way.'

'Never too tired to see new things!' Felka exclaims, and adds, 'What a beauty you are, my dear! You must fight off the men with a broomstick!' Mizumi smiles shyly. Rachel is embarrassed once again by her grandmother's lack of discretion.

'Well, if you have the energy to go sightseeing, you could drop your bags in your room and I will show you around the city? If there is anywhere you would like to go in particular today, I would be happy to take you. You are the first to arrive.' Her English is perfect, with the lightest American accent around the edges. Rachel wonders where she might have learned it.

She turns to Felka, who looks almost hesitant.

'Do you know the Jewish cemetery?' Felka asks Mizumi.

'Yes. It is easy to get to from here.'

Rachel eyes her grandmother, confused. Felka's face is unusually neutral. 'I have memories of something important from a long time ago. I want to see if it is still there.'

'Of course,' Mizumi says, inclining her head. The man behind the counter offers them two room keys and gestures towards the staircase.

'No lift?' Rachel says, thinking of Felka's lungs.

'It is only one flight,' Mizumi says. Perhaps she sees how Rachel is glancing at Felka, because she adds, 'I will help you with your bags.'

Rachel takes her own bag, and Mizumi takes Felka's, ignoring her ensuing protests. Mizumi must be stronger than she looks; Rachel knows for a fact Felka's bag is quite heavy, but Mizumi doesn't make a sound, simply hefting the bag as they begin to ascend. After three steps, Felka stops to cough. She catches her breath, and they continue. She pauses again. Another cough. Mizumi waits patiently.

Rachel tries to make light of it. 'They are pretty steep – I'm sweating. It's been a long day.'

Felka pats her on the arm, and after a few more minutes of stopping and starting, they reach the landing. The moment the suitcases are stowed, Felka turns to Mizumi.

'I am starving,' she announces.

'Grandma doesn't just get "hungry",' Rachel says to Mizumi, by way of explanation.

'I'm *really* hungry!' Felka agrees. Mizumi laughs. 'You don't understand. If I don't eat now, I will die. Right here. On this spot. And then you will have to deal with the consequences! I am dizzy. Can you see?'

'You can't *see* dizzy, Grandma. It's not that type of symptom.'

'You're not looking close enough. Look!'

Mizumi is clearly amused. 'So, what would you like for lunch?'

Felka, already lit like a bulb, somehow gathers a further surge of energy. 'Miso. Udon. Sashimi. Sushi. Everything!'

***

The small eatery Mizumi suggests just around the corner is decorated simply, traditionally, featuring a dented wooden countertop, well-used wooden stools, rows of sake jars and small tumblers arranged on shelves behind the counter.

There's only one staff member in the entire place. He's elderly but clearly fit: wiry brown arms protrude from a simple checked shirt, covered by a clean but yellowing apron. His arms look like nobbled branches: an extension of the lined, aged wooden counter, as though they have grown out of it over time. Most of the patrons are men in their forties, who politely glance at the foreigners before turning back to their food. Rachel can't make out what it is they're eating. There's some rice, but the accompaniments are unfamiliar. Some kind of charred soybeans in an oily sauce, maybe? Some raw seafood with tentacles – octopus, perhaps?

Mizumi orders for them as Felka gratefully takes a seat at a table. Between Mizumi's excellent English and Felka's own varying levels of language mastery, Rachel is feeling inadequate. She learned a few words of Latin at school, but it's not exactly relevant in day-to-day life.

The owner/waiter/chef brings them three bowls of steaming noodles in soup, then returns to deftly slicing salmon into wafer-thin morsels. Rachel stares at the chopsticks and deep, oddly shaped spoon before her.

How exactly is she going to get food into her mouth with these two sticks of wood?

Her grandmother laughs, picking her own up. 'Like this, pupelle.' She clacks them together; though her fingers are old, knobbly, she handles them with ease. 'Hold them higher up!'

Rachel fiddles with them, blushing as Mizumi watches on. She can't get a good grip; either the chopsticks clatter from her fingers or she feels her hand cramping up. She can't imagine how she's going to be able to finish her bowl of noodles. The fish arrives.

'Here. Look. Watch.' Felka takes one piece of salmon sashimi with chopsticks – she adds nothing – and gifts it to her palate. 'Start with this, not the noodles. This is easier to learn on.'

Mizumi agrees. 'Your grandmother is correct.'

Rachel tries with a piece of salmon, but a dip in soy sauce goes awry. It drops from her grip and splashes black dots of sauce – testament to her failure – around the small dish.

Felka laughs. 'No, no – like this.'

A demonstration doesn't help; there's another plonk of fish into too much sauce, and a bigger laugh from Felka. 'Do you want to try again?'

'No,' Rachel says grumpily. She can feel her stomach rumbling.

'May I?' Mizumi asks, reaching out. Rachel nods, and Mizumi gently corrects her grip.

'Now, like this,' Mizumi says, picking up her own chopsticks. 'You should feel how the bottom chopsticks rests between your knuckle and thumb.'

Rachel gathers herself for further embarrassment, and is surprised when she picks the sashimi up easily. 'Oh!'

'Well done,' Felka praises.

'Thanks,' Rachel mumbles to Mizumi, who nods, before turning to her own food. Bolstered, Rachel tries with the noodles, one at a time, pleased that she's no longer making a fool of herself.

'Mr Nishri mentioned to me that your group all came to live in Japan during World War II,' Mizumi says to Felka. 'He did not explain, though. Do you mind telling me more?'

Never one to turn down the opportunity to weave a story, Felka begins talking. Rachel has heard it all now, of course, but Mizumi is completely transfixed – not just by the tale itself but also by how Felka tells it with such colour and description. Rachel finds herself enjoying Mizumi's enthusiastic reactions almost more than the story: she responds at exactly the right moments. A laugh, a gasp, a lean in. Her eyes sparkle with it; at one point she leans over to Rachel and says, 'Your grandmother has such a way with words!'

Rachel does her best to give Felka her attention too, despite her fatigue. She doesn't know how many times she'll get to hear this, how Felka punctuates and accentuates every word to such a degree. A German is not simply a German, he is a filthy kraut! They didn't just walk in the snow, they trudged in the freezing, icy muddy slush! Though Rachel doubts the other patrons can understand too much of her grandmother's story, they still seem drawn in by the emotions on show. Felka could have been an actress. Rachel can't imagine a world without her.

***

The afternoon streets of Kobe are alive in a way Rachel has never seen – the sheer volume of people in Japan feels a little overwhelming. And, of course, it looks so different from Sydney; traditional houses with upturned roofs sit side by side with tall, modern apartment and office buildings, hemming them in.

Businessmen zip past them. Women dart by with the same urgency: workers, mothers, nurses. Some men are dressed for the docks. Interspersed among them are older men and women – sitting and chatting, running stores, moving about slowly with canes. And some younger people – in jeans and t-shirts – drift past at a more measured pace.

Felka takes great pleasure in pointing out the Japanese characters she recognises on signs. 'That's a chemist's,' she says of one. Another hangs above a shop a few doors down. 'Laundry. It's a laundry,' she says proudly. She is right. The heat from the dryers seeps out onto the street and the scent of freshly washed clothing hangs in the air as they pass. Mizumi praises each of these, and Rachel listens as she explains other characters that Felka is unfamiliar with. She would never have thought so much meaning could be taken from these characters that Mizumi calls 'kanji'; that they can be broken down and built back up so efficiently.

Felka's arm is entwined with Rachel's as they walk. Rachel is still hurt by the revelations of the last few weeks, of course, but the excitement of being here in Kobe pushes it to the back of her mind. So much is different and interesting: little children on their way to school wear uniforms that almost look like army clothing, consisting of a peaked cap and black blazer done up to the neck with round brass buttons; several women pass by in traditional dress, wearing wooden sandals and lush, colourful kimonos that seem to have leaped straight out of one of her grandmother's woodblock prints. Even the dog breeds are unfamiliar, Rachel marvels, as they pass by a short-haired dog with a sandy coat and curled tail. And it's all just less than a day's journey from home. As they meander, Rachel finds herself placing these things on canvases in her head, already wondering how she can re-create this new world as a piece of art.

As they stroll, Felka points out places she's been. Places that have changed. Places they should return to later. Mizumi is impressed she remembers so much.

'Oh!' Felka says suddenly, coming to a stop. 'I think my old apartment is down this street.'

The further they go along this street, the more the air seems to change. Sounds rise from a parallel street on their right: shouting and the chanting of slogans. Rachel tries to stay engaged as Felka resumes pointing out places she remembers. But what is it, this noise? The voices are young. As they pass a narrow adjoining street, they hear even louder voices. They're chanting, shouting, singing.

Felka's curiosity pulls them further down the road. They finally see the source of all the noise: it's a protest.

'Vietnam?' Rachel asks. Mizumi shakes her head as Felka pauses to read the signs and listen to the chants.

'Students,' she tells Rachel, straining to listen, to understand the words being shouted. Rachel glances at Mizumi, who clearly wants to explain, but is restraining herself as Felka pushes her linguistic ability. More and more protesters rush past in jeans, t-shirts, overalls.

As they move towards the chaos, Rachel feels the tension of it, the gravity.

Felka translates some words: 'They are protesting about ... money?'

Mizumi elaborates, 'About university fees.'

'They want a ... a...' Felka can't finish her sentence; she begins coughing.

'They want free education,' Mizumi finishes for Felka. More coughs. Six. Seven.

Rachel manoeuvres Felka away from the crowd. Mizumi follows.

'Are you okay, Mrs Margolin?' Mizumi asks, looking between Felka and Rachel. Rachel doesn't even know how to answer that.

'I'm fine,' Felka wheezes, recovering somewhat. She points further down the road, through the crowd. 'My apartment. It's that way. We need to go that way.'

'We can't go that way,' Rachel says, thinking about her own recent protesting experience. 'It's chaos.'

'We must,' Felka tells Rachel. 'I must.'

'We're in no rush,' Rachel counters. 'We can come back when it's not dangerous.'

Felka looks at Rachel – a deep, searching look – and says simply, 'Please.'

'If we are careful, it will be okay,' Mizumi says. 'We will move quickly and try to shield your grandmother from the worst of it.' She smiles knowingly at Rachel.

'Besides, I do not think it is an argument you are going to win, Rachel.'

Though the crowd is chaotic, many of the people see that Felka is old and foreign and try to make way for her – except for two young men caught up in the protest, who earn a snapped 'Sumimasen!' from Felka when they bump her. They move aside quickly, apologising profusely. Rachel is relieved when they make it through relatively unscathed, despite the clear anger and energy in the air.

***

Felka is doing her best not to let Rachel see how much she's struggling when they finally arrive at the early 1950s apartment building. Felka stares up at it. This is not the house she came to see. She backs away slightly from Rachel and Mizumi, looks around.

'It should definitely be here,' she tells them. '6 Yamamoto Dori I Chome.'

Rachel frowns. 'Are you sure?'

'Of course I'm sure! I—' She stops before she starts coughing, looks up the street, down the street. 'This is definitely it.'

Mizumi waves to an old man smoking on his balcony in an apartment across the street. He waves back.

'Excuse me,' she calls in Japanese. 'Is this 6 Yamamoto Dori I Chome?'

He yells back, and Felka sighs at his words.

'It was bombed.' Mizumi confirms Felka's own translation.

Rachel puts her hand on Felka's shoulder. 'Are you okay?'

Felka turns to her granddaughter and smiles wearily. 'You can't have everything. But it was such a beautiful house.' She pauses, nods at a bench across the road. 'Can we sit for a while?'

She sees how Rachel looks worried but, blessedly, she says nothing as Felka all but falls onto the seat.

Rachel sits next to her, and Mizumi perches on the armrest.

'I'm sorry about your house,' Mizumi says gently. 'A lot of this area was bombed during the war. When I was a child, my brothers and I played games among the rubble. It was a part of life, along with the GIs and military police.'

'Does the rest of your family still live in Kobe?' Felka asks.

Mizumi goes quiet, pensive, then says, 'No.'

Felka doesn't push her. She understands. They sit in silence, enjoying the street. Cherry blossom trees frame the identical traditional wooden houses lined along the street like those on a Monopoly board. Felka sees a past that stops at the footpath across the road.

There is no testament to where she lived – the world really does move on. But at least it's still intact in her memories.

'It's not far to the cemetery from here,' Felka says after a few minutes, looking to Mizumi for confirmation.

'Yes,' Mizumi nods. 'Shall I accompany you?'

'No, thank you,' Felka says. 'This is ... personal. A family matter.'

'Of course,' Mizumi says, standing. She removes a pen and small notepad from her bag, and writes a note that she hands to Rachel. 'It was nice to meet you. Here is my phone number and address. If you need anything at all, please do not hesitate to contact me. Otherwise, I will see you at 8am the day after tomorrow in the hotel lobby.'

She bows, and then heads back up the street.

'Come on, then,' Felka says, and allows Rachel to twine an arm through hers.

***

A breeze blows quietly through the leaves, bending the tall green grass. It whistles around headstones, chiselled from porous rock and trailing moss from holes and cracks. Some are very old, and the Hebrew lettering, once deeply etched and legible, has been faded by the elements over decades and is now barely decipherable.

Rachel follows Felka as she slowly walks uphill along a gravel path. The silence is palpable, punctuated only by Felka's suppressed coughs. Finally, Felka takes a turn and then comes to a stop. She gazes down at a small headstone near the end of the row, a Star of David engraved above the text. All the headstones here are partially overgrown with grass and weeds, long unattended. Felka takes a deep breath.

'Grandma?'

Felka closes her eyes as she exhales, then opens them. 'They were true to their word. They gave you a stone.'

She carefully bends down to pick at the stalks and strands of grass that conceal the headstone's name. *Rachel Adele Margolin,* it reads.

Felka is crying, Rachel realises, but her voice is steady. 'I'm sorry, darling, for not coming back sooner. For leaving you alone. My Japan-born daughter.'

Bewildered, Rachel wraps an arm around Felka. 'Grandma? What happened?'

'I was pregnant when we left Lithuania. She was stillborn. Here.' A cough. Another cough. More tears.

Rachel imagines, again, Felka's flight from her home in Poland across the border, through the deathly cold – but this time, carrying a fragile life. Rachel's seen how badly wrong pregnancies can go. She's seen the aftermath of patients losing their babies. She knows the taboos of stillbirth and miscarriage. She can't fathom how Felka has lost so much and yet remained the vibrant, life-loving woman Rachel knows.

Unlike the lies about Rachel's heritage, this revelation prompts no anger; she hugs Felka close, crying herself – a completely involuntary response to Felka's pain.

'Oh, my darling! Don't you cry too.'

Rachel hiccups a laugh. 'I can't help it!'

Felka laughs, and then her crying intensifies; she lets out a guttural wail and covers her mouth. They stand like this a while, until the sobs turn to shaky breaths and their tears dry.

Eventually, Felka steps back, dabbing at her eyes. 'You know, pupelle, I couldn't cry for years. It is a big release.' Felka pats Rachel's arm. 'Thank you, Rachel, my darling, for being with me.'

'Of course,' Rachel says, and then frowns. 'But I wish Dad was here too. He should be.'

'Your father ... your father saw things, terrible things, that no child should see. What can I say? His pain is my fault.'

'No, it's not,' Rachel says fiercely. 'He's an adult. He's responsible for his own actions.'

But Felka just shakes her head, and they find a place to sit on the soft grass on the hill overlooking Kobe Harbour. Ships come and go; tiny cars sputter along. It's peaceful up here, beneath the shining sun.

'Little Rachel was watching over your harbour for you, Grandma,' Rachel says, gesturing back at the grave; it has a perfect view over the water. She regards the grave and takes in the detail. She runs her fingers along the etched lines that form the star. There is nothing like this on her mother's headstone – *Shirley Margolin, concealed Jewess,* she thinks with a sad smile.

Felka looks calm now, despite her make-up-streaked face. She notes Rachel's interest in the symbol. 'A Star of David; a *Magen David* in Hebrew. I can buy you a gold one for around your neck. On every Jewish grave.'

'Except Mum's,' Rachel returns.

Felka guiltily avoids the prompt. 'I want to be buried here,' she tells Rachel, who blinks. 'I had to abandon my husband's body, and my daughter's. I don't want to leave her again. Michael has Shirley to spend eternity with – he doesn't need me. This little angel has nobody. And your father was so excited about his little sister when she was due. He was so looking forward to being a big brother. And then, more loss.'

Felka coughs. Harder and harder – deeply, from her chest. Between breaths, Felka continues trying to explain. 'Darling, I had a loving childhood. I had a normal life until I got married, until we had to say goodbye to ... but your father, he saw so much. The only way to survive was to push it all down. Marrying your mother helped, until she died, too. It's all still inside of him, pupelle.' One more significant, chesty hack. 'I have a lot of regret. But so much to be grateful for.'

'I know,' Rachel says. 'I know. And I'm going to make sure you get to thank the man who saved you. I'm excited to meet him. But Grandma – he's just a stranger, really. He can't fix us. He was the medicine that sustained life, not the cure.'

Felka wipes at her running make-up, and sighs. 'It would help your father to meet him. I wish he were here.'

She yawns. Rachel yawns too, and says, 'I think we've earned a nap, don't you?'

'I could do with a lie-down,' Felka admits. 'Between the walking, the eating, the walking, the crying...'

And so they retreat to the hotel, too tired to contemplate anything except their comfortable mattresses. As Felka enters their hotel room, the mandatory safety check ensues. 'Quick, pupelle, turn on the lights! Go check under the beds for me while I stay here.'

Rolling her eyes, Rachel dutifully performs the task, though not without a little commentary. 'Grandma, it's a hotel room.'

Felka snaps back, 'Keep searching. Plenty to steal. Cleaners, housekeeping, you can't trust anyone!'

Finally, Felka is placated, and Rachel, a little more understanding now, accepts the ritual for what it is and falls onto her bed, fully dressed.

Chapter 10

Rachel, snugly wrapped in her quilt, watches as morning creeps into Kobe. It makes its way up the hotel's facade and slips in between the gap in the curtains in their room.

Their hotel room displays a clear divide between the two sections. Felka's side is fastidiously ordered: her clothing has been folded and meticulously arranged in the room's compact but adequate wardrobe space. Toiletries are lined up like obedient schoolchildren in a row on her bedside table, ready to be on duty when needed, next to many small canisters of various medications, and an asthma inhaler that Rachel seriously doubts she's ever used. Felka, comatose thanks to the time difference, sleeps in her thick crimson bathrobe and matching eye mask, earplugs still in place.

Rachel's side is marked by a distinct *lack* of order. Rachel has discarded her clothes unconsciously overnight – overheating from having fallen asleep in her daywear – onto the floor in a pile, crumpled, inside out and unbuttoned practically concealing her rucksack. Hungry and keen to explore, Rachel sorts through them quietly and gets dressed, brushing her teeth. As she comes out of the bathroom, she notices something glinting from Felka's open wardrobe, swaddled in tissue paper. Rachel carefully crosses the room and opens it: the shards of Felka's vase. Rachel is confused before she remembers that Felka mentioned someone could repair it in Kobe. She shoots a glance at Felka, who is very much still asleep. A question for later, perhaps.

Before Rachel heads downstairs for breakfast, she sits cross-legged on the floor at the coffee table and writes postcards to Kate and Susan. It feels surreal, spending her twenty-first birthday in Japan. They told her they had wanted to give Rachel a surprise party, before the trip got in the way. Rachel wishes they were here; she can only imagine the fun they could have. And the trouble they could get into, of course. She addresses a third postcard to Yanni but, guiltily, isn't sure what to write. If she's being honest, she hasn't thought about him too much, a realisation that makes her chew on the inside of her cheek. She decides to write it later. There is so much going through her head. This one requires way more attention.

She stows the postcards in her bag and tries to wake Felka. 'Grandma.'

No response. She tries again, a little louder. Still nothing. She touches her shoulder. 'Grandma?'

Felka half wakes up, with a slight snort. 'Pu ... Pupelle?'

'Yes, it's me. Happy birthday, Grandma,' Rachel says, feeling a little guilty for waking her.

'Mmm. Happy birthday.'

'I'm going for breakfast and a walk. Do you want to come?'

'What's the time?'

'Around seven.'

'Oy! No, my God!' Felka rolls over and hugs her pillow.

'Grandma...'

'Kids these days – you're meant to be lazy,' she mutters. 'Go – have a good time! My purse is by the window, get something nice for yourself!'

Rachel rolls her eyes, smiling, and leaves without taking a cent.

She heads downstairs and asks the receptionist for the phone, taking out Mizumi's number. It's odd, seeing such a different string of digits, an utterly unfamiliar pattern. She hesitates – is it too early? – but she can see people already streaming through the gardens beyond the hotel.

Mizumi picks up after the first ring, answering in Japanese. '*Moshi moshi, Mizumi desu.*'

'Hi Mizumi,' Rachel says. 'It's Rachel Margol ... Margolin. Sorry to bother you so early.'

'Rachel! No, it is no bother. How can I help?'

'I forgot to ask – where's the nearest post office from the hotel?'

She could have asked the receptionist, but Mizumi's confidence with speaking and giving directions is so apparent, so reassuring. Unsurprisingly, the route she describes to the post office is very clear; head along the harbour, turn into this main street, take a right at this landmark.

'I was planning to go there myself,' Mizumi says. 'If you'd like, I can meet you there, and we can get breakfast together afterwards?'

'Are you sure? You don't need to change your plans.'

'Not at all. If you leave now, you will get there in forty minutes or so. I will see you soon!'

***

Rachel walks along the harbour, enjoying the brisk breeze as she follows Mizumi's directions to the post office. She can sense the business bustle will start soon; the dockyard hustle, though, probably started and finished before sunrise. At this early hour, the harbour is dimly lit and peaceful. Very different to the harbour back home, she thinks, where Sydney's waterways seem to be designed for pleasure – yachts dotting the horizon, a majestic bridge arching over natural beauty, the partially completed Opera House with its shiny white wings beginning to emerge from steel and mesh. Rachel vastly prefers this tranquillity. Everything is so different, so new. She wishes she had the time and materials to paint this scene, bathed in morning light.

Some dishevelled young men in black pinstriped suits stumble past Rachel in the opposite direction. They've clearly been up all night; their ties are loose, their shirts haphazardly buttoned. She smiles at them automatically, despite the alcohol reeking from their clothes.

A mistake: one whistles and catcalls at her. The other two laugh. She turns away, keeps walking. The whistler turns around and follows her. She doesn't respond. One of the other men says something. She doesn't understand the words, but she knows the tone. Flirtatious, brash, disrespectful. She's pulled to a stop as the whistler grabs her by the shoulder. Her heart is pounding as the other two catch up. She smiles again, the sort of smile she's given to drunken men who can't take a hint before. Will it work here? She glances around, but this stretch is quiet, just far enough from the busy main footpath that she's easy to miss.

The whistler reaches out and slides her hair behind her ear. She shudders.

'Supein? Su—' He turns to one of his friends. 'Supein?'

'Spain,' his friend replies.

'Oh, oh ... Spain. You Spain?'

Rachel shakes her head, trying to step back.

He leans closer. 'You look Spain.'

She's had that before, with her complexion. Greek too, of course.

He smacks his lips and licks them. He leans in close to Rachel. 'Where you from?' The alcohol from his breath is overpowering.

'Rachel?'

They turn; Mizumi stands a few feet away next to a deep-blue bicycle. She's looking at Rachel in concern. 'Are you alright?'

'Mizumi,' Rachel says, unbelievably relieved.

Mizumi wheels her bike over. One of the men waves his hand at her rudely, says something quickly that Rachel can't hear over the thumping in her ears. Mizumi says something coolly to him. They have a brief whiplash of a conversation; the man flinches with each of Mizumi's words, and one of the others holds up his hands as if to say *take it easy!* Mizumi turns to him next, giving him what is clearly a good telling-off. They skulk away like chastened little boys.

'Good to be rid of them,' Mizumi says as they go. 'They should be ashamed. Are you okay?'

Rachel presses a hand to her chest. 'Yes. They were very ... pushy.' She glances at Mizumi. 'Lucky you came by.'

'I thought I might run into you,' she explains, brushing her hair behind her ear. 'It is a nice day to cycle along the harbour. Only a little detour.'

In the morning sun, her eyes turn almost a liquid gold, and her skin all but glows. Rachel can't help but look at her admiringly; for all her recent confrontations, standing up to three drunk men in a quiet place is another matter. And she could never have spoken to Thomas so calmly, so coldly.

'I can take you the rest of the way.' Mizumi smiles. She climbs back onto her bicycle, gestures at the handlebars. 'Hop on.'

Rachel has never felt more grateful to be so small; she climbs on, settling her feet on the two small bars extending from the middle of the front wheel, and Mizumi pedals back into the street. She steers the bike well, maintaining a tolerable speed for Rachel, who hasn't done this since she was a kid.

'Thanks again,' Rachel says. 'Can you see?'

'Yes,' Mizumi says. She's puffing a bit, but seems unbothered. 'The post office is just a few streets away. I was heading there to pay some bills, so it is fortunate you called me.'

'Bills? You live by yourself?'

'Yes,' Mizumi says, and doesn't elaborate. Instead, she says, 'Are you excited to meet the other group members? They are travelling from all over.'

'I suppose,' Rachel says. She waves at a couple of kids who are pressing their noses to the window of their school bus to look at her. 'I'm mainly here for my grandma, though. And to meet Sugihara.'

'Family is important,' Mizumi says, taking a right turn; Rachel laughs as the wind goes through her hair. 'Very, very important.'

They stop alongside an official-looking little building. No big red postbox, of course. Another difference. Rachel hops off the front of the bike as Mizumi wheels it into a rack. Sweat dews on Mizumi's forehead, but she smiles at Rachel, unbothered, as they go inside.

Mizumi helps her send the postcards and put the correct stamps on them, before attending to paying her bills. Rachel waits for her outside, enjoying the warmth of the sun, the general pleasantness of being in an unfamiliar place with no pressing responsibilities.

The cafe is clearly a favourite; people come and go and come and go around them even as they sit down. Mizumi orders for them both, a bowl of warm rice and grilled fish, and a small bowl of savoury-smelling soup. It's far from the breakfast fare Rachel is used to, but it smells so homey and comforting that after her run-in with the drunks, it's just what she needs.

'I am sorry about those men,' Mizumi says, picking up her chopsticks. 'That is not how we Japanese usually behave.'

Rachel remembers how unflappable Mizumi was, facing them down. 'Weren't you scared?'

Mizumi shakes her head, rolls her eyes. 'Businessmen party all night long, and then wander home in the morning. They are usually too drunk to be dangerous. They probably tried their luck with you because you are not Japanese. They will not do that again in a hurry, I think!'

'Well, I'm grateful you were there,' Rachel says, carefully using her chopsticks to pick up a piece of fish; it's perfectly salty, and melts in her mouth.

'What are your plans for today?' Mizumi asks, sipping from the small bowl of soup.

'I was thinking I might try and find a birthday gift for Grandma after this,' Rachel muses. 'I have a few hours to kill, and she likes to sleep in.'

Mizumi nods. 'Mrs Margolin likes Japanese art, yes? Shall I take you to some artist studios?'

'That would be amazing, but you can't carry me all the way there,' Rachel protests.

'There is a bus a few streets over that we can take,' Mizumi says. 'I will take my bike with me. It is no big deal, as you say.'

'Are you sure? I can probably get there myself,' Rachel says. She can't imagine that Mizumi wants to spend her free time wheeling her through the city.

'I insist,' Mizumi says firmly. 'I don't want you thinking that Kobe is full of men like from earlier. We are very nice people!'

She looks so determined that Rachel has to laugh. 'I know you're very nice people! *You're* very nice.'

Mizumi gives her a little smile then, one she hasn't given before. Rachel catches herself blushing, not entirely sure why, and tucks into her food so that Mizumi can't see it.

Chapter 11

When Rachel returns to the hotel room several hours later, Felka is in the bathroom, taking a shower. She goes to knock on the door as a courtesy, but pauses at the sound of what she thinks might be sobbing. Is Felka crying?

She knocks. 'Grandma?'

Something clatters, a shampoo bottle perhaps, and then: 'Oh – Rachel? You are back earlier than I thought.' The shower turns off.

'Are you alright?' Rachel says hesitantly. There's silence for a bit, the sound of Felka pottering around. A few minutes later, the bathroom door opens, and Felka steps out, wrapped back up in her red robe. She's clearly been crying.

'Grandma,' Rachel exclaims. 'What's wrong?'

Felka waves at her. 'I am fine, it is fine. How was your morning?'

'I thought we weren't going to keep secrets anymore,' Rachel says pointedly. She takes a seat on her bed. 'Tell me.'

Felka sighs, sitting next to her and unwinding the towel wrapped around her hair. Rachel rarely sees her like this: bare-faced, hair not perfectly coiffed.

'I did not cry for so many years,' Felka says eventually. 'And now, the tears! They will not stop coming.'

'Is this about your daughter, about Rachel?'

'Yes. No.' Felka sighs.

'Losing a baby is so hard,' Rachel tries. 'But it happens often, Grandma, you'd be surprised. In the hospital I saw so many women recovering from miscarriages, or whose babies came too early. It wasn't your fault.'

'I know,' Felka says quietly. She goes to speak, but shakes her head.

'Grandma? What is it?'

'When we found that hut,' Felka tries, and then falls silent. Rachel takes her hand, rubs it. Felka takes a shuddering breath, then closes her eyes. 'After wandering through the snow. I knew they had left only recently. But we took the risk. We had no choice. It was a case of survival. We fell asleep. We had to. But the soldiers came back in the middle of the night. They ripped your daddy from my arms, locked him in the bedroom. He screamed so, so loud.'

Rachel doesn't dare say a word.

Felka's lips quiver. Her voice goes shaky. 'I thought they were going to kill him in front of my eyes. It felt like my beating heart was being torn out of my chest.'

She falters.

'You don't have to tell me, Grandma,' Rachel says softly, squeezing Felka's hand.

Felka exhales. 'They pushed me. Pushed me to the floor. Drunk, stinking monsters. One climbed on top of me, then his friend, then another.' She opens her eyes, looks at Rachel. 'You know what I am saying. You are old enough.'

Rachel nods, swallows.

'They hit me,' Felka continues, then shakes her head. 'No, "hit" is too gentle – they beat me. I was unconscious for a while, thank God. I tried to be quiet, not moan, cry, scream. I didn't want to scare Michael any further. I could hear him crying. I hoped that he might not understand. Finally, after they were done, they fell into a drunken sleep. I unlocked the bedroom door – the key was still in the door, stupid Nazis – and escaped. Again. And we ran, and ran, and ran. The stress, the trauma – your daddy saw so much.'

Felka is staring at the blank wall ahead. Rachel dares not prompt her. She can see that her grandmother needs time to repackage these horrible memories, to put them back where they belong, well secured in the recesses of her mind.

Finally, Felka comes back to 1968. 'We were rats. Filth to be thrown out with the garbage. And that's what we will always be if gentiles want to blame someone for their troubles. Don't you ever forget it.'

190

Felka coughs. It's a deep, racking thing that no inhaler will fix. Rachel gently rubs her grandmother's hands until the fit subsides. There's nothing she can possibly say, and so there's a long silence as the two of them sit together. Their band of two. The Margolin women.

After a while, Rachel dares to ask, 'How did Mum survive? Leaving her surroundings and being on the run. She was so young. Do you know if anything happened to her?'

'I don't know,' Felka admits. 'Many of us didn't talk about the things that happened. Couldn't talk about them. We were just so thankful to be alive. We didn't want to spend time on the terrible memories. Perhaps that was a mistake. It became a rot.' She pats Rachel's hand.

'But whatever happened to your mother, she was a ray of sunshine. She loved you more than anything in her life. As for your father ... I failed him.'

'Grandma, what you went through – you did your best. You didn't fail him.'

'I am his mother.' She smiles at Rachel. 'One day, please God, you will be a mother and you will understand the weight of knowing that everything you do has an impact on your child. That you are responsible for how they turn out. I couldn't be there for him in the way he needed at a time, as it turned out, that was most important, that made him who he is. And when I was ready to be there again, the damage was done. I learned that I could survive anything, as long as I let life in. He learned how to survive by shutting life out.

'He coped by building a new life in a new land and never turning back,' Felka continues. 'He left the weight behind, Rachel, because I never taught him to carry it. He tried, he felt he had to – at such a young age, not even a man – to be one. To be the man, for me. To protect me, my boy became the man of the house. He lost his childhood. And I shouldn't have let that happen. It toughened him. And now you suffer.'

Rachel blinks away tears. 'Not as much as I could have, Grandma.' She squeezes her hands. 'Thanks to you.'

Felka pulls her in for a hug, clumsily kisses her on the cheek. 'A fine start to our birthday,' she tuts, dabbing at her eyes. '*Oy vey!* Enough of this, we cannot spend our special day crying on each other's shoulders.'

She stands up and opens one of the wardrobe drawers, taking out a little box. She passes it to Rachel. 'Happy birthday, my darling.'

She removes the elegant wrapping and opens the box. It's a platinum ring with an elegantly set solitaire diamond. Rachel gasps, slipping it on; it fits perfectly.

'That used to be my mother's,' Felka says. 'I was going to give it to my own daughter, but – well. From Rachel, my mother, to my beautiful Rachel.'

'It's gorgeous, Grandma,' Rachel says, holding it to the light, marvelling at its beauty and history. 'Thank you.'

'I thought to myself, well, Rachel may not be getting married anytime soon, but she still deserves a ring!' Felka laughs.

'Let me get yours,' Rachel says, turning to her bag.

'Pupelle,' Felka says very seriously. 'You simply being here is gift enough.'

'Here,' Rachel says, taking out a cardboard tube. She passes it to Felka, who, raising her brows, carefully prises the lid open and slides out the thick hand-made paper.

'What's this, darling?' she begins to ask, and then falls silent when she unfurls it. Rachel watches her anxiously. Mizumi, determined to help, had taken her to several different painters before they found this piece. The painter lived in a tiny house down an alleyway near the harbour, but his studio had been full of colour. Even then, the piece had stood out among the others: a detailed, loving depiction of the view of the harbour from the graveyard, as if standing at baby Rachel's grave.

Felka's lip trembles, and she reaches out to pat Rachel's hand. 'Thank you, my darling,' she manages. 'Beautiful. It's beautiful. Perfect. You're going to make me cry again!'

'I'm glad you like it, Grandma.'

'Of course I do. How could I not? All these emotions, oy. Enough. It's making me hungry.'

Rachel laughs. 'Shall we go find something to eat?'

KAUNAS, 1940

July in Kaunas is warm, pleasant. It could almost be like home, if Chiune closed his eyes and imagined Japanese architecture rather than Lithuanian. He and his family have been here for nearly two years. He had hoped by now that he might end up somewhere more permanent, where he and Yukiko could raise their sons. And perhaps, in another world, Kaunas could have been it.

'It is beautiful here,' Yukiko says almost every morning as she opens the curtains to let the light flood the house.

'Yes,' he replies almost every time, sliding an arm around her waist, marvelling at how his wife's skin glows in the sun.

But one morning, when she opens the curtains, she gasps.

'Chiune,' she calls as he makes a pot of tea in the kitchen before returning to work. 'Chiune, come here, quickly.'

He abandons the pot – she sounds afraid, confused. Have the Soviets finally attacked? Have the Germans turned on Japan? – and when he comes to the front room, expecting to see sun streaming through the windows, he gapes at what he sees instead.

Hundreds of people, mostly men, crowd outside their front gate. They look bedraggled, harrowed. Chiune and Yukiko stand there a moment, just looking at them all. Enough to form an army battalion. But they do not look like soldiers.

'What are they doing?' Yukiko murmurs to him.

'I will take care of it,' he assures her, pressing his hand on her shoulder. 'Go check on the children.'

She lays her hand over his and squeezes, before nodding. As she leaves the room, he steels himself and opens the door.

The noise outside of people talking is low, urgent, frenzied. Like cicadas in the summer months. They all fall silent as he closes the door behind him.

'Excuse me,' he says in Lithuanian to the nearest man. 'May I ask what you are all doing?'

'Please,' the man says. 'You must help us.' He introduces himself as Zorach Warhaftig, and a man beside him as Nathan Gutwirth. They are from the Mir Yeshiva, a Jewish learning centre that has moved from one European city to another as the Nazis progressed. They explain the plight of the Jewish refugees pouring into the country, from Poland. They have nowhere else to go, but Lithuania is barely safer than home: anyone can see the violence brewing. It seems there is nowhere in Europe that is safe for the Jewish people.

He asks Chiune if he remembers a couple, Pesla and Izaak Lewin, to whom he recently gave transit visas through Japan to Dutch Curacao. Word has got around quickly about their success. Impossible to believe. They had all swiftly approached the Dutch consul, Jan Zwartendijk, and he had issued all of them papers to enter Dutch Curacao – even those who were not themselves Dutch, like Pesla Lewin. Now they, too, each needed the all-important Japanese transit visa.

Their desperation is palpable. He knows that they tell the truth – he has seen it on the streets, the way the locals find any excuse to beat the Jewish population. He and Yukiko have changed the routes they take to the market, hoping to avoid exposing their sons to it. But it is clear it is no longer something they can ignore.

It reminds him of Manchuria. Should he really be so surprised that his country has allied themselves with this?

He scans the forlorn faces of these weary men, resignation and destitution etched into their blank expressions, his mind racing through the logistics of what will be required.

'Please give me some time to discuss this with my family,' he says, and returns inside. He stands there a moment, hand still on the doorknob. He had fled Manchuria, but he does not think he can flee Kaunas.

He explains everything to Yukiko, including the fact that issuing so many visas will fly in the face of Japanese law. It will have repercussions not only for him, but for his family, too. But what is the alternative? He became a baptised Christian because he believed in the core tenet of Christianity: kindness.

'I may be disobeying my government,' he confesses to her. 'But if I do not do what I feel is right, then I am disobeying God.'

Yukiko looks at him solemnly and says, 'We must help them if we can.'

And so Chiune begins the gruelling task of processing hand-written visas for what is at first dozens of people, and then hundreds, and then thousands. The crowd outside his house swells and ebbs like the tides, but never completely dissipates. A few weeks later, he has already issued nearly two thousand visas. He must contact his superiors in Japan; he can put it off no longer. The first of three telegrams to his superiors in Japan, requesting permission to issue visas to these individuals, gets a simple reply: No. He wires them again. No. A third attempt warrants a terse, clear response: 'Under no circumstances are you to issue visas to these Jewish refugees.'

He reads the telegram a second time, just to confirm he has read it correctly, and then writes a further forty visas that day.

Chapter 12

By the time they get back from lunch and dessert and wandering around, Felka barely has enough time to touch up her make-up and change clothes before they go to meet the rest of the group.

Rachel simply slips into a dress, but for Felka, changing an outfit is an event. She settles on a navy skirt and matching woollen cardigan with gold buttons, a maroon-coloured blouse with a big bow at the neck, and dark red leather pumps with sensible heels. She checks her mascara and rouge, applies some more lipstick, and then Rachel drags her off. Still, Felka is glad for it when they arrive at the restaurant, full of beautiful people wearing beautiful clothes, the walls decorated with traditional art. A little touristy, Felka thinks, but still very nice.

Joshua Nishri sees them the moment they enter, and waves them over. Felka recognises him now, remembers his face, even if he's got quite old – not that she can talk! – and presses a kiss to his wrinkling cheek after he introduces her to the group. Felka is last to arrive. Oops.

They embrace each other, one by one, two by two. They are comrades together, once more. Judit and Chaim. Roman and Anna. Adinah and Benjamin. Yitzhak and Ida. Ette. Felka. It's only a small selection of those Felka remembers from the time, and some she doesn't know. Everyone looks older and greyer. Most have put on a few pounds – except poor Adinah, of course, always a bag of bones. But the eyes don't change, and these faces take Felka back thirty years.

She proudly introduces Rachel. 'This is my granddaughter! Beautiful, yes? Smart, too!'

'A little doll, Felka!' Judit says in her rich, warm voice. 'The petite figure, the olive skin, the big, round eyes.'

'And who is this handsome boy?' Felka asks the only other young person in the group, as Rachel blushes. He couldn't be much older than Rachel, Felka thinks approvingly. A handsome young man with nicely cut hair and good cheekbones. And, most importantly, Jewish.

'This is Reuben, our son,' Ida says.

'Ida, Yitzhak! What a prize! Lucky will be the woman who steals his heart!' Felka ignores Reuben's outstretched hand and embraces him as she does the rest of her friends. 'See, Rachel? You two youngsters will have each other while us oldies ramble on.'

'It's so wonderful we are all together again after so long.' Joshua beams. 'Nearly thirty years! It took some searching to locate him. Mr Sugihara is quite overwhelmed; he says he hoped maybe one or two would reach Japan and safety. But not so many of us.'

Ette interrupts. 'When can we see him?'

'Tomorrow. He knows we are grateful to have been sheltered by Japan and embraced by her people. He knows how thankful we are. He is very much looking forward to seeing all of you.'

'Where are his family?' Ida asks. 'I remember his wife, Yukiko. And his little boys. They were there, at the consulate, when we got the visas. Are they with him?'

'No. They are back at home in Yaotsu. One of his sons unfortunately passed away in 1947, but the others have grown up to be fine, healthy young men who have completed their studies. Nobuki, the youngest, is about to start university – the Israeli government has offered him a scholarship to study at the Hebrew University in Jerusalem as small thanks for what he did for our people.' They are all delighted to hear such news. 'But all of this can be discussed tomorrow. Tonight is about seeing old friends!'

'I still can't believe you found him,' Anna marvels. 'What of Jan Zwartendijk?'

'The Dutch diplomat?' Joshua shakes his head regretfully. 'No, no word. Perhaps he does not wish to be located. It is so difficult to get hold of any confirmed records these days. So many cover-ups ... people are scared because they defied orders, even after all this time.'

Seeing that Reuben is talking to Rachel, Felka pulls Joshua aside. 'Joshua, darling, tell me – is anyone coming with the name Schagrin?' She keeps her voice low, urgent.

Joshua looks down the list of participants. 'No, not that I can see.'

'I see,' Felka smiles, relieved, and takes her seat. The food arrives soon after, a veritable feast. A myriad of dishes, from soybeans to sushi, yakitori to sukiyaki, cover the large, circular table. Felka couldn't be happier.

***

Rachel is pleased with how easily she uses the chopsticks; Mizumi's guidance has made all the difference. She can't stop thinking about how helpful her new friend is, how lovely the Japanese are.

'Where did you learn to use chopsticks?' Reuben asks her. 'You seem a master. It took me ages.'

They exchanged a couple of pleasantries earlier, but she senses he's been mustering up the courage to have a proper conversation. He's cute enough, she thinks, close to her own age. But he lacks Yanni's masculine beauty. And besides, can't she just have a conversation with a man without it having to mean anything?

'Thank you, but it's hard-won,' she replies. 'I think I'm a Westerner at heart – I much prefer a knife and fork!'

He grins. 'Yes, they're far easier.'

'Were you born here, or...?' She's curious; he has an American accent that sounds like those in the movies.

'Washington. My folks were among the lucky few who got a visa to the US.'

'My family managed to get to Australia.'

'What's it like? Kangaroos everywhere?'

She laughs. 'No. Everyone seems to think that we live in huts, with wildlife hopping down the main streets! It's not like that, not in Sydney at least. But I've not left home before – except now, to Japan – so I can't compare it to the rest of Australia.' An uncomfortable pause. 'What do you do?'

'I graduated last spring. From NYU.'

'NYU?'

He's surprised. 'New York University? I studied business. I work for an investment banking company. You?'

'I'm a nurse. Who loves to paint.' She laughs nervously.

He smiles awkwardly. The silence is thankfully interrupted by an avalanche of more food. Lots of food. Just in case they run out. And lots of drinks.

Around the table there is endless singing. Songs of Polish youth, Yiddish songs. Stories from their time in Japan, stories from before the war, places they had in common, people they knew. Rachel observes, absorbs, listens and learns. She knows there is limited time to ask her grandmother all she wants to know. It feels intoxicating, this atmosphere of lifelong friendship, camaraderie, heritage, culture and ritual. She deeply regrets that she doesn't understand Yiddish or Polish; they speak in English solely, she feels, to include her. Reuben may have been brought up in America, but he at least speaks enough of their languages to understand.

More sushi arrives, and a very thin, angular woman in a neat pink suit – Adinah, Rachel remembers – sighs. 'Sushi, sushi, sushi! We need some good Jewish food. Matzo balls, kreplach, boiled beef, chopped liver, herring!'

Across the table Anna breaks off a monologue about her children in Canada to answer. 'You won't find those in Kobe, Adinah!'

They laugh. Adinah turns to Rachel, leaning across Reuben to talk. 'I hope your nana has taught you to cook properly.'

Rachel, not sure what to say, looks at Felka, who appears stricken.

They turn on Felka. First Anna, 'Felutkah! Really?' Then Judit, 'Surely she knows the basic dishes. No?'

Felka shrugs.

Adinah announces to the group. 'Okay, tomorrow – cooking class! I will organise with the kitchen in my hotel!'

'Good luck finding the ingredients,' Anna says.

Adinah looks crestfallen, and Felka pipes up, 'Don't worry, we can improvise!'

As the women discuss ingredients, Rachel is taken back to the scene in Maria's family's kitchen, with the Greek women pressing her about what she can cook and how she had to admit she couldn't. Judit, who sits on Rachel's other side, leans in, bringing her back.

'I'm so glad to meet you, Rachel, though it does make me feel quite old – your father was a little boy the last time I saw him.' Judit must be Felka's age, with dark hair set in slightly old-fashioned waves around a striking, well-formed face. Most intriguing is her rich, deep voice. Rachel noticed that whenever she joined in a song, the rest of the table would quieten a little, the better to hear her. Judit asks about Rachel's life in Sydney, her profession, her friends, her pastimes. She seems genuinely interested, but Rachel thinks her life pales in comparison to those of the people sitting around this table, and she tries to keep focus on Judit. 'So you and Chaim were in Kobe with my grandma?'

Judit corrects her. 'Chaim was. But I met him in England after the war. I was very lucky to make it there.'

Rachel wants to know more, but tries to be respectful, patient, thinking of Felka's and Hannah's tears. 'Would you mind telling me about your life? Before the war, I mean. During it, too.'

Judit looks hesitant, but seems to understand.

'I knew your nana in Warsaw,' she begins. 'She was a friend of my older brother, a real beauty, as I'm sure you know.'

Rachel smiles. She's been told as much.

'She was Miss Warsaw Judea.' That much Rachel didn't know. 'We had such a beautiful, rich life,' Judit continues. 'I was training as a singer – opera, of course. My family were all musicians, and very well regarded. Nobody really noticed the changes at first. A little thing here, another thing there. But we all thought, what could they really do to us? We are important to society, respected members of the community. It will pass. But it got worse. They began taking our basic rights.'

Rachel stops her. 'What kind of rights?'

'Think of everything you take for granted in your daily activities. First, it was our right to be on the streets.'

Rachel interrupts her again. 'What do you mean?'

'They made it illegal for us.'

'To just be on a street?!'

'And parks, public spaces. Outside after dark, cafes ... even to move house required special permission. Then they took our right to work, to travel. My parents could no longer perform publicly. It broke their hearts. They blocked our bank accounts. Synagogues were closed, of course, and praying was forbidden. We couldn't even take public transport with everyone else; we were forced to ride special streetcars only for Jews. We were banned from school, university.'

Judit pauses, a dark expression on her face.

'I knew Grandma stopped studying,' Rachel says after a moment.

'Your grandmother was very academic,' Judit says. The table is too loud for Felka to hear their conversation, but she still speaks quietly. 'I don't believe she would have stopped of her own accord.'

'She said she was forced to...'

'That's correct. They implemented a rule called "Numerus Clausus".'

'Numerus ... what?'

Judit pauses, and they both glance at Felka, who is swept up in the chorus of an old song with the rest of the group, who clap and clap and clap to the beat.

Satisfied they aren't bringing the mood down for the rest of the table, Judit continues. Rachel listens intently.

'They limited the number of Jewish students,' she explains. 'And then they separated us from the others, from the gentiles. Then we were banned from universities altogether. Finally, they took our possessions, our homes, and crammed us into ghettos; then they started transporting people to the camps...'

Judit falls silent. Rachel realises she may have gone too far. 'I'm sorry. You don't have to go on.'

'No,' Judit says. 'It's okay. Sometimes it is good to talk. For some of us, it helps. For others ... most here won't share ... anyhow. Have you met any survivors in Sydney? There are many in Australia.'

'I met two. A patient in my care, and a rabbi. But the patient I knew – she couldn't really talk about it.'

Judit empathises. 'Poor thing. What can you talk about when you went through this hell? They took our clothes, the gold from our teeth, even our hair ... our hair! To stuff cushions!'

It's a horror so beyond her comprehension that Rachel can't quite grasp it. This happened not even thirty years ago. She feels nauseated, and it's clearly painful for Judit to continue – but it seems it's cathartic, too.

'Then finally, all they had left to take was our dignity. They took our names, and we each became a number.'

Rachel responds. 'The patient I knew – she had a tattoo. Numbers. She said something about that.'

'Only those who were so fortunate as to be sent to the Auschwitz concentration camp were tattooed like that. Branded like cattle. It was a place I hope we never see the likes of again on Earth. If the starvation, lice or disease didn't get you, the torture did – or the gas chambers. Huddled in concrete enclosures, the doors locked, thinking they were going to have showers, but gas came out of the shower heads instead.'

Hannah. The shower. Now it finally makes sense to Rachel: the fear she had evoked for the poor woman. Guilt engulfs her.

'Were you...?'

Judit shakes her head. 'No. I was one of the lucky ones. I was in the Warsaw Ghetto, and I escaped.'

'How?'

'A stroke of good fortune. Stupid krauts,' she chuckles, but it's a dark sound. 'Certain workers were allowed to leave the ghetto to do certain tasks for the gentiles outside. Every day, these workers would line up at the gate to be let out, you see. It was the only way in or out.

'I was quite pretty, despite the dirt and starvation. I still had my figure. I was a performer. I knew I could use it to my advantage, if I could just wait for the right moment. One day, I saw a woman was lying dead in the gutter down an alley no one ever used. She must have been quite sick when she entered the ghetto. The very sick had no chance, of course. In or outside of the walls. And it was a heatwave, too; she must have been so dehydrated. Poor thing.'

Rachel tries to picture it, these walls. Tries to imagine walking past them every day on the outside as a gentile, knowing that people were suffering inside for no reason.

'I decided to see if the clothes beneath her coat were salvageable,' Judit continues. 'I know it sounds awful, but when you have little or nothing, you have to take anything you can get. It was a free-for-all. So I looked. Her shirt and pants were ragged, but she was wearing beautiful lingerie beneath that. I don't know how she had hidden it from the Germans, but it gave me an idea.'

Rachel is on the edge of her seat.

'I took the bra, then dressed her back in her shirt and coat. That poor woman. I still feel ashamed for leaving her there like that, but I had no time to waste. I hid in a dark corner and put the bra on beneath my blouse, which was still in okay condition. I kept the blouse open beneath my coat, so if I opened it, you could see the bra very clearly. I needed something for my face, though. I cleaned it as best I could, pricked my finger and used the blood for rouge. It would have to be enough, I hoped. Many of these men's shifts were long. They were tired, foolish. I had nothing to lose.

'When those workers lined up that morning, I approached the soldier on duty who was checking their permits. I fluttered my eyelashes at him and said that I was terribly sorry, someone had stolen my work permit in the night. I made sure he could see the lovely bra. He looked down at my cleavage hungrily and told me to go, so long as I reported back to him that evening for a new one. Pig. I walked right out of that ghetto, right under their noses, and I never looked back. After I ripped the Star of David armband off my sleeve, I was free; I found an old family friend, who concealed me for two years.'

'Two years?' Rachel says in awe.

Judit nods. 'An old boyfriend. I hid in his attic the entire time. But what I remember most is one day, just after the Germans had retreated. It was only a matter of time before the war ended. The Russians were approaching, and the streets were deserted. I went outside, the first time in two years. I lay on a small patch of grass – God, you can't imagine how it was to smell grass again – and then I heard buzzing. I thought it was bees in some bushes. But I looked up at the sky and saw the American planes. Soldiers parachuted out, quietly falling, drifting, like in a dream. It was the most beautiful sight I'd ever seen.'

'I didn't know you were in the ghetto,' Felka murmurs. Rachel starts; the entire table has fallen silent, listening to Judit's story. Felka pulls out her wallet and takes out a yellowed, dog-eared, black-and-white photo of a middle-aged man. He wears a jacket with the Star of David armband, and sits on the steps in front of an old building.

'My parents...' Felka swallows a lump. 'They ... my daddy...' She shows Judit the photo. 'Shmerl Szput. Did you ever see him? Do you know what happened to him?'

'Felutkah – I'm so sorry, but—'

Felka interrupts. 'He lived on Tlomackie Street, number 3, you knew it, yes? Next door to the Great Synagogue of Warsaw. Or with my parents-in-law, around Nowolipie Street, number 54. Szput. Shmerl. Maybe you saw him once, maybe you know when – where...' She looks to Judit for closure, for answers that everyone seems to know she is not going to get.

Judit just looks at her with tremendous compassion, speechless. Yitzhak wraps an arm around his wife, Ida, as Felka nods, eyes watering, and puts the photo back in her wallet. Rachel watches on, tears in her eyes, as the group descends upon Felka, murmuring sympathies.

After Felka has dabbed away her tears, she stands up, holding her sake glass high. 'To what was lost,' she says. 'To those who were lost. To survival. To life.'

'To life!' Adinah crows. 'To Sugihara!'

'*L'chaim!* To Sugihara!' Anna adds.

Rachel does not know that word, but she can gather the sentiment. The camaraderie is so clear here, so natural, that Rachel can't believe Felka could ever hide it: a faith, a past, a community to which she belonged, one she clearly adores being part of.

Their Polish heritage was celebrated, of course. Rachel's upbringing was different to her Anglo-Australian contemporaries. She was the daughter of refugees, after all, and her friends always regarded her as a little 'exotic' – the accents of her family, their clothing, the food they ate (sliced meats from a delicatessen, pickles, piroshki). She has always felt more continental, more European, than her friends. Now she sees that being Polish is one thing, but Jewish, well, that is an entirely different matter.

And though she has so much to learn, between the languages and the cultural references and the emotions, Rachel feels welcome here in a way she never did with Yanni's family. They have embraced her as their own. As family. Effortless, natural. They will teach her to cook. Pass on treasured recipes. Educate her on her people. She didn't know she could feel like this in a room full of strangers.

***

The night continues. At one point, Rachel comes back from the bathroom to see everyone standing around a huge cake with twenty-one candles. She's swept up by kissing and congratulations, until she says, 'Thank you, everyone, but did my grandmother not tell you it's also her sixtieth birthday today?'

The attention shifts to Felka, which feels more natural for them both, and 'Happy Birthday' is sung loudly in English, then Polish. This is Felka's cue. She stands up on her chair, supported by her friends, and they begin to sing something in Yiddish. A traditional song, Judit tells Rachel, as they clap along. The Japanese patrons clap with them. The waiters clear the table, and Felka steps up onto the table with Ette. Rachel gasps, half-expecting the table to collapse, but it's sturdy enough; holding hands, they dance joyfully among the rice grains, squashing them into the soles of their high-heeled shoes. Their feet thump the red tablecloth, and they link arms and sing. The group is all standing now, encouraging the excitement.

Rachel stands there, watching. This is everything she admires about Felka, and it reminds her of everything she is not. That Felka can even summon the strength to get up in the morning, let alone feel joy like this – Rachel can't believe it, knowing what she does now. She thinks about what Felka said about her father's reaction to the same trauma, and decides she will not be like him. She will not go down that path.

'Come here!' shouts Felka. Roman and Ada pull Rachel to the table and help her up. She flushes as she sees the waitstaff poking their heads out from the kitchen to watch the scene. But she resolves to follow Felka's example. Tonight, she is going to dance on a table with her grandmother, even if she's a little terrified she's going to fall down and make a mess of herself.

Her grandmother, who shouldn't be getting drunk and dancing on tables. Her grandmother, who should be spared the awful, untimely death that is imminent.

At first, Rachel feels unsure, but Felka shows her the steps. The tablecloth is crumpled. Bits of rice and vegetables are strewn across the table. But Rachel lets herself go, and she finds she really enjoys it. She's laughing with Felka as she sees Mizumi enter the restaurant, how she stops and stares in surprise at the scene.

Only a month ago, Rachel would have clambered off the table immediately. But instead, bolstered by her new family and a little bit of sake, she continues on. When Mizumi catches her eyes, her expression isn't of disgust or anger or confusion, but delight.

And then Felka wobbles, stumbles, and drops to her knees, laughing but also coughing. Panic rises in Rachel, and she stops, helps Felka get down off the table and back into her seat as Mizumi approaches them.

'Is Mrs Margolin okay?' Mizumi asks.

'I'm fine, I'm fine,' Felka wheezes, grinning. 'It's just all the excitement.'

'Well, I'm glad to see you are all enjoying yourselves.'

'Perhaps a bit too much,' Rachel says, passing Felka some water. 'Why didn't you join us for dinner?'

'Joshua told me that it would be a very emotional reunion,' Mizumi explains. 'I thought it best that for this event, at least, I was absent.'

'No, no,' Felka protests. 'You're more than welcome!'

Mizumi smiles. 'I just wanted to stop by to make sure that dinner went well, and to speak to everyone about their plans for the next couple of days.'

'Sit, sit,' Felka says. 'Have some sake. We have all the time in the world!'

Rachel leans her head on her hand, pleasantly drunk, and listens as Mizumi talks to Judit about her plan to take a tour of the local temples. She's wearing another perfectly chic dress beneath her coat. Rachel thinks of how delicate she looks: like the artwork of Japan, like the cherry blossoms.

Minutes later, Adinah pulls up a chair and begins talking. She has a nervous energy about her, an intensity that makes Rachel feel suddenly much more sober. Without prompting, Adinah leans forward and begins to speak in a long, unbroken monologue.

'I had a little boy,' she says through tears. 'Less than a year old. The Germans came looking for us. We were hiding under the floorboards. My baby started to cry. What can you do? I covered his mouth to stop the noise. So he would live, so we would all live. But instead, I accidentally suffocated him.' Rachel's heart wrenches. At least with Judit, she was prepared to hear such horrible things, but this – unexpected and so unbelievably horrible – sends her reeling. Adinah strokes Rachel's hair, saying, 'We were so lucky to be saved.'

What is it they say? Rachel thinks. *In vino veritas?* With wine comes truth. Adinah weeps. Rachel, incredibly uncomfortable and unsure how to console the woman, looks about for help. Mizumi comes to her rescue once again.

'Excuse me, Adinah,' she says gently. 'You mentioned you wanted to see some of Kobe's gardens. Judit was thinking she would do the same – perhaps you should talk with her about what time might suit the two of you? Then I can organise transport and so on.'

'Oh,' Adinah says, wiping away her tears. 'Yes, that's a good idea. Thank you.'

She gets up and goes over to Judit, and Rachel turns to Mizumi.

'You have the most amazing timing,' Rachel says. There is only so much she can bear to absorb in one evening.

'Mr Nishri told me it might be an intense evening,' Mizumi nods. 'Did your grandmother like your gift?'

'Yes! She loved it. Thanks again for pushing me around like that.'

'Any time. I was wondering – do you like going to nightclubs? I thought once I am done speaking with everyone, I could take you and Reuben to one. It's a side of Kobe I don't think most of the group will be as interested in.'

'That sounds great.' Rachel beams. Mizumi returns to speaking with the others, and Rachel lets Reuben know. As he goes to update his parents, Felka – who has obviously been eavesdropping – leans over to Rachel.

'He's a nice young man,' she says pointedly.

'Yes, Grandma.'

'Yanni is nice, of course. Handsome. But very old.'

'I know, Grandma. You told me a few times.'

'And Greek.'

'Uh huh.'

'Reuben is very good-looking, too. And Jewish.'

Rachel takes Felka's hand and says, 'It's a bit early for me to be making a decision like that, Grandma.'

Felka relents. 'Have a good time, darling.'

Rachel plants a kiss on her grandmother's cheek.

'Ah! My medicine.'

Rachel wishes a kiss would be sufficient to fix her, but tonight was a start.

***

'Hey! That's the Beatles!' Rachel exclaims. A young crowd races onto the dance floor as 'Sgt. Pepper's Lonely Hearts Club Band' wafts through the speakers. She and Reuben watch the response of the partygoers, astonished that the Japanese youth have embraced Western music so readily.

The nightclub Mizumi has led them to – down some stairs in a dingy basement – could be any cool club in Sydney's Kings Cross, Rachel thinks. Go-go dancing, thigh-high boots, miniskirts. Same atmosphere, largely the same music, even the same dance moves.

Reuben, Mizumi and Rachel sit at a small table on the edge of the dance floor. Reuben looks like he wants to get up and dance, but Rachel is peppering Mizumi with questions about Japanese pop music – who else from the West has made it big here? Does she know about David Bowie? How about the Doors?

A man comes up to Mizumi, and they quickly converse in Japanese. She turns back to the two of them. 'A friend – excuse me, I'll be right back.'

Rachel watches her go, a little deflated.

'Did you want to dance?' Reuben asks her.

'Uh,' she says, surprised. 'Sure.'

Technically she is engaged. Was engaged? And despite Felka's pushing, she just doesn't find Reuben attractive as she does Yanni. Shit, she thinks, stumbling a little as he leads her into the throng of people. She needs to call Yanni. But in any case, there is nothing wrong with a harmless dance.

Reuben is trying to talk to her, but she just can't hear him over the Beatles. She shakes her head, pointing at her ear, and he gives her a good-natured shrug as they dance on.

Mizumi's friend pulls her onto the dance floor. She's only a few metres away, but with the room this packed she may as well be unreachable.

Rachel watches her, how the flashing lights slip across her fine cheekbones, how her dress gathers at her waist. Mizumi is beautiful, Rachel thinks, and everyone surrounding her on the dance floor sees it. She shines. Rachel feels a strange longing that she can't quite pin down – an anxious need to be seen, to have Mizumi *like* her. She sometimes feels this way about Kate when they're out together: how confidently her friend strides out into the world, how easily she gathers people around her. Though they're different in so many ways, Kate and Mizumi share a fearlessness, a confidence in their own skins, that both attracts and intimidates Rachel.

When the song ends, replaced by an unfamiliar tune – a local hit, Rachel assumes – Reuben points at the bar, lifting his hand to mime a drink. Rachel nods and they retreat until Mizumi is lost among the many heads bobbing in the red and purple lights.

'You looked a bit spaced out there,' Reuben says, grinning at her.

'Just taking everything in. It's a bit of change from dinner!'

'No matchmakers in Kobe's nightclubs, huh?'

Rachel feels herself blush and is grateful for the darkness. 'Felka's not exactly subtle.'

He snorts. 'Standard Jewish grandmother behaviour.' He sways a little, and she realises he's quite drunk. *In vino veritas* strikes again.

She laughs. 'I've never been part of a bigger Jewish community. I guess I haven't had much exposure. You don't mind it?'

Reuben pauses and narrows his eyes as he considers it. 'They're just trying to help, I guess. But it's hard sometimes, figuring out where the family stops and you start. We're so tied up in our community back home, it's like there's nothing else out there. Some of my friends are fine with it – just get your degree, get a good job, marry someone from school or temple and never leave Washington.'

Rachel considers this as Reuben pauses to order their drinks. Once more she finds herself thinking of Yanni, and before she realises it, she's speaking again. 'Would you ever marry someone who isn't Jewish?' she blurts out as he hands her a glass.

Something in Reuben's face tells her he's thought about this question before. 'A year ago, I would have said no. You know, at college, you meet a lot of girls. One I was quite involved with – a Catholic. Seemed pretty obvious that wasn't going anywhere. But now ... it's hard to explain. I mean, how amazing is Japan? I'd never have come here if this Sugihara meeting wasn't happening. So what else am I missing? I guess I'm just not feeling so sure about anything.'

Rachel smiles to herself: that she can understand. The crowd briefly parts and Rachel spots Mizumi. The man she was speaking to is nowhere to be seen, but Mizumi is still dancing. For a moment, Rachel and Reuben quietly watch her, her thick, dark hair catching spots of light from the disco ball above, her eyes closed as she spins alone in her own world.

Chapter 13

The next morning, Rachel lies in the bed, watching the dawn light filter through the curtains and across Felka's sleeping form. Her eye mask is opulent and the most sensual red satin. Her hair has exploded across her pillow. Some drool, though, has made its way down to her chest. How does someone have this much character when they're asleep?

Rachel wishes this trip would last forever, so she wouldn't have to face losing Felka one day soon. She isn't getting any better; Rachel heard her coughing at several points across the night. And once Felka passes – even the thought brings tears to her eyes – she'll only have Michael. Notionally, at least, but who knows for sure after the last week? She'll be alone. She can't even say whether or not she'll have Yanni.

First love is a curious thing. Felka warned her once that it has an intensity that she'll likely never experience again. She told Rachel (because she tells her everything, with no filter) that the experienced lover will eventually overcome the longing, the breathlessness, the sensation of not being able to eat, sleep, function, the electric shock to the chest like a defibrillator at the mention of their partner's name. The intensity eventually settles into intimate companionship.

Lying here, separate from Yanni, alone in her head, Rachel is surprised to find that she doesn't miss him like she thought she would. She longs for his touch, for his face, for the release of their furtive storeroom meetings. Yanni is fun; Yanni is safe. Or was, at least, before she found out she was Jewish. To marry Yanni now has connotations she never thought she would consider. After the weighty joy and sorrow of last night, she isn't as sure that Yanni's family is the one she wants.

The idea of him still brings flutters, of course. He's the only person she's ever been intimate with; there's a pact between their bodies, a knowledge of each other's scent. His fingers are the only ones to have softly, purposefully traced the lines in her skin to their end destinations, like braille.

But now, she remembers how there have been other women before her. Other women his family have met. How different is Rachel from them? Does he still think of his first love, and, if so, how does Rachel measure up to her? If she leaves him, how long before he finds a nice Greek girl to marry?

And if she *does* marry him, does give up this new-found heritage and family, will she ever really forgive him for it? Will she be able to let it go? Or will it haunt her, as it clearly haunts Michael and Felka?

Rachel's eyelids feel impossibly heavy. Damned jet lag. Probably a good thing, though, she thinks, drifting back to sleep. It's too early to be thinking this hard. And even if it doesn't work out with Yanni, she won't be alone, she reminds herself sleepily. She'll have Kate, and Susan, and...

What feels like seconds later, Rachel opens her eyes to the bright sunlight slicing through the air, creating glittering dust particles. The curtains are open. Felka's bed is empty.

What time is it? Rachel fumbles around for the bedside table's alarm clock. It's almost nine o'clock.

'Shit. Shit!' The horrendous sensation of going from sleep to fight-or-flight in an instant. Where's Felka? 'Grandma?'

A shout from the bathroom. 'In the toilet, sleepyhead! Get ready! Quick! I let you sleep in, you looked so tired...'

Everyone is meeting in the foyer downstairs in twenty minutes. Of all the days to sleep in while they're here, this is the worst. They're off to meet Hiroshima survivors today. Mizumi will be there. She needs to look halfway presentable. There is a palpable pressure on her given Mizumi's beauty and presence. She doesn't want to be invisible.

Rachel strips off her pyjamas, throws on one of her nicer t-shirts and climbs into her favourite pair of overalls. They're all creased. They look, of course, like they've just come out of a suitcase. She tries to smooth the wrinkles out with her hands. No time to iron. She clips one side, aiming instead for fashionably dishevelled, and slides on her sneakers without undoing the laces.

Felka emerges and exclaims, 'Oy! *Cholera psiakrew!*' Rachel knows that Polish expression. It's a swear word her grandmother uses often. Loosely translated, it means *I hope you get cholera.* She knows there is no ill intent behind it, though. 'You look like a drowned rat! What, you don't own a hairbrush? There isn't a coathanger in the cupboard?'

They make their way down the single flight of stairs. Each time they ascend or descend, fear pricks Rachel as she watches Felka struggle. Her cough is getting worse. Is it just the pollution, or—?

Felka coughs hard. Perhaps she sees the fear on Rachel's face, because she lets Rachel help her down the stairs. When they get to the ground floor, Rachel hugs her grandmother and Felka plants a kiss on her forehead. How many moments like this do they have left? The thought has Rachel grabbing Felka's hand as they approach the group, who are busily chatting away.

Rachel cranes her neck for Mizumi, who is of course looking intimidatingly perfect and chatting with the receptionist and checking off the members of the group, when Reuben interrupts her. 'How are you feeling?'

'Better than you, I'm guessing,' Rachel responds with a grin.

Reuben looks away awkwardly. 'Yeah, I'm sorry about that. Too many sakes.'

She wants to tell him she enjoyed their conversation, but as he launches into a detailed description of his breakfast, it becomes clear that the honest Reuben of the nightclub has been packed away.

It's a relief when Mizumi interrupts, directing the group to board the bus outside, and they file out of the lobby. When they are all seated, the bus lurches forward and Mizumi stands at the front, portable microphone in hand, and begins to relay the story of Hiroshima to them.

'As you all know,' she begins, 'what happened in Hiroshima on Monday, August 6, 1945, changed Japan and the world forever. When America dropped the atom bomb called "Little Boy" on Hiroshima, it killed at least 70,000 of my countrymen. The Americans did the same once more on August 9, this time hitting Nagasaki. Six days later, our Emperor Hirohito had no choice but to announce Japan's surrender.'

Rachel knew of this in the abstract, but hearing the numbers – realising that Mizumi's parents would have heard this news in real time, may have lost family members to it – brings a weight and reality she hadn't considered. Sighs of sadness rise from the group and the Americans all seem to shrink a little in their seats. Rachel hears Reuben clearing his throat.

Mizumi continues: 'By the end of the year, however, the number of casualties had risen dramatically because of the resulting injuries and radiation burns. Some say the number of deaths is actually more like somewhere between 90,000 and 140,000.'

Felka takes Rachel's hand and squeezes it.

As Mizumi continues, speaking about the memorial monuments for the disaster, Rachel finds herself remembering a patient she had last year. An old man, succumbing to kidney disease, who told her about the horrors he had endured as a prisoner of war in a Japanese camp. Felka had raised her with an appreciation for Japan and its art, but she knew little about the place besides what she was taught in school. The old man still had scars, and she could see the fear in his eyes when he spoke of it. The horrors visited upon him.

But she can't reconcile that with the Japan she has seen, with the kindness its people have shown her family, with the sweet, sad smile on Mizumi's face as she registers her audience's reaction. How can such cruelty and kindness coexist? And was that cruelty really reason enough for the carnage of Hiroshima and Nagasaki, the destruction of so many innocent lives?

'Hiroshima was officially named a City of Peace in 1949,' Mizumi concludes. 'May we always have peace.'

The crowd is silent: not only as a mark of respect, but simply because there is nothing further one can say. These people, in particular, know that.

The bus pulls up outside a local school. Teenagers in tidy uniforms – military style for the boys, sailor-style for the girls – peer curiously at the tourists as they disembark. The group is guided into a small hall where rows of chairs are set out in front of a low stage. A few other tour groups are there as well, their guides settling them into their seats. Mizumi hands out pamphlets about the history of Hiroshima and Nagasaki, and the black-and-white images of burnt-out building shells sear into Rachel's mind just as a middle-aged Japanese woman steps up onto the stage.

The woman wears a patch over her right eye, the puckered, discoloured skin surrounding it suggestive of what is beneath. As she begins to speak, her friendly expression jars with the darkness of the words Mizumi translates into English.

'I was fifteen when the bomb hit Hiroshima. I remember the day very well. There was an explosion of intense light, then total darkness. Poisonous, choking smoke surrounded me like a thick blanket and suffocated me.'

Mizumi's voice is shaking a little. The audience is silent, but as the woman goes on, Rachel turns to see tears trickling silently down more than one face, especially those in her own group. Judit is pressing a carefully folded handkerchief beneath each eye, again and again, trying and failing to preserve her meticulous make-up. She soon gives up and lets a trail of black run down each cheek.

The woman on stage explains how she endured uncontrollable vomiting for many hours after the explosion. For weeks, her family refused to allow her to see her reflection in a mirror. When she finally managed to get hold of one from a local shopkeeper, she could not believe the monster that stared back at her. Her right eye resembled a pomegranate, she said, and her face was completely scarred with deep wounds. Though the wounds have healed, the remnants are still there. And the emotional scars have never healed. Soon after, her father began suffering from diarrhoea and constant high fevers, his hair began to fall out in clumps, and he developed huge, dark, unsightly blotches all over his body. He passed away very soon after.

Reuben is sitting with his parents directly in front of Rachel, and she sees him placing a hand on his mother's shaking shoulder. She realises that the members of her group have all slipped back into their own memories, their own personal hells reanimated by this story of another violence, another large-scale wave of destruction. She glances at her grandmother beside her, but Felka's face is steady. She is concentrating intensely on the Hiroshima survivor, but

Rachel can see the distress in her shallow, quick breaths.

More survivors of the bombs step up onto the small stage and speak. One tells of the discrimination against those who were affected by radiation. Known as the Hibakusha, these people were marginalised. There was little understanding of the long-term effects, and fellow citizens were fearful they could contract illnesses from those who had been exposed. Marriage with the Hibakusha was discouraged because women, it was believed, would bear children with defects.

When the speeches are over, a few of Rachel's group approach the speakers to pay their respects. Felka takes the hands of the woman who spoke first and looks directly into her face, meeting her remaining eye as the pair exchange a steady gaze. Something passes between them – something that Rachel suspects there would be no words for, even without the language barrier.

Rachel notices Mizumi hanging back near the stage, observing, her face inscrutable.

***

Lunch is a sombre affair. Mizumi hands out pre-prepared sandwiches and drinks in a nearby shady park, where they sit to get some respite from the heat, but nobody has much of an appetite. Instead, they enjoy the simple pleasure of sitting in the shade on a warm day. Of being alive.

Sagely, Mizumi has organised a lighter event for the afternoon: a tour of Kobe, focusing on the history of the Jews there.

Mizumi talks as they walk. They break up naturally into smaller groups of two or three to navigate the laneways. Mizumi remains at the front and turns to address them every now and then, pointing out buildings of interest.

'Kobe has been a vital port since the thirteenth century, eventually becoming a major container port so much so that it is now recognised worldwide for its significance,' Mizumi explains. 'We are a diverse city. Jews started coming back in the nineteenth century; businessmen around the world were attracted to Kobe when Japan opened up to trade. They particularly preferred living in Yokohama and Nagasaki. By the early 1900s, the Jewish community here was already quite sizeable – large enough that they constructed a synagogue, which was completed in 1912.'

They pass the current synagogue. Nearby is a stone wall that looks very old and out of place next to the other well-kept buildings.

'You will all know this area, I think,' Mizumi continues. 'It is the Kitano District. These are the remaining stone walls of the Kobe Jewish Association.'

Chaim calls out to the crowd, 'Yes! This was the relief centre for the refugees! When the Jews arrived before World War II, before us, they used to gather here.'

They all stop to regard the wall, murmuring among themselves. Mizumi calls to a couple of stragglers to catch up and gather around her. Then she continues: 'Has anyone heard of the great earthquake that occurred in Yokohama in 1923?'

Chaim again: 'Yes! It forced much of Japan's Jewish population to relocate to Kobe.'

Mizumi smiles. 'Yes, Chaim, that is correct. The majority of Jews there identified as Sephardi – is this how you say it?' The group nods, and Felka quietly explains to Rachel that Jews originating in Spain, North Africa and West Asia are called Sephardi, as opposed to families in Europe like her own, who are Ashkenazi.

Mizumi concludes, turning to the group, 'This Jewish community of Kobe came to be known as...?'

The all-knowing crowd answer in unison: 'JEWCOM!'

'Yes. This community was treated without prejudice by the Japanese government. Does anyone know exactly why?'

This, the group has no answers for. Rachel herself is intrigued.

'So, the Japanese invaded Manchuria in 1931 – in fact, you may not know it, but Mr Sugihara spent many years working there,' Mizumi explains. 'At the time, Harbin already had quite a large Russian-Jewish population who had fled there from the pogroms. Many of these Jews were capable businessmen. This was very desirable to the Japanese. And so, when the numbers of Jewish refugees began to increase, they were happy to have more Jews in Manchuria in order to develop local industry. It was hoped that Jews would repay the Japanese for their kindness by helping them to influence Jews in the US and Britain to be pro-Japanese and more open to dealing with us.'

'Did the Germans ever try to get us when we were here?' Judit asks.

'The Nazis did naturally want the Japanese, their ally, to adopt their anti-Semitic policies,' Mizumi replies. 'But on December 31, 1940, Japanese Foreign Minister Matsuoka made a statement that while he was responsible for the alliance with Hitler, he never promised that he would carry out anti-Semitic policies in Japan. He even made a point of specifying that it was not just his personal opinion, but the opinion of Japan, and he had no concerns about announcing it to the world.'

The crowd applauds loudly, causing such a commotion that locals going about their business pause to work out what the fuss is about.

Yitzhak interrupts with some extra detail. 'Did any of you know about Josef Meisinger, the Butcher of Warsaw? I was doing some reading.'

They all shake their heads, Mizumi included.

'My husband, always reading,' Ida says, and they laugh.

'In 1940,' Yitzhak says, 'the bastard tried to convince the prime minister of Japan to kill all of us. The rabbi went across to meet the prime minister and you know what he said to him? He said, "We Jews are different. Look at yourselves. Do you follow the template for the Master Aryan Race? You are not fair-skinned and blond with blue eyes, either. You are next!" So, the Japanese decided they had nothing against us.'

Rachel considers this. In her mind, Japan had simply been an ally of Germany, an enemy of Australia. It had turned a blind eye to the crimes of the Nazis as well as committing many atrocities of its own – she knows this, and has seen its effects. And yet, this same government also defended Jews at times. And even when it didn't, people like Sugihara listened to their consciences and acted. It's so much more complicated than she originally thought: the brutality, the aggression, the kindness, the integrity. The pain always inflicted on ordinary, innocent people. She's not sure if she'll ever be able to untangle it all.

The group laughs as one. Yitzhak continues. 'This pig tried again in 1941, hoping the Japanese would murder about 20,000 Jews who had escaped from Austria and Germany to Shanghai.'

Ida is shocked. 'I had no idea – once we landed in America, we didn't hear much about what happened. But here, we were closer to tourists than refugees.'

They all agree. Adinah adds, 'We didn't work, we travelled ... to Kyoto, I remember. We went to resorts. We walked, went into the mountains. Did any of you? Do you remember?'

Judit remembers the exotic fruits they were offered on their arrival; Felka remembers Michael playing baseball with the local children and going to the movies to see Western films.

'JEWCOM was an amazing group,' Anna muses. 'We all had food, shelter and security...'

Mizumi chimes in. 'This was thanks to funding from the.'

Felka murmurs to Rachel, 'These Americans funded many rescue efforts for Jews throughout the war.'

Yitzhak, the avid reader, adds one last piece of information for them all. 'Did you know that the Japanese government even ignored petty crimes like littering and shoplifting when committed by the Jewish residents? I even remember a Japanese farmer who had heard there were over sixty children among the refugees, who gave them free fruit as a gift.'

'I remember this!' Felka cries with delight.

Mizumi is clearly touched. 'I hadn't heard this, though I think there was a local Kobe doctor who refused to accept money for treatment of a child when he found out he was a Jewish refugee.'

The group confirms this happened more than once.

Chaim says, 'Do you remember how the locals even helped us source matzo for Passover in 1941?'

Judit laughs. 'We tried to make it out of rice flour, but it was a disaster!'

Rachel is so absorbed that she isn't even noticing the scenery; she has no idea where they are in the city. The survivors take delight in visiting familiar places and remembering the kindness of the locals in their temporary home. They visit the synagogue and neighbours who lived near where the refugees were housed. Reuben looks perpetually stunned. Clearly many of these stories are as much news to him as they are to Rachel.

Eventually, it's time to board the bus back to the hotel. On arrival, the group unanimously decides that they will go their own ways for the evening, physically and emotionally spent. The women make plans for their cooking class, which is to take place the following morning at Adinah's hotel at 11am. The hotel staff have very kindly sourced some groceries for them to use, she assures them.

Felka is doubtful – 'Are we really going to try again with rice flour?' – but Rachel can't wait.

***

Felka can tell that the hotel's chefs are a little overwhelmed by the noisy, exuberant Westerners overtaking their kitchen; they hover as the head chef uses polite but limited English to show the women around the facility. Judit and Ette tip out the bags of groceries they have managed to secure that morning at the local market. Chicken livers were fine, as were vegetables for the soup stock. But how does one explain to local Japanese merchants the unleavened bread in the form of crackers called 'matzo' – symbolising the rushed departure from slavery in Egypt by the Israelites – which is ground into crumbs before being combined with water, egg and chicken fat to form dumplings called 'matzo balls', which are then boiled to accompany the soup?

Instead, as predicted, the ladies could only salvage rice flour. But first things first.

'Chopped liver, girls!' shouts an elated Felka. 'We need onions, hard-boiled eggs, a skillet, and ... *oy vey,* how do you say "food grinder" in Japanese?'

Rachel laughs as Felka plays charades with the chef, her Japanese not extending to culinary vocabulary; she simply pretends to hold a handle and turn it. He has no idea what she is doing, apologetically shaking his head. Never mind.

The ladies conclude they will have to mash the fried livers by hand. Judit sets about chopping the onions to fry, Adinah simmers a saucepan of water for the eggs. Rachel, standing awkwardly on the fringes, is given the unenviable task of removing the membranes from the livers. Rachel can't stop gagging between the smell and the feel, even though Felka would think that she's handled far worse at the hospital. Perhaps it's different when it's separated from the context of caring for a patient. Her granddaughter is holding her breath, squinting, barely able to see what her hands are doing. Felka and the others laugh when she quits mid-task to run out for air.

'She will be back,' Felka says confidently, taking up the livers. And, indeed, Rachel returns only minutes later with freshly soaped hands.

Meanwhile, Judit attempts to produce matzo balls from rice flour. Everyone can tell the texture is off, but they swap words of encouragement as she drops the raw, tightly formed dumplings into the boiling broth. They immediately fall apart, forming a sea of frothy sludge that floats to the surface. The group grimaces sympathetically as one.

Felka takes control. 'Here. Let me try.' She scoops up a bundle of the dough, squeezes the life out of it and places it into the soup. For a moment, it holds together, but then it meets the same fate.

Adinah huffs. 'Let the master chef have a try. If I can't be successful, there's no hope for any of us!'

She takes over; it is a disaster, of course.

'How about latkes?' Ida suggests.

'Latkes?' Rachel asks.

'Potato pancakes,' Felka says. 'We eat them during Chanukah. Well, I don't mind starting the festival early if it means eating latkes!'

They begin grating the potatoes, and Felka listens guiltily as Judit gives Rachel an abridged version of the history of the festival.

'Chanukah lasts eight days, and usually happens around the same time as Christmas, sometimes a little earlier. When the Temple in Jerusalem was desecrated by the Syrians in 165BC, the Maccabees – Jewish fighters – stepped in. At the time, there was a small vat of oil in the Temple that was burned for light and was only expected to last one day, but it miraculously burned for eight days instead. So we light candles for eight days to celebrate this miracle of light.'

'But what about the latkes?'

Judit grins. 'We deep-fry them in oil. Latkes, doughnuts, fried food – it's symbolic of that vat of oil all those years ago.'

The latkes come out golden-brown, crisp, perfect. They offer one to Rachel, who is impressed.

'Like hash browns,' she says, going in for more.

Even the head chef, who has returned to politely hurry them along, decides he will sample one and is very satisfied. He even asks if he can use some for his dinner menu that evening.

KAUNAS 1940

Days after the order not to issue any more visas, Chiune and Yukiko watch on as Lithuania is annexed into the Soviet Union. On the rare occasions he takes a break from writing visas to accompany Yukiko to the market, the streets are full with Russian soldiers. Embassies begin to close. It is only a matter of time before the Japanese embassy does the same.

In August, Russian soldiers knock on the Sugiharas' door.

'You are to close the consulate immediately,' they tell him in no-nonsense Russian. The Japanese authorities issue him a directive to go straight to Berlin to await further orders.

'But I like it here,' one of his sons says. Chiune doesn't know how to say to him that he won't like it much longer.

'We can come back when you're older,' Yukiko says soothingly.

And so the Sugiharas move into a cramped Kaunas hotel room. There is no room for Chiune to talk privately with Yukiko; they communicate exclusively in glances during the day, and hushed whispers when the boys sleep at night. Chiune does not discuss with Yukiko what may become of them, but it threatens to suffocate him. The stark reality is that Japan is an ally of Germany. Germany is exterminating Jews. Chiune is allowing Jewish refugees to escape to safety and enter Japan. He can't entertain the consequences and ramifications of this act. It is done. He has no regrets. But the fate of his family is in his hands, and he cannot think about it for long.

The refugees follow the Sugiharas to their new abode. A long line that never seems to shorten runs around the block. He glances out the window at them every now and then. Some stand, shuffling forward painfully slowly to advance ever closer to freedom; others sit in the dirty gutter awaiting their turn. Mothers try to contain restless toddlers while the elderly are comforted and supported. Each of them enters his tiny makeshift office and leaves one step closer to escape.

It's been eerily quiet outside ever since the annexation. Russian guards patrol constantly, even though the majority of locals remain indoors.

'So long as they do not interfere,' one of the Mir Yeshiva members says. Chiune doesn't know what he would do without these volunteers, the members of the Jewish learning centre who assist him with the visa processing. They help him carve stamps with the Japanese characters required for the visas, so that others can take over when his fingers become too cramped and his back too sore.

Even with others to help, he refuses to succumb to fatigue for long. Every day that passes is a day closer to him being officially recalled to Berlin. Every break he takes to close his eyes and rest his heavy head on the desk, or ease the cramping in his now crippled hand, is one less soul to be saved from the hell that is unfolding. On the one day he takes a walk outside to feel the sun on his face, he sees the brutal butchering of a group of Jews in plain sight of onlookers.

Manchuria, all over again.

He cannot stop. He's barely paused in days, writing visas almost in a trance, night and day. At several points, he glances at his watch and calculates he has not stopped writing for almost twenty hours. Between him and his helpers, they are producing a month's worth of visas in a day.

At one point, he becomes feverish. Droplets of sweat run from his brow and occasionally fall onto the freshly formed letters, splattering the words and smudging the ink. Yukiko enters from time to time to mop his brow with a cool, damp cloth.

'You need to sleep, recover,' she begs.

'I can't,' he says simply. She looks at him, through him. He thinks of the day he met her, not even five years ago, at his friend's picnic. She was so beautiful. She paid such solemn attention to his thoughts of Japan's role in Manchuria. She never said a single dismissive thing about it. They married two weeks later. He has never regretted it.

Has she? Look at the risk he is putting them under. Yet she never mentions it.

'I understand,' she says eventually, and he closes his dry eyes as she places her cool, gentle hand on the crown of his head.

The day draws closer, ever closer. Chiune does not stop. He issues visas, while the refugees begin the daunting task of trying to secure the outlandish price that has been applied to tickets for Jews travelling on the Trans-Siberian Railway. One hundred and fifty dollars in US gold coins that they need to wrangle on the black market. Many cannot afford this exorbitant amount, and Jewish agencies from around the world begin to step in with funds.

Chiune does not think his hand will ever recover, and still, he does not stop. Even as he stands on the station platform, waiting for the train to take him to Berlin, he writes visas to the refugees still hoping for freedom.

And when he sees, through the fog and steam, those he helped, calling out in thanks as his train departs, and the other desperate faces of those he could not, he wonders.

Was it enough?

Chapter 14

They travel to meet Sugihara at a warm bar in the middle of Kobe. The lively Jewish group stands out among the crowds of Japanese businessmen, who sip their sake quietly in corners, fascinated by the unusual new arrivals. There are so many businessmen everywhere. What do they do all day? Rachel wonders. Do they ever work? Today, however, the suits are outnumbered.

Japanese music floats through the air, winding between shelves and shelves of alcoholic beverages. The group orders a variety of drinks from a confused bartender, who's not entirely adept at English. They point to the bottles lined up, choose, change their minds, order something else. This continues until Felka orders in Japanese for them all, allowing the poor bartender to get on with it.

'I'm glad you, at least, kept your Japanese, Felka,' Judit says.

The beginning of the affair is sombre. But it's a reunion that stands testament to the failure of Nazism, to Sugihara's bravery.

'How lucky we are to be here,' Felka toasts. Rachel watches as she single-handedly lifts the mood of the room, making bawdy jokes and telling darkly funny stories of escape. When a familiar jazz number from the late 50s comes on, Felka claps, sings, pulls up reluctant friends to dance. Rachel doesn't wait for her grandmother's invitation this time; she knows this is an opportunity she may not have many more of.

When Felka, tired and sweaty, goes to the bathroom, Rachel picks the others' brains.

'Tell me about Poland,' she says. 'Before the war.'

Ette raises her brows. 'Your grandmother hasn't spoken of it? What is to tell – a cosmopolitan society. Culture. Ballet. Opera. Intellectuals discussing politics in cafes, expensive restaurants.'

Anna, sitting near Rachel, interjects. 'And elegance. Beautiful boutiques with the finest clothing and shoes from all over Europe. And hairstylists.' She takes Rachel's locks and gathers them up into a ponytail and twists it into a bun. The ladies laugh and Rachel smiles.

Ette continues, 'And cakes: rugelach, babkas, pastries, piroshki!'

Felka comes back to find them weaving tales of Poland's beauty and grace. Before she can add her own, Joshua Nishri arrives; attention turns to him as he takes a seat.

'It's lovely to see you again,' says Felka. 'Such a great thing you have done.'

Yitzhak is all business, 'So Sugihara is in Kobe? We will see him here tonight, yes?'

Joshua shakes his head. 'Friends, I'm so sorry.'

'He isn't coming?' Ida says, crestfallen.

'We came all this way.' Adinah sighs. Rachel takes Felka's hand.

'I so appreciate the time you have taken away from your lives to make this momentous journey,' Joshua says. 'But Sugihara is a busy man, and divides his time between Japan and the USSR. His work is unpredictable. He has just been called back to Moscow on unavoidable, urgent business.'

Anna's emotions spill over. 'You mean we came all this way, and we won't see him?'

One of the other group members, Benjamin, says, 'That's crazy. We will wait. He will be back soon, no?'

Joshua's expression says otherwise. 'He will not be back for a year or so. He sends his deepest regrets and said he tried his hardest to delay his return. He didn't elaborate, but I get the impression you do not argue with the Russians.'

Felka matter-of-factly says, 'So, Mohammed can't come to the mountain? Then the mountain will go to Mohammed.'

Roman, one of Benjamin's friends, pipes up. 'Felutkah! Are you suggesting we go to the USSR?'

Felka has a glint in her eye. 'I am indeed. What is wrong with a little adventure?'

Roman doesn't buy into her blind enthusiasm. 'We can't go to Moscow! I have a business to run. A visa can take weeks to be approved by the Communists. Especially for Americans. Maybe for Australians, they are more lax. I'm as grateful as the next person, that is why I came, but I need to get back to the US.'

Yitzhak sighs. 'We must return home soon as well. We'll have to come back to Japan another time, when we know it is a certainty. We were all so looking forward to this. Please make another time soon, Joshua.'

Ette shakes her head. 'Can we at least see the family? Yukiko, his wife?'

'I will speak with her,' Nishri promises.

'Well, I'm going to go behind that Iron Curtain,' Felka says defiantly.

Rachel isn't surprised. There won't be a next time for her dying grandmother; it's now or never. They can't know that.

Nishri cautions her. 'Getting to the USSR is a bit of a process. And it is not easy to be a tourist there.'

'I've been to Moscow,' counters Felka. 'We spent a week there on the way on the train to Vladivostok. I speak the language like a local. They better not mess with us!'

'If you're sure,' Nishri says uncertainly. 'I can direct you to the appropriate authorities and a good travel agent tomorrow. But you must be prepared for the red tape.'

Ette asks, 'Felutkah, are you not a little frightened? It's the Soviets, for God's sake!'

'What are they going to do with an old Polish woman?' Felka retorts. 'Lock me away? Let them try!'

***

The group do their best to make the most of the evening. They're deflated but resigned. They've been through worse. There will be other opportunities now they know he is alive. More survivors arrive across the evening, people who came only that day from various locations in Japan and beyond. Their faces all fall when Nishri greets them with the same information. The group try to bolster each other, to salvage what should have been the highlight of the trip. Slowly, the mood lifts as more and more alcohol is poured, and the group swells in numbers, taking up the room.

Reuben wanders over to Rachel and she can see he's loosened up again, a few sakes in. 'Can you believe it? We came all this way and Sugihara isn't even here! What a letdown.'

Rachel smiles. 'Maybe you should come to Moscow with us. You said you wanted to see more of the world – and you know what a fan of yours my grandmother is.'

Reuben's face briefly lights up, then falls. 'That's tempting. But no. I have to fly home in the morning, get back to work. You know – real life.'

'Yes, of course. Real life,' Rachel says, her chest tightening. Her own real life is in tatters. With no Sugihara to meet, this trip is essentially over, and she still doesn't really have any answers for what she'll do next. She looks around the room, her mind racing, when someone catches her eye: a woman in a long-sleeved orange paisley dress, dark hair piled onto her head, is standing in a shadowy corner of the bar. She's strangely familiar, but at first Rachel can't quite place her.

Then it's unmistakable. *Shirley* – the woman looks just like Rachel's mother. Rachel tries to convince herself that she must be wrong. The low lighting, the packed room, the sake she's had. But the woman has seen her too; she's staring, the look of someone seeing an old, unexpected friend.

The woman begins crossing the room, and Rachel feels a moment of sudden, intense panic. Felka is out the back, getting some fresh air with Judit. Rachel's heart is beating out of her chest.

The woman comes to a stop in front of her. Up close, she doesn't look quite the same as Shirley – a slightly different nose, thinner lips, thicker brows. But the similarity is undeniable.

Rachel can't speak, but the woman does.

'Hello,' she says hesitantly, her Polish accent light but discernible. 'Can I ask your name?'

Rachel swallows. 'Rachel. Margolin.'

The woman's lips part, and she shakes her head, then pauses. Reuben is still there, staring blankly at her. 'I'm so sorry, could you please excuse us?' she says to him.

'Oh, yeah, of course, definitely.' He makes a graceless exit as Rachel stares, stunned.

'Let's sit down somewhere quiet,' the woman says to Rachel, who follows her outside onto the street, where they sit on a nearby bench. The warmth and noise spilling out from the bar feel a million miles away.

'My name is Loretta Shineberg,' the woman says.

Loretta. Rachel begins trembling. She clasps her hands tightly.

'I had a feeling you would be here,' Loretta says. 'Or at least, some members of your family. You don't know who I am, do you?'

She smiles sadly when Rachel shakes her head.

'I see. Then this won't be easy for you to hear, to understand.'

'What is it?' Rachel manages.

'My maiden name was Schagrin. I am your late mother's sister. Your aunt.'

Of course. This makes sense, as Rachel explores every inch of this woman's face. Every crease, every blemish. The outline of her mouth, her fine, slim nose. Her dark eyes, her thick, black hair. Her mother. Slightly aged, slightly different, but nonetheless – her mother. But how? Why? Her trembling has turned to shaking. Is it anger or is it fear?

Loretta waits patiently as Rachel tries to find words, any words. The arguments, the secrets, her mother's perpetual, inexplicable melancholy. Only one word comes to mind. Only one word comes out of Rachel's mouth.

'Why?'

Loretta opens her mouth.

'Ah, pupelle!' Felka calls cheerfully, stumbling down the street. Rachel and Loretta turn. 'There you are. It is so cold, what are you doing out here?'

As she comes closer, she sees Loretta, and stops. The colour drains from her face.

Surrounded by deceit, yet again, Rachel can't breathe.

'Felka,' Loretta says. 'How are you? It's been a long time.'

Felka's eyes are wild. Rachel has never seen anything like it, and wonders if the sheer shock will be what kills her, right then and there, not the cancer.

'Loretta!' Felka says after a moment. 'Darling! How ... how is everything? How is life? You look wonderful!'

Rachel stares at her grandmother, who carries on as if Rachel isn't even there. Flirting is her default. Her cloak.

'I'm fine, thank you. Life is good.' Loretta doesn't buy in.

'And your parents?'

Loretta picks up for her. 'My mother passed away some years ago. My father is doing well, though. Thank God.'

Felka nods mechanically. 'And your husband?'

'He is well. As are my kids.'

'Kids! Well, ah. Kids! Wonderful! Our reason for living!'

'Grandma,' Rachel says slowly. 'You told me my mother's parents were no longer alive. And you never told me about having an aunt.'

'Well, we just assumed ... I mean, there was never any contact, ever again ... after Shirley—' Felka stumbles, as if trying to walk over large pebbles in heels, starts coughing. Rachel doesn't move to help her.

'Shirley's death was too much for my mother to bear,' Loretta says quietly to Rachel. 'She fell into a depression and passed soon after. But your grandfather is still alive. He lives near me, in Tokyo.'

Rachel stares at her grandmother. Felka closes her eyes, is silent.

'This all must be so hard for you,' Loretta says gently yet purposefully with Felka in earshot. 'I'm so sorry.' She shares her late mother's passion: gentility.

Rachel almost succumbs to a wave of all-consuming nostalgia before regaining her composure. She shakes her head at it. At the lies. She thought – she trusted – no. She can't be hearing this. It's not true. No. Felka wouldn't conceal this from her. Surely.

But, damningly, Felka says nothing. Felka, who once went to small claims court because of a parking ticket incorrectly filed against her, has nothing to say in her defence.

'Didn't you tell her, Felka?' Loretta asks.

Felka ignores her, looking only at Rachel. 'Your mother's parents were devastated when Shirley left them to move to Australia. And when Michael and Shirley announced their decision to turn their backs on their faith, because they said religion only brings heartache, her family vowed never to contact them again. Loretta, you agreed with them! You cannot pretend—'

'I promised no such thing,' Loretta says quietly. 'I rang her every week. Michael was furious about it. He wanted me to stop, said I was trying to get her to turn back to her faith. But she was my sister, and she was alone with a baby and a man who hated himself. I would not.'

'And you went along with this?' Rachel says to Felka, who is shocked by Loretta's words. She didn't know, clearly. But it doesn't lessen the fury.

'I had no choice if I wanted you in my life,' Felka says, unable to meet her eyes.

'But what if I wanted *them* in *my* life?' Rachel says loudly, hating how high-pitched her voice is. She's not prone to hysteria. But she's at her limit. 'Has anyone ever thought about what *I* want?' And then she turns to Loretta, in tears. 'And you knew about me? You knew she died. Why didn't you ever reach out to me?'

'I tried, several times,' Loretta replies, her face twisted. 'Your father picked up. He never let me speak to you. I even sent letters. He destroyed them, I suppose. I gave up. I didn't know what else to do.'

Rachel doesn't know what to say, so she leaves, ignoring Loretta's and Felka's calls, striding headfirst into the blurry, inky night.

✳✳✳

It takes several locals pointing her in the right direction to get to the address; almost an hour later, at around eight thirty, she arrives – flushed cheeks, sweat running down her back, feet sore. She barely notices it. Her mind is a blank, shell-shocked daze as she goes to knock on the door, but it swings open before she can.

Mizumi stops in surprise, halfway through fixing her earring in place.

'Rachel?' she says.

'I'm sorry,' Rachel says. 'I just didn't know what to do, where to go.'

Mizumi reaches out, places her hand on Rachel's arm. 'Is everything okay?'

'I just discovered that—' She can hardly form the words. The grief of what was taken from her is too difficult to bear. 'My late mother has a sister here I didn't know about.' She begins weeping; the words hiccup out of her, in staccato, becoming almost incoherent. 'And my grandfather is still alive and living in Tokyo. They lied to me my entire life and when ... they told me the truth, they ... were still lying!'

Mizumi shepherds her inside. Rachel can't see through her tears, relying on Mizumi to steer her to a seat before she collapses. A few seconds later – a few minutes, maybe, Rachel can't tell – she comes to sit next to Rachel, setting something on the side table next to her. The smell of something herbal and calming is in the air.

'Have some tea,' Mizumi says.

Rachel wipes at her eyes. She can feel how swollen her face is, that her make-up is running. She must look foul.

'I should go,' she says thickly. 'I'm so sorry.'

'Have some tea,' Mizumi repeats. Rachel obediently picks up the teacup – a simple pale blue porcelain with no handle – and sips from it. Bitter, but not unbearably so. The warmth spreads down her throat. She wraps her other hand around the cup, feeling its heat.

'Thanks,' she says after a moment. 'It's nice.'

Mizumi nods. 'It is very calming. I often have a cup just before I go to bed.'

'It's not like the tea back home,' Rachel says. It feels nonsensical to be talking about tea right now. She clings to it, the semblance of normality, and casts her eyes about Mizumi's home. It's a cosy traditional apartment, with art both Japanese and Western hanging from the walls. A little television sits in front of a small, low table that has some sort of fabric hanging from the edges, surrounded by thick pillows.

'What is that?' Rachel says, gesturing at it.

'A kotatsu,' Mizumi replies. 'Underneath, there is a heater. So you can sit on the cushions there in winter, with your legs under the quilt, and stay warm.'

Rachel can imagine sitting there, surrounded by family and friends. The thought makes her burst once more into tears.

'Sorry, sorry,' she splutters.

'Tell me more about what is happening,' Mizumi says soothingly. 'You did not know about your aunt?'

So Rachel tells her, all of the lies, how her life came undone in a matter of weeks, and how just as she thought she could begin moving forward, the past, yet again, ensnared her.

Mizumi is an excellent listener. She's patient, kind, prompts Rachel when she falters, refills her teacup before it ever empties. And when Rachel is done, she places a hand on her shoulder.

'I am so sorry,' she says simply. 'You deserve better.'

If Rachel had any tears left, this would have sent her into a fresh spasm of crying. Instead, she sniffs. 'I can't face them right now,' she says.

Mizumi checks her watch. 'I was on my way to an exhibition with some friends,' she says. 'It should be going for a few hours yet. Why don't you join me?'

'I've already ruined your evening,' Rachel begins, and Mizumi cuts her off.

'Caring for a friend will never ruin an evening,' she says.

'Oh, well – okay. If you insist.' She touches her face, feeling the mascara tracks clumped there. 'Do you mind if I use your bathroom first, though? I don't want to frighten anyone.'

***

Mizumi's three friends wave from across the room when they arrive. Mizumi speaks to them, gestures at Rachel – presumably introducing her, possibly complaining about this no-good Australian woman who's made her run terribly late – and they smile, greeting Rachel in stilted English. Their words are awkward, but their tones are warm. The three of them move off after a few minutes, though. Rachel can't blame them; Mizumi having to translate everything for both parties makes for prolonged conversation.

The descriptions are all in Japanese, so Mizumi offers to translate. Her soft voice is an anchor, stopping Rachel's thoughts from drifting back to the bar. To Felka, to Loretta.

They stop before a work depicting a crowd gathered on a subway platform, the perspective directed along the tracks and towards the train emerging from the tunnel. The figures, all gathered on the right of the image, wear a mix of traditional kimonos and elegant 1920s fashions. The shapes are flat and clean, the colours bold, the postures and gestures of the people natural and yet perfectly composed. It's exquisite.

'This is by Sugiura Hisui,' Mizumi explains. She points to a sign near the painting. 'It's to commemorate the opening of the first subway in Tokyo in 1927. This exhibition is all about the period between the Great Kanto Earthquake of 1923 and the war, around 1943. This art would have been popular when your grandmother lived here,' she adds.

Rachel forces a smile, but the mention of Felka makes her stomach churn.

Mizumi turns back to the painting, her admiration clear on her face. 'I love this period. In the 1920s, the youth in Japan took pride in working all day and partying all night. The boys were known as "mobo" and the girls "moga" – it's short for "modern boy" and "modern girl". This was the first time Japanese women were represented as liberated career women, capable of doing just what the men could do. They were the inspiration behind the modernist movement. Thanks to their spirit, the print, textile and ceramics industries flourished – for a time. After the war, it's like we went backwards.'

They continue walking along the line of paintings and Rachel regards the works carefully. There is something distinctly Japanese about them, but also some Western influence: they are bright, bold, colourful, flat, their compositions perfectly balanced. She thinks, with slight embarrassment, of her own art: her scrambling for a new style between Matisse's paintings and Felka's woodblocks, her experiments with perspective. And the whole time there was an entire art movement she never knew existed, combining everything she adores with a grace she can only strive for.

'A tasteful melding of European and Eastern art, very much influenced by Cubism and Fauvism,' Mizumi says, as though reading Rachel's mind. She looks up at Mizumi's profile, clean and bright against the white gallery wall, and suddenly itches to be at her desk with her pencil and paints.

Behind her, Rachel notices one of Mizumi's friends – Sakura, Rachel remembers from their earlier introductions. She's a tall, slight woman with long hair and thin lips, and she keeps glancing back at them, brows furrowed, mouth tight.

'I'm sorry again for interrupting your evening,' Rachel says to Mizumi after she catches Sakura staring several times. 'I think I've upset your friend.'

'Sakura?' Mizumi says, surprised. 'Ah. We grew up together. We were neighbours and she lost her family very young. She has relied on me to fill this loss in her life.' She pauses, and gently lays a hand on Rachel's forearm, gazing at her steadily. With great deliberation, she says, 'She can be possessive. But I do not approve of it. I am happy to have you here with me.'

Rachel nods. She can empathise with Sakura. She feels a return of the longing she felt at the nightclub.

Rachel can feel her cheeks are warm. Mizumi's fingers are soft on her arm. She feels confused.

Oh, Rachel thinks as it suddenly falls into place. She's attracted. To Mizumi.

As Mizumi returns to talking about the art, Rachel is barely listening. This kind of thing, this kind of attraction, is unfamiliar. She watches Mizumi glide from work to work, inspecting them, voicing her thoughts. When Mizumi suddenly looks and smiles at her, her heart jumps, the same sort of jolt she got when Yanni first noticed her. This surprises her.

'Rachel?' Mizumi says half an hour later. 'You are very quiet.'

'Just ... thinking,' Rachel says, and manages an approximation of a smile.

'Of course. This has been an eventful day for you. Would you like me to call you a taxi?'

'No, no,' Rachel blurts. 'This is lovely. Being here with you and your friends. These works are amazing.'

Mizumi blinks, the faintest hint of pink on her cheeks, and Rachel has another thought: that Mizumi might feel attracted to her too. She thinks back on their interactions, moments that she couldn't quite read and had put down to cultural difference. In this new light, they look a lot like flirting. Has Rachel been misreading the signals and brushing it off? Now she's

262

got to wondering – is this real? And if it is – what then?

And then a nagging idea intrudes – what would Felka say? But she boldly pushes this thought away. Why should she care what Felka thinks, especially after what she's learned tonight?

'This one is lovely,' Mizumi says, breaking Rachel out of her trance. She feels awful for being so absent, especially after showing up at Mizumi's door with no warning. Feelings aside, she owes it to Mizumi to at least be present.

Sakura comes up to them, and – ignoring Rachel entirely – has a brief, low conversation with Mizumi. Sakura looks at Rachel several times, and Mizumi seems exasperated, guilty and sad all at once. It's jealousy, Rachel realises. Sakura is jealous.

Sakura abruptly leaves and Mizumi appears a little embarrassed. Rachel desperately wants to question her, but holds it in until a couple of hours later when they're back at Mizumi's house, sipping tea.

'Do you have anybody in your life?' Rachel dares to ask. 'A special somebody?'

The lack of specific gender is deliberate, and she can tell Mizumi picks up on it from how she searches Rachel's face again, taking her time to answer.

'I had a boyfriend when I was younger,' she says eventually. 'We were very close. But he moved away for work, and we decided it was best to part ways. Since then, not really.'

'Sakura and you seem very close,' Rachel presses.

'We were once. Not so much anymore.' She pauses meaningfully.

'I understand,' Rachel says.

Mizumi looks at her for a moment, then smiles. 'And you?'

'I am...' Rachel pauses then responds, '*was* engaged to a doctor. Yanni. A Greek guy. But we're taking a break while I work myself out.' She gives a half laugh and shrugs. 'I'm not sure I'm working much out, though.'

Mizumi shows no reaction, just sips from her cup and tactfully changes the topic. 'How are you feeling about your aunt?'

'Angry,' Rachel admits. 'I don't even know what I'm going to say to Grandma.'

'I would be angry too. But I'm sure they didn't mean to hurt you.'

'Perhaps not,' Rachel says. 'But they still did.'

'I can see your grandmother adores you,' Mizumi says. Her voice has an undertone. Envy, Rachel thinks in surprise. 'You are her everything. Seek truth, yes, but ultimately, try to forgive your family.'

'What happened to yours?' Rachel blurts. 'If you don't mind me asking.'

Mizumi pauses, as if weighing up how much to tell, how much to reveal. 'They were killed by the events of Hiroshima,' she says quietly. 'When I was just a baby. So were my grandparents. My aunt raised me.'

'Oh,' Rachel says, embarrassed. 'I'm sorry.'

'It is okay. You didn't know.' Mizumi looks at her teacup. 'But family is very important to us Japanese. Very, very important. To not have parents, or grandparents ... it is difficult, here. Freeing, in some ways. But difficult. This is why I think you should try to forgive your family.'

'You're probably right,' Rachel says. But it's not that simple for her. She can't stop thinking about the years she spent with a hole in her heart, a wound that could have been healed by the people kept from her.

Chapter 15

It's just after midnight when Rachel finally returns to the hotel. Felka and Judit are the only people in the lobby besides the night staff, speaking to a couple of police officers. At the sound of the door opening, they all turn to her hopefully; Felka's face crumples in relief, and she crosses to Rachel, arms outstretched.

'Where have you been? It's past twelve! I was worried sick about you!' She tries to wrap her arms around Rachel, who shrugs her off. Felka searches her face. 'Pupelle, I didn't know. I didn't know she would ... I didn't know Michael hid her from you.' She starts coughing.

Rachel is so, so tired. 'Why should I believe you?'

'Rachel—'

'All you and my father have ever done is lie to me. Were you ever going to tell me about Loretta, or my grandfather?' Felka is spluttering, coughing. Rachel watches her dispassionately. 'If Loretta hadn't come to the reunion tonight, I don't think you would have. I think I would have spent the rest of my life not knowing. Christ, even you telling me about being Jewish was only because you couldn't stand the idea of me marrying a gentile. Lie after lie after lie after lie, and for what? To protect me? The only thing you've protected me from is having a loving family!'

Rachel's screaming, she realises. Judit looks on in shock. The police officers are staring, as are the hotel staff. Blood is pounding in her ears and her chest is heaving. And then Felka coughs, spraying blood down her front, and collapses.

Rachel reaches out, sinking down with her to the floor. Judit gasps in horror, and she and the police officers rush over.

'Call an ambulance,' Rachel tells Judit. 'Quickly!'

'I am fine,' Felka protests, but her voice is thick, almost a gurgle. Rachel pulls her into a sitting position, trying to keep her airways clear. 'I do not need the hospital. So ... so much fuss...'

The receptionist suddenly sprints out the front as Judit comes to kneel beside Felka, helping to support her weight. Rachel can't breathe, she can't get the oxygen in.

'They're going to flag a taxi to take you straight there,' Judit explains. 'Quicker than waiting for an ambulance.'

'Alright. Did you hear that, Grandma?' Rachel says desperately.

Felka smiles at her granddaughter. Her eyes are half-shut. The blood splattered down her chin matches her lipstick. Rachel wants to throw up.

'You are my millions,' Felka manages. 'I'm sorry, darling ... I shouldn't have ... concealed the truth from you ... yet again...'

'We need to get her outside,' Rachel manages. The police officers help Felka up and out onto the street, where the receptionist waits next to the taxi, urgently instructing the driver.

Rachel and Judit sit either side of Felka, propping her up. The taxi feels like it's crawling, like it would have been faster to just walk. The taxi radio is playing something just loud enough that Rachel can hear the drums. She wants to rip it out, wants to scream at the pedestrians still out and about.

Felka weakly grabs Rachel's hand, interlocking their fingers.

'Grandma?' Rachel says, bewildered as she starts swaying their hands from side to side.

'Dance with me, pupelle,' Felka says. Her chest sounds wet, and she stifles a cough. 'Like it's your wedding day.'

Rachel starts crying. 'Don't you do that to me!'

'Dance with me,' Felka insists, and begins humming 'Sunrise, Sunset, Sunrise...' Felka saw *Fiddler on the Roof* in Sydney last year and since then Rachel's heard her sing it many times, often while cleaning. She's said several times that she's going to dance to it at Rachel's wedding.

'You need to save your energy, Grandma,' Rachel tries to tell her, but Felka shakes her head, limply forcing their arms to move as one in time with her humming, as if they're waltzing across a dance floor. And then, wheezing, breathless, Felka stops humming, her arm dropping down just as the taxi pulls into the hospital.

***

Judit sits next to Rachel in the hospital's waiting room. It's stark, white, full of people all waiting for news of their loved ones. A frail, ancient woman – tiny and grey – sits opposite, her face expressionless. A younger woman, presumably her daughter, sits beside her. No words pass between the two. A mother sits a few rows away, holding a baby who is sleeping in a blanket. A restless toddler climbs under the seats and mumbles to himself, immersed in his imaginary world. He occasionally surfaces to peer up at his mother. She doesn't react, clearly too distracted by her thoughts to care about his behaviour. He continues on his merry way.

Rachel watches him listlessly, envious of his youth and freedom. She wishes she could crawl under a chair, immerse herself in an imaginary world and start life again.

'Is there anyone I can call for you, sweetheart?' Judit asks Rachel. She's clutching Felka's coat and handbag. They both look deflated, the bright reds turned rusty in the hospital lighting.

Rachel shakes her head.

'Not even your father?'

Rachel looks at her – there's a difference between *can* call and *should* call. She just shrugs instead, and Judit pats her knee.

Rachel should be pacing, crying, screaming, but she just feels cold. Hungry with no appetite. She doesn't have the energy to move. She saw the doctor's expression when she informed him of Felka's condition. She knows that look.

The same doctor enters from the emergency department, and immediately approaches them. Rachel's chest tightens.

'Rachel, isn't it?' he says. His English is good. A small mercy.

'Yes. Is she – has she—'

'No. But the cancer has definitely spread to her liver, and she has fluid in her lungs, as you suggested.' He pauses. 'We have given her morphine for the pain and will keep her comfortable. But she doesn't have long. Hours at most. I am so sorry.'

Rachel nods. What else can she say?

'I will take you to her room,' he says. 'So you can say goodbye.'

Judit gives her a warm, one-armed squeeze, and she follows the man through the doors and down the hallway to Felka's bedside. He leaves her just outside the door. Rachel has never been so petrified in her life. She musters every ounce of strength that she has left, and tentatively enters the hospital room.

Even in her final moments, Felka is majestic. Elegant. Not a hair is out of place. Even as the ominous rattle of her breath intensifies, it is somehow dignified, not ugly, not overdramatic. But it breaks Rachel's heart to see her like this, lying in the simple, plain hospital gown, without a hint of red in sight save for the tiny prick under the plastic strip where the cannula pierced her skin and went into her vein. An oxygen mask is strapped to her face, and the IV drip, Rachel notes with a distant satisfaction, has been perfectly inserted. The morphine must feel gentle, Rachel thinks, hopes. Pleasant, even.

Felka can barely speak, but she sees Rachel and smiles through the mask. Rachel pulls up the visitor's chair and takes Felka's hand in her own. They gaze at each other for a moment. Rachel knows that deep down, somewhere in her soul, she is still angry with Felka. But it no longer feels important. Her grandmother's hands – usually so strong, gesturing and cooking and conducting a song – feel limp. Her breaths are a struggle.

'I'm sorry,' Felka croaks. It's barely audible above the wheeze of the oxygen machine. 'Should have ... told you...'

'You need to save your strength,' Rachel tells her sternly. She can feel the tears running down her cheeks.

'Love you,' Felka manages, takes in a breath. 'So much.'

'I love you too, Grandma.'

Felka gives her a small nod, barely a tremble. 'Forgive ... him...'

'Dad?'

Another nod.

Rachel swallows. 'I'll try.'

'My millions,' Felka says, and Rachel feels the lightest of pressures as Felka tries to squeeze her hands. '*Finita la ... commedia*...'

She closes her eyes, and Rachel presses her forehead to Felka's hand, tears soaking through the pressed white hospital blanket.

In the end, it takes two hours. Felka's fight for breath turns slow, resigned. Each breath is a little shallower, the pause between each inhale and exhale a little longer. Rachel finds herself breathing in time even as the tears stream down her face, as if she can transfer her strength, her oxygen to Felka. Just a little longer. Just another breath.

And finally, Felka simply stops breathing. Her chest is still. It's over.

***

Michael lies in bed next to Betty, staring up at the ceiling. He usually spends the night at her apartment, but with Rachel and Felka gone, he is afforded the rare opportunity of certain privacy in his own home.

He's finding it difficult to sleep tonight. Visions of Kobe pass through his head. Have they met Sugihara yet? Does he remember them? His stomach has felt leaden ever since he waved them off at the airport. Guilt, he realises. Melancholy. The thought makes him furious.

He flinches when the phone rings, checks the clock on his bedside table; it's almost four. Who on earth is calling at this time?

He climbs out of bed – 'Where are you going, darling?' Betty mumbles sleepily – and picks up the phone in the living room.

'Who is this?' he snaps. 'It's four in the morning, for God's sake.'

'Hello? Is this Michael?' The woman's voice is unfamiliar, timid. A Polish accent.

'Yes,' he says tersely. 'Who am I speaking to?'

'My name is Judit,' the woman says. 'I'm one of your mother's friends. I'm calling from the hospital in Kobe.'

Michael doesn't say anything to this. He just waits. It's an easy guess as to why Judit is calling him.

'Your mother has passed away,' Judit says gently. 'I'm so sorry.'

Of course she has. He ignores how his breathing has suddenly become laborious. 'Is Rachel there?'

'Yes, I'll put her on.'

The sound of scuffling. He waits, and someone whose breaths are hiccups comes onto the phone.

'Rachel,' he says.

'Dad?' she says. She's been crying, clearly. Of course. The image of her standing in a Japanese hospital, alone and out of place, unexpectedly moves him.

'I'm – I'm—' He takes a breath. It feels like the air is siphoning out of him, and he starts again. 'I'm in the middle of a huge deal. The major department stores want to take on our brand. I can't just up and leave. I'll arrange for the body to come back. Do you have enough money to reschedule your flight?'

Rachel takes a moment to reply. 'She wants to be buried here.'

Michael wants to throw something. 'Don't be ridiculous.'

'Next to her daughter.'

'What?' Michael says.

'She had a stillborn daughter. When you both came to Kobe.' Rachel's voice is harsh. Cold. 'So you had better make arrangements to come. If you intend to come, that is.'

He gapes, blindly staring at the dark outline of the couch. He doesn't know what to say; he can't seem to connect his brain to his mouth.

A scuffling sound again. 'I can't talk to him,' Rachel says from far away, 'I can't, you do it.' And Judit is back on the phone.

'Michael, you know we cannot start the funeral without you,' she says gently.

Michael knows, of course, from his father's funeral. A Jewish burial must happen as quickly as possible. He feels overwhelmed. There is so much to organise from so far away.

'We – Felka's friends – will make all the arrangements,' Judit says soothingly. 'All you need to do is get here as quickly as you can.'

'Three days,' he croaks. 'I will be there in three days.'

Judit pauses. 'Three days?' Her tone is disapproving.

'Yes.'

'I see. Three days. We will organise things for then. I will be in touch to confirm your arrival time and so on.'

'See you then,' Michael says, and hangs up. He stands there for a moment, in the darkness, and then returns to bed.

Betty stirs. 'Is everything okay?'

He doesn't answer her, rolling away from her. She starts snoring again moments later. It takes him much longer to drift off.

He's in Warsaw. A thirteen-year-old Michael is skipping along in the newly fallen snow with his grandfather, Shmerl, as his parents, Felka and Myetek, walk proudly arm in arm behind them. Shmerl is neatly dressed in a smart dark suit, tainted slightly by the white cotton armband bearing a large Star of David. He flicks a coin into the air and catches it, teasing his grandson.

'Grandfather, let me see!'

Shmerl smiles and gently answers, 'Ah, this one is special. A gold sovereign given to me on my bar mitzvah by my grandfather, may he rest in peace. And this – this I will soon give to you, now that I have just had the joy of seeing *your* bar mitzvah. But not just yet.' He pockets it with a cheeky smile. Michael grabs at this arm, begging to have it, then grins, lunging for the pocket. As Shmerl playfully dodges his grandson, in front of them, an old lady falls while trying to cross the street. Shmerl rushes to her aid as Michael hangs back, watching. A German soldier approaches, shouts at Shmerl, reprimanding him. He hits Shmerl hard, over the head, with the butt of his rifle. Shmerl falls into the snow, face-down. The soldier begins kicking him in the guts.

Michael is petrified, only tangentially aware of his parents pulling him away, urging him to move quickly, fear thick in their voices. The last they see of Shmerl, he's curling into himself as the soldier yells at him – and then he disappears behind the crowd of people going about their day as if a man weren't being beaten right in front of them.

The pulling on his arm is now from Betty. 'Michael! Shh, it's only a dream.' She tugs him free from the nightmare and strokes his forehead.

He stares at her blankly for a few moments as she comes into focus. In the dark, he can make out her sleep-mussed hair, the concern in her eyes.

He pulls her to him gruffly, abruptly. A warm body. Her arms circle him, hands drifting. Then they're having sex – fast and rough – and his eyes are tightly closed as he thrusts over and over.

Afterwards, he lies on the bed next to her, completely spent, drenched with sweat and breathing hard. His clenched fists cover his eyes, concealing them, lest Betty see they have welled with tears.

He hears her shifting beside him. 'Michael … is everything okay?'

He stands and retreats to the bathroom, hating the worry in her voice.

At some point, back in bed, sleep finally claims Michael. But there is no distraction strong enough; his grandfather's face, terrified, follows him into sleep.

The next morning, as Betty applies her make-up, he casually tells her. 'My mother passed away.'

She stops, stares at him. And then his words seem to sink in; she sets the blush down and comes over, hugging him tightly. He lets her. It's not unpleasant.

'Oh, Michael, I'm so sorry,' she says. 'In Japan! I didn't even know she was ill. Was that what the phone call was about?'

'She wants to be buried there,' Michael suddenly offers, unasked. 'I ... I'll need to go. Rachel is there alone. My daughter.'

'Do you need me to organise anything?' Betty asks. 'What can I help with?'

He doesn't know. Comfort. Company. But he senses a hesitation from her, like she's not willing to engage too much with him. It makes sense; their relationship isn't deep. He gives her sex. Great sex. Physical, unemotional, disconnected. And denim. Lots of denim. What more can a girl want? He knows he has never been there for her, but he needs her to be there for him. He needs her to understand.

'It's just like my mother to do this, to complicate things. Why Japan?'

'It sounds like it was an important place for her. After all, you—'

Michael cuts her off. 'Silliness. Inconvenient. How am I supposed to just stop everything?'

Betty pauses then. He can see he's lost her. She turns back to her blush, adding the final touches.

'I'm sure you'll manage, darling,' she says, turning her face as she checks the mirror. 'You're a very organised and capable man.'

She gives him another hug and a kiss, but it feels a little cooler than when he broke the news. Then she grabs her coat and leaves.

Michael is left alone, alone with his thoughts. For the first time since his father's death, he wishes he wasn't.

Chapter 16

The Ashkenazi Synagogue of Kobe is splendid despite being smaller than the churches Rachel is used to: it has bright white walls, polished wooden pews and a red-carpeted platform for rabbis to read from. A lectern, or *bimah* – Judit tells her that's what it's called. She can appreciate none of it, not a thing, because the only reason she is even there is that her grandmother's funeral will soon take place within its walls.

Rachel sits in a dimly lit side room, doing her best not to think or feel. It's a welcome distraction when Judit enters, sits next to her and takes her cold hand.

Rachel was too young to be involved when her mother died – not that it would have mattered, as it was a nondenominational funeral – and so has no clue what needs to be done in normal circumstances, let alone Jewish ones.

Judit explains to her the Jewish rituals for burying the dead, starting with sitting *shemira:* acting as a guardian of the dead. A Jewish body is not to be left alone at any time before burial, while the soul ascends to heaven. Prayers and psalms are recited softly. Judit has volunteered for this, as have several of the group's members.

'Shouldn't I do it?' Rachel asks.

'No,' Judit says gently. 'Relatives aren't expected to. It would be too much, I think.'

Rachel is as relieved as she is disappointed. Felka was there when she was born; it feels like she's missing an opportunity to complete the journey, somehow. Still, she's glad that Felka won't be alone.

Judit continues: 'They will begin the process called *tahara.* Her body will be completely cleansed with only water and a cloth. Nothing else, unless nail polish needs to be removed. Then they will use some acetone.'

Rachel pictures the red being wiped from Felka's fingernails. Her signature erased from the world.

'Then there is the *mikvah* – you know what a *mikvah* is?'

Rachel shakes her head.

'It's a ritual bath. The body is dipped vertically into the water until it's entirely submerged. Her body will then be dressed in what is called *tachrichim* starting with linen pants that are tied and secured with a special knot in the front in the shape of a Hebrew letter called a *shin* which represents God – this is an art that has to be mastered. This knot can be very easily undone, because the spirits need easy access to the soul. Then a long shirt is placed on the body and a hood on the head and a light piece of cloth covers the face. Then the body is laid in a pine box with wooden nails – not metal. Everything used has to be biodegradable. Finally a flap of cloth is folded over, one from each side, and the lid closed.'

'The cloth should be red,' Rachel murmurs. 'She'd like that.'

Judit smiles. 'I will see what I can do.'

'They do this for every Jewish person, even foreigners?' Rachel asks.

'Yes. Ritual is the glue that keeps a community together. Every Jewish life is precious. It is said in the Torah that if you save one Jewish soul, it is as if you had saved the world. That's why Sugihara, what he did, is so precious to all of us. There will be memorial prayers in the evening after the burial. There will be no headstone erected yet. You need to decide on the wording and it will be instated sometime before the end of the first year after the funeral.' Rachel can't imagine at this stage what she should insist on for the wording. But it has to be unique, bold and positive, like Felka. And there has to be a Star of David on the grave. She knows that now.

When Judit leaves to sit *shemira* at the Chevra Kadisha nearby – the building where the body is kept and prepared for burial., Rachel retreats to the main sanctuary and sits on a pew. The room is largely empty, but the rabbi still prays. She finds comfort in his soft, almost whispered dialogue. She closes her eyes for a while, hovering on the blessed precipice of sleep, reality pushed back to a manageable distance.

282

She could sit here for hours, but she can't: she needs to return to the hotel to pack her suitcase. Felka's suitcase, too. The thought fills her with dread.

A door opens and the sanctuary fills with tungsten light. Anna enters, walking down the pews to Rachel. She must be sitting *shemira* next, Rachel thinks, Or perhaps she's simply here to worship.

Anna rounds the bench and sits next to Rachel. She puts her hand ever so gently on Rachel's and squeezes it tightly. Rachel closes her eyes and imagines the hand to be Felka's: the soft, wrinkled skin, the arthritic, knobbly knuckles. But it's not. However soft and kind the woman is, Rachel can't maintain the delusion. She opens her eyes. Anna is gazing at her patiently.

'I shouldn't have convinced Grandma to come here,' Rachel croaks. 'She was so unwell. I should have realised how bad it was.'

'I understand your remorse,' Anna says. 'And the burden you are carrying. But it is not your fault, sweetheart. You did not know she was so close to the end. Who knows these things?'

'But I'm a nurse,' Rachel protests. 'I should have known.'

Anna shakes her head. 'You know how Felka was! She was stubborn, so stubborn. You didn't lead Felka to her death. You helped her live the last of her life.'

Rachel tears up. Another flood. How can one person create so much water? She can't bear to eat or drink, and yet her body continues to function. Her body knows she needs tears, and so it produces them from a reservoir gone dry.

***

Rachel sits in the pew for several hours, until the evening sun is beginning to stretch through the window.

She can't think clearly. Felka would be furious at how she's still sitting here. *What are you doing? Crying? What for? Where will that get you? Puffy eyes and a red, swollen nose. No time for sadness. Up! Up!*

With all her remaining strength, she takes a heavy breath, lungs struggling, and then stands. She collects her thoughts. She must snap out of this before she is dragged down so far there will be no crawling out of the hole she is digging for herself. The sun warms the back of her head. Like Anna's hand, the sensation is familiar, welcome. It's as if Felka is cupping the back of her head. *Come, pupelle. You can do it.*

***

She returns to the hotel, retreats upstairs to begin to pack her belongings. But she is surrounded by Felka. The perfectly folded clothes, the precisely made bed. Her toiletries in the bathroom; the red dressing-gown draped over a chair.

One battle is enough for today, Rachel decides, and falls asleep, wrapped in one of Felka's scarves, still smelling of her perfume.

The next morning, Rachel procrastinates until she can't anymore. She brushes her teeth, showers, washes and dries her hair, does her make-up, and then there's nothing left to do and she must confront the fact that every nook and cranny of the room is flooded with Felka. Felka has melted and crept into every crevice. Every surface has been touched by her, is sticky with her presence. It's an unbearable, excruciating task, to try to avoid the reminders of her. But she must. And so, once she's packed the majority of her own clothes, she turns to her grandmother's. The woollen skirt, the thick tights, the eye-wateringly bright blouses. She folds them all with a care she would never assign to her own belongings, stripping the room of the last traces of Felka, creating tidy piles on Felka's bed. Rachel must eventually decide what will return to Australia and what will be disposed of. The idea of this makes her cold.

She is just placing the last item of clothing on the bed when a call comes through to the room's phone.

She picks up, expecting it to be Michael, perhaps Kate or Susan. 'Hello?'

'Rachel,' a voice says, masculine and lovely and sad. 'Michael ... your dad just told me the news. I'm so sorry.'

'Yanni,' she says. She doesn't know what to say. He feels a world away, a lifetime away. And her father actually made the effort to call him? To think maybe she would want him to know. To comfort her. How extraordinary...

'Are you okay? Can I do anything to help?'

'Yes. No. It's – fine. The Jewish community here is wonderful.'

'I'm glad. I've been so worried about you.'

She nods, remembers he can't see the motion. 'They're taking good care of me.'

'I want you to come back,' he says. 'I miss you so much.'

She doesn't know what to say. It feels as if everything outside of Kobe is something she dreamed. How can she explain it?

'Rachel? Are you there?'

She misses him. Even more so at hearing him. But more than him, she misses the person she once was. The person who didn't know any of this, who had no curiosity or confusion. But the sound of his voice is so comforting. She could just take the next plane after the funeral. No one would think any worse of her for it. But she can't. It would be a thing to regret for the rest of her life, she knows.

She tells him briefly of her discovery, of her aunt and grandfather. Of Sugihara being in the USSR. He is shocked. He wants to know more. She doesn't have the energy to recount it all. She's depleted, wrung out like a used facecloth. She needs time to say goodbye. Time to forgive.

'But when will you come back?' Yanni asks eventually.

'I don't know,' she says. 'I need to go to Moscow.'

'Alone? Behind the Iron Curtain? Rachel, you can't.'

'I can. I have to.'

'Rachel...'

She cuts him off. 'I want to.'

'I – okay. Promise me you'll be careful.'

'I promise.'

'Call me. The moment you get there?'

Abruptly, the strength leaves her. She can't even reply. Doesn't he understand?

'Hello? Rachel? Are you still there? Can you hear me?'

'I have to go.'

'I love you,' he says. She ends the call.

For a moment, Rachel just sits there. The light eases through the windows, warm on her skin.

Is it the physical distance or the emotional distance? No matter how Yanni feels, the truth will always be there for her, lingering. She is Jewish. She is not like him, or his family. It's a similarity she no longer wants, either. A similarity that would require sacrifice.

Rachel opens the hotel window. The warm breeze and smell of the gardens drift in: grass, flowers. Fresh, and old, too. Smells that have been on the earth long before her, and smells that will be there long after her. Rooted in the past, and in the future, too.

No. She can't go back to Sydney in the way Yanni wants her to.

She can't give up what she's found here, this past and future of her own.

***

When Rachel opens the small hotel safe to retrieve her passport, she notices an envelope with Felka's handwriting on it, addressed to Chiune Sugihara. She holds it for a long while, desperately wanting to open it. But she knows that would be a betrayal. It's personal. For the eyes of one person only.

The passport is so Rachel can begin the difficult process of entering the USSR, a gruelling administrative process that Mizumi offered to assist Rachel with the moment she heard of Felka's passing. Rachel needs a visa to enter the USSR, and an airline ticket to Moscow.

But Mizumi's assistance comes with a price: a homemade dinner at her apartment. Rachel agrees readily. She can't imagine being in a restaurant right now, surrounded by people living their lives, heedless of her grief. And she needs to escape the hotel room, if only for a little while. She suspects Mizumi might think the same thing: that this dinner is as much an intervention as it is an invitation. Her feelings, her uncertainty about what exactly is between her and Mizumi, now feel irrelevent. She will take what kindness, what comfort she can find.

She leaves early so that she can walk there. Her legs are numb, coiled things; her whole body has curled in on itself. The fresh air does her good, even if the city is rudely colourful and noisy. *Life goes on,* Felka might have said. *And so should you.*

When Rachel arrives, Mizumi is just finishing up with the cooking. She wears an apron in a pale blue gingham pattern with smears of flour and recent stains. Rachel can't explain it, but the sight soothes her.

'You are just in time.' Mizumi smiles, opening the door. Her apartment is flush with sunlight, the windows thrown open. A deeply savoury smell is in the air.

'I made us udon soup and dumplings,' Mizumi says, ushering Rachel to the kotatsu, which has had its quilt removed. Now, it is just a low table. Rachel sinks onto the thick cushions sitting on the floor, surveying the feast Mizumi has made. The bowls are filled with thick noodles, greens and eggs, the dumplings pleasingly arranged in a pyramid next to soy sauce and vinegar. Rachel's mouth waters; it's been over a day since she last ate, she realises.

Mizumi comes in from the kitchen with a pot of tea, and takes a seat opposite her, pouring her a cup.

They talk easily as they eat, Rachel trying not to eat too quickly. It's delicious. As Mizumi finishes the last of the dumplings, it occurs to Rachel that she hasn't asked Mizumi how she came to be a guide.

'When I grew up, many Americans were still in Japan, occupying it after the war. They were ... difficult. We did not care for them. But I picked up English here and there from them, and studied it in school and university.

'I worked as a translator and English tutor for quite a while,' Mizumi adds. 'A friend of mine asked me to act as a guide for some American clients once, and then everybody started asking me. It pays very well. Tourists like to learn about our history – good and bad.'

'But how can you do it – revisiting the past? Why do you want to put yourself through that?'

'It helps me,' Mizumi says. 'I feel it is my duty to remember those who died. I am considering going back to university, actually. I would like to study more history, and educate others about my country's past as a full-time occupation, not simply as a tour guide.'

They shift to the topic of Vietnam, and Rachel tells Mizumi about the protests, and her friends' conflicting feelings about the war, then to the political struggles in Japan about university debt. They talk away into the early hours, and at some point agree that it's too late for Rachel to go back to the hotel, a decision that makes her glad. They talk some more as the clock ticks on, voices lowering to avoid disturbing the neighbours, and at some point, Rachel falls asleep.

***

Rachel wakes to the dawn sun slipping into the room, gentle and delicate. She's on some sort of mattress in the living room – a futon, she remembers Mizumi called it. Mizumi sleeps on the sofa. Rachel has kicked the blanket off in the night, and the air is pleasantly cool on her bare skin. She remembers talking late into the night, borrowing a shirt from Mizumi to sleep in so she wouldn't crease her clothes. She looks across to Mizumi now, still sleeping. Her hair fans over the pillow like an ink stain, black and glossy. Even in sleep, Mizumi is beautiful. A study in chiaroscuro, Rachel thinks, the contrast of her dark hair against her porcelain complexion. Her lips, pink, have parted slightly in slumber; her breathing is even and deep.

Rachel gazes at her for a few minutes. She almost feels guilty for it, as if she's invading Mizumi's privacy.

It feels the same as when Yanni occasionally stays the night with her; she wants to reach out and run her fingers along the curve of Mizumi's cheek. As if to see whether she's real or a piece of fine art.

Yanni. These thoughts must be a betrayal to him. Or they would be, if she was sure she would be returning to him. Here, in Mizumi's apartment, her time with Yanni feels dreamlike. It feels like another time and place. Another life.

Rachel's gaze scans the rest of Mizumi. Her pyjama shorts have ridden up, and Rachel takes a sharp breath at an enormous round scar on the top of her left thigh. It must be at least the size of Rachel's hand, a puckered crater long healed. She can tell from the way the scar has stretched, its faded, purple colouring, that the wound must have happened when Mizumi was a child. A burn, she suspects from the rippled pattern.

'The aftershock of Hiroshima caused much destruction,' Mizumi says quietly, catching Rachel by surprise. 'Even beyond the range of the nuclear fallout.'

Rachel looks up. Mizumi is watching her, eyes half-lidded.

'It must have hurt,' Rachel says quietly.

'I do not remember the wound,' Mizumi says. 'Only how long it took to heal.'

Rachel can only imagine. The cycle of cleaning, bandaging, cleaning again. Burns are, she knows, the most terrible wound. Prone to infection, the awful pain difficult to anaesthetise.

They both lie there, thoughts drifting on their own trajectories. Eventually, Mizumi asks, 'What do you remember of your mother?'

'She fell ill when I was only seven, then she died a couple of years later,' Rachel says.

'But you remember her?' Mizumi presses.

'Yeah. She used to read to me. I remember her telling me so many stories.'

'I do not remember my mother,' Mizumi murmurs. 'I was so young. Nobody would tell me about her. Perhaps it is better that way.'

For the first time, Rachel feels grateful for the time she had with Shirley. Despite the lies and the illness, for a brief, shining moment, she had a mother. Mizumi looks so vulnerable and small, a world away from the confident tour guide, the serene, independent woman Rachel saw dancing in the lights of that nightclub only days before. Her eyes are sparkling with unshed tears, and Rachel gets up, goes to sit next to her and draws her close, enfolding Mizumi as the woman comes apart. In all her watching Mizumi, marvelling at her freedom, her strength, she failed to see her loneliness. Mizumi sobs, just once.

They hold there like that for a while. Rachel closes her eyes, finding her mind empty; feeling the sensation of the sun and Mizumi's warmth. She feels the strength in her own body, its ability to comfort: something Mizumi's mother never had the chance to do for her. Rachel, at least, has some memories of that feeling – from Shirley. From Felka. It's only right that she shares it now.

Eventually, Rachel releases and rests her fingers on the scar. Mizumi stiffens, then exhales and relaxes. It's smooth and cool, a texture that would feel almost pleasant beneath Rachel's fingers if it weren't for the pain she knows is attached to it.

'I hate it,' Mizumi confesses.

Rachel's fingers are still at the border, where scar tissue turns to the soft skin of Mizumi's thigh. 'It's part of you,' she says. 'Part of your history. The trauma you overcame.'

'It is hideous,' Mizumi whispers.

Rachel shakes her head. 'It's beautiful. *You're* beautiful, Mizumi.'

She looks up and sees the flush staining Mizumi's cheeks, how she's watching Rachel's hand. Rachel has surprised herself with this brash, instinctive manoeuvre – such intimacy with someone she hardly knows. Something told her it was right, though, almost necessary. She pulls her hand back slowly and looks at Mizumi, wondering if she's crossed a line. She doesn't think so, and Mizumi confirms this when she leans in, gently kissing her. Warmth rushes through Rachel – it should feel strange, she's sure, but it doesn't. They both pull back, and Rachel strokes the scar once more. It has taken on a beauty of its own, the morning sun painting warmth down Mizumi's exposed leg.

They should be getting ready to leave, to go to Tokyo, to the consulate and the travel agent, but they linger just a minute longer. They smile and compose themselves, taking stock of the moment that passed between them and processing it each in her own private way. A first for Rachel, probably not for her friend. They dress in silence.

***

The train ride to Tokyo is quiet, companionable; Rachel sleeps through most of it, and Mizumi reads a book. They still haven't discussed what happened that morning – the kiss. Rachel isn't really sure what to say, or, on reflection, what it means, and only once has Mizumi let a glance linger long enough to ask a question. Something has been dislodged in each of them, but they silently agree to let it be, for now.

Tokyo is a shock to the senses after Kobe's relative quiet. Streams and streams of people take up space no matter where they are, even though it's long past the morning rush. It's noon before Rachel and Mizumi arrive at the USSR embassy, and the shock continues when the armed USSR embassy guards stop them before they can even enter the building. Rachel shows her Australian passport to one of them, and they take their time looking at it, scrutinising them thoroughly. They are finally permitted entry when Mizumi explains she is acting as Rachel's interpreter, and they step inside. Rachel thinks it seems more like a prison than an embassy.

The expansive lobby is adorned with Communist posters and a bronze bust of a man with incredibly thick eyebrows – *Leonid Brezhnev,* the plaque reads. The information desk and booths are made from mahogany, edged in polished bronze. It feels imposing, just foreign enough that Rachel is on edge.

They approach the information desk and are handed a number by a very threatening-looking, buxom woman who appears to be in her fifties. She's dressed in drab dark grey, in such an unbecoming jacket and matching skirt that it appears to have been deliberately chosen to offend the eye. She gruffly advises them to take a seat.

Away from the warmth of Mizumi's isolated apartment, reality seeps back in: Rachel carrying out Felka's final wish depends entirely on this appointment. If she fails here, she will have come all this way for nothing.

It's a small mercy that Rachel and Mizumi don't have to wait very long; a loud, shrill voice shouts Rachel's number after only five minutes. They approach the right counter, and the woman on the other side says, still in a shout, 'Passport!'

Rachel isn't sure why the woman is screaming when Rachel is standing directly in front of her. She hands her passport across.

The woman flicks through it. She speaks in Russian first to Rachel, who stares blankly at her; she then turns to Mizumi and says something in Japanese.

Mizumi replies, then says to Rachel, 'She is asking why you want to travel to the USSR. I told her it is for personal reasons.'

The woman says something else. Mizumi translates, 'Is your family originally from Russia?'

'No,' Rachel says, and Mizumi translates. 'My family emigrated to Australia from Poland during the Second World War.'

'Nobody will accompany you?' is the woman's booming response. Rachel couldn't imagine someone could make Japanese sound so aggressive, and the combination of tone and words brings tears to Rachel's eyes.

'No,' Rachel says again. 'I'm going alone.'

Mizumi places an arm around Rachel to comfort her. The woman sees the tears, but doesn't react. She scribbles in her book, then she flicks through Rachel's passport again and says something to Mizumi before returning Rachel's passport and waving them both away.

'You can come back in three days,' Mizumi says.

'That's it?' Rachel says in surprise. 'No other questions?'

'I suppose not,' Mizumi shrugs, bemused. Clearly a twenty-one-year-old Australian girl isn't much of a threat to Russian national security.

The train ride to Kobe lulls Rachel back into sleep, and she feels a little energised by the rest and Kobe's familiar streets. The experience at the travel agency is easier. It's a tiny, hole-in-the-wall, one-man-show of a business, set up close to Mizumi's home and run by Mizumi's good friend, Riki.

They decide on a flight that departs in four days or more, to give extra time in case there's a delay with the visa. Riki also advises that the flight needs to be organised via an official USSR travel agency called Intourist. She will hand the documents over to them and take care of the back-and-forthing that will ensue. The tickets will be ready just after Felka's funeral.

As Rachel and Mizumi walk back onto the street, it's time for them to part company. Rachel doesn't know what to say. There's no excuse for her to see Mizumi again before she goes, as she'll pick up the visa before she flies out of Tokyo.

Mizumi speaks first. 'So, Rachel. What will you do next, after you meet Sugihara? Will you go back to Australia?' There is no sign of the vulnerability from that morning; her face is clear and calm as she watches Rachel, a smile playing at the corners of her mouth.

Rachel shakes her head. 'I don't know. I have to get to Moscow first. After that ... I don't...' She laughs awkwardly. 'I'm sorry, it's been a really strange time and I feel like I'm...'

Mizumi holds up a hand. 'I understand. There is so much for you to do. You are welcome to leave luggage with me. I've enjoyed meeting you. Spending time with you.'

Rachel finds her cheeks growing warm. 'Me too.'

'I hope you will come back to Kobe some day, then. And Rachel, thank you.'

Rachel laughs, looking at her feet. 'I'm the one who should be saying thank you,' she says, but she knows what Mizumi means, and she is glad to hear it.

They hug each other goodbye, and Rachel watches Mizumi walk away until she's out of view.

***

Back in the hotel room, it occurs to Rachel that the other survivors might like to write letters for her to take to Sugihara. She'll speak to Joshua Nishri about it. But in the meantime, there is so much to do. Though she has organised the majority of Felka's belongings, she needs to decide which to keep and which to discard. A task that she should have weeks, not days, to do. But Rachel needs to vacate the hotel room soon, and although there aren't scores of possessions, and few of them hold any material value, each one is precious to Rachel, now that Felka is gone.

The synagogue auxiliary has offered to store Felka and Rachel's belongings, a gesture which Rachel realises the pragmatism of and decides to take the offer. All Rachel needs to do is decide what to leave behind.

And so, she begins the task. Felka's jewellery is first: a small collection that is the most valuable of all Felka's belongings here, Rachel reflects. But aside from the ring her grandmother gifted her, the pieces mean nothing. What creates emotion and evokes memories of wonderful moments for her? The scarves that Felka wore with such flair. Her beloved red-satin eye mask and matching bathrobe. The reading glasses. The make-up. Her hairbrush, still carrying silky strands of her beautiful, pepper-grey locks. Her embroidered hanky, still streaked with mascara stains from crying.

Rachel weeps as she collects these things that are so truly Felka – her uniform, in a way. She doubts Michael will have any sentimentality about what is thrown away, so besides these things, she holds on to the jewellery, if only because she can't bring herself to dispose of such expensive pieces, and the painting she bought for Felka.

She checks the wardrobe, just in case, and is glad she did; resting in the back is the bag filled with the pieces of the vase Michael broke. She touches one of the shards. Felka never had the chance to fix it, of course. It sparks a determination in Rachel: she stows it in her luggage, vowing to repair it. She stares at the neatly folded items on the small hotel room shelf in the cupboard and is transported back to Sydney, to Felka's apartment, one morning a few months back:

'Careful, the cord!' Felka shouted, just in time for Rachel to duck under the line stretching from the lounge to the power point beside the toaster in the kitchen. Felka was carefully ironing a pair of silken underwear. She folded and placed it atop a perfectly aligned pile of matching specimens, and set to securing them with a pink satin ribbon.

'Grandma, is it really necessary to iron underpants?' Rachel asked. But of course she knew the answer.

'Necessary? Pupelle, when I'm dead and someone comes looking through my drawers, *I* will have nothing to hide!'

Rachel gently lifts the pile of undergarments and stands there, not sure where to put them. She returns them to the shelf. Hopefully, the housekeeping staff will know what to do with them.

The last thing she packs is Felka's letter to Sugihara, set with the utmost care in her handbag.

Later, Joshua Nishri meets her in the cafe nook tucked into the hotel lobby.

He tells her how devastated the survivors are about Felka's death: 'Most of them have arranged to stay longer so they can attend the funeral. They asked me to say that if there is anything you need, anything at all, let us know.'

'I don't know what I would have done without you all,' she says. 'I was thinking, there's not much I can do for everyone, but if anyone wanted to write to Sugihara, I could take letters with me?'

'That is a wonderful idea.' Joshua smiles, clasping her hand. 'I will let them know. All the arrangements for the funeral have now been made. Your father's flight has been booked. He will be here tomorrow.'

Rachel is glad that he's coming; at least he won't be missing his own mother's funeral. But she hasn't thought much about him the past few days. The anger at him concealing Loretta's existence is dwarfed next to the grief. There is still so much to do. But he hasn't even called her once, she realises, and the thought hardens her.

'Joshua,' she says. 'You went to Moscow to find Sugihara – you've been there. What can you tell me about it?'

Joshua is hesitant. 'It's not a nice place, the USSR. I would not want my daughter going there, alone.'

She waves this away. 'The flight is already booked.'

'I know. I cannot stop you. But it is not a place for a girl on her own, let alone a foreign girl, a Jewish foreign girl. Are you sure it is not enough to meet Sugihara's wife with the others instead?'

'It's not the same,' Rachel says. 'Please, Joshua. The travel agent had a very outdated map. Is there anything you can tell me?'

Joshua shakes his head. 'Follow the signs, and keep your head down, that is all I can offer. You will have an official tour guide with you the whole time anyhow. It's mandatory. But I wish you would at least wait for your father. It is much safer for you to be going with a man.'

Rachel laughs. 'He can barely make it to his own mother's funeral. I'm going to go, and I'm going alone – with or without your help. At least give me the name of a good hotel. Please.'

Joshua sighs, and writes down an address. 'Take taxis where possible. It's easy to make your way to the Kursky Train Station, but from there, take a taxi straight to this hotel, and your guide will meet you there. If you need me, it may be difficult to call me, but I will do what I can to help.'

'Thank you, Joshua,' Rachel says, standing up.

'Do not stand out,' he tells her. 'Do not draw attention to yourself. Do not give anyone a reason to single you out. Do you hear me? There are no simple misunderstandings behind the Iron Curtain. And above all – remember – you are a Jew.'

'I'm Jewish, yes, I know.'

'Not Jewish, Rachel,' Joshua says deliberately. 'A Jew.'

Joshua says 'Jew' in a charged way, the way Thomas said it. She pauses, then nods once more, and only then, Joshua stands up. As she follows him outside, she feels uneasy, but pushes it down.

She can do this for Felka. She must.

Chapter 17

On the morning of the funeral, Rachel is not sure how she should be feeling. What is the correct way to feel? The fact that this day's cloudy start has given way to clear weather and bright sunlight has tempered the melancholy a little for her. It feels as though Felka has organised fair skies for her own send-off – very, very in character for her.

But still, Rachel finds that preparing to bury the person who was closest to her is far from easy. It was Felka's presence – so ample, gargantuan – that filled the hole left behind by her mother, after all. It's a compound pain, this feeling. The pain of losing the person closest to her, yet again.

Rachel cannot get back to sleep. She fusses around the hotel room, packing and repacking. Then she fixes her hair. Sheds a few tears. Reapplies her eye make-up. Tears up again. She changes her dress, a new, chic cut with a mid-thigh hem, worried it's not respectful enough. Better? No. Now she looks dowdy, which she knows Felka would hate. She changes back again.

She can imagine Felka's commentary:

All this fuss over me? What are you doing? Are you crazy? Stick me in the ground, and poof! *Forget it. Go live! Life's too short. I'm dancing up here with your grandfather. We're having a ball! You think we care? Pupelle – you have a wonderful life ahead of you, full of promise and possibilities. Go. Enjoy. I love you, I kiss you, I hug you.*

She smiles, despite herself, and then there's a knock on the door. She peers through the viewer.

It's her father. Her smile disappears.

Rachel composes herself, takes a deep breath and lets him in. She promised Felka she would try to be more compassionate. To forgive him. And she will. But she's already steeling herself for the lack of reciprocation that will surely follow.

She eases the door open very slightly, as though she might let him in but keep out his surly demeanour. It doesn't work. His gloom enters before he does, and envelops her. Michael looks tired. His usually pristine Brylcreemed hair is loose, falling onto his face. His tie is rumpled, his jacket slung over his forearm. He sets his suitcase down and awkwardly moves to embrace her. She hesitates – it's a gesture born of duty, she's convinced – but allows it.

'Rachel,' Michael says awkwardly. 'Are you ... well?'

'It's been difficult,' she says. She won't lie to him. 'But the Sugihara group have been incredible to me.' She pauses, wanting to bring up Loretta – but now is not the time, she knows. Not if she's wanting to avoid conflict.

'I see,' he says, and they fall silent. Rachel fusses unnecessarily with the hem of her cardigan as he works up to saying something. An apology, she hopes. But she isn't optimistic.

'I know you are angry with me,' he says eventually. 'With Felka, too. About hiding your heritage.'

'Yes,' she says levelly. 'You hid an entire side of me from myself. A side that I'm really glad to have connected with. Especially before Grandma died.'

She pauses, and adds, 'It's a beautiful religion, Dad. I don't understand how you could have just ... left it behind.'

'I hid our faith to protect you,' he snaps.

Rachel takes a deep breath. She will not be drawn into his problems. 'I don't believe you,' she says slowly, as gently as she can. 'None of the survivors I've met shied away from Judaism. *Fuck Hitler. We won. We are proud to be Jewish.* That's how they feel.'

Michael shifts uncomfortably. 'Rachel...'

She waits.

'I know you're ... I'm...'

He trails off.

And then, he shakes his head. 'You shouldn't leave the room in such a state. It's an upmarket establishment. It's embarrassing.'

There's hardly any mess; Rachel's long since bagged the things to be thrown away, packed the rest. The only feasible issues are the unmade beds and the wet towel slung over a chair. But his baseless nit-picking doesn't strike the usual blow.

'I'll tidy it up,' she shrugs. 'Don't worry.'

He's clearly thrown by her calm response, and he softens. 'Well ... good. I'm glad.' He clears his throat. 'My room is just down the hall. I'm going to shower and change before we leave. I'll meet you downstairs in fifteen minutes.'

He nods, reaches out, then changes his mind and instead pats her on the shoulder. Then he leaves, closing the door behind him.

Rachel sits down on her bed. Why must she be the more mature one? Taking that pause to think before she replied didn't come naturally, but it certainly avoided the fight they probably would have had otherwise. Maybe, if she leads by example, he will eventually learn to meet her halfway. God, she hopes so. She doesn't know how much of this she has in her.

But still, she did it. She shifted their dynamic. Just a touch.

$$***$$

In a small building off to one side of the graveyard, Rachel stands next to Michael. The rabbi stands before them, running them through the event to come. Preparing them to bury their loved one. When the rabbi directs Rachel and Michael to rip part of their clothes, Michael does it without hesitation, but Rachel is confused.

If the rabbi is confused by her ignorance, he hides it. 'We are recognising your loss, accepting that your hearts are irreversibly torn,' he explains. 'But in Judaism, we understand that the body is only a garment worn by the soul. At the time death is upon us, we strip off one uniform and dress in another. The garment may be torn, but the essence of the person covered by it is intact.'

'Oh,' Rachel says inadequately, lost for words. At her mother's funeral, Rachel had been afraid to cry, in case Michael scolded her. And now, she is not only allowed, but expected, to embrace her pain?

'The loss of someone we love is always tragic,' the rabbi says kindly. 'But I hope that through the pain, you can find an even deeper truth: that the soul never dies.'

Even though Rachel's eyes are dry, his words shift something in her, ease the pain just a little. They follow him outside, where he begins the service with the graveside prayers in English. Afterwards, Michael begins to recite Kaddish in Hebrew – the memorial prayer for the dead, Judit softly explains to Rachel. 'It is traditionally recited by the son, by men only,' Judit murmurs.

Rachel is annoyed by this. That her father is the one to say Kaddish, even though she was far closer to Felka at the end. If the roles were reversed – if Felka were here, and Rachel in the ground – she thinks that Felka would fight to say it for her. So she interrupts her father and asks the rabbi if she can also say the memorial prayer.

The rabbi hesitates. 'It is not the done thing,' he says awkwardly. It's obvious he does not wish to hurt or upset her.

'My grandmother was no ordinary woman,' Rachel protests. 'She would have wanted me to say it with my father.'

The rabbi looks at Michael. Rachel expects him to argue, but he just nods at the rabbi, who relents and offers the phrases for her to repeat after him. Michael joins her, and they speak in unison. As she utters the unfamiliar words, mispronounced in a shaking voice, holding back tears, Michael surprises her when places his hand on her shoulder, steadying her.

At the end of it, the rabbi hands a shovel to Michael, who drops the first load of dirt onto the open grave. He passes it to Rachel. She steps to the mound, takes a shovel-load of dirt and drops it in. The noise of the soil hitting the wooden lid is dull, mournful, heavy. She passes the shovel on to Judit, stepping back, watching as the others step forward, one by one, passing the shovel between them as they do the same. Some opt to drop in the dirt with their hands.

Once everyone is done, Rachel takes the shovel back, continuing the work herself. The labour feels good in a way she can't explain. The blisters forming on her hands, the burn in her arms. Some of the men try to help but she shrugs them off. Tears run down her cheeks. She hardly notices them.

Michael watches her – she can see him from the corner of her eye – until the grave is two-thirds full. He holds out his hand for the shovel. She shakes her head, continues by herself. Her hair sticks to her cheeks, hampering her vision. The other mourners look on, wearing expressions of sympathy and pity. She notices none of it until, finally, Felka's grave is full. The earth covers her, embraces her; she lies next to baby Rachel at last.

The attendees file past them, one by one, offering their respects. 'I wish you long life,' several say. Many embrace Rachel warmly, despite her sweat-damp, dirt-streaked clothes. At the end, there is only the rabbi, Michael and Rachel left.

In another world, Michael would put his arms around Rachel and pull her close to him. But Rachel knows she must continue to build the bridge, brick by brick. Slowly, as they gaze at Felka's grave, she places an arm around Michael's waist. She feels his body turn rigid, but she doesn't flinch away. Just waits. After a moment, he puts a tense arm around her shoulder.

'I'm going to stay here a little while,' Rachel says.

'I'll see you back at the hotel,' he says, and then offers her a small smile before he goes. It's barely a twist at the corner of his lips, but she can't remember the last time he smiled at her. Rachel doesn't turn to watch him go, still staring at the grave. The rabbi bids her farewell, and then she is alone.

Rachel sits on the grass next to the fresh dirt, picks up a handful and lets it fall from her hand back onto the pile. She repeats the action mindlessly, trying to cause the dirt to fall as slowly as possible in a gentle, steady stream, guiding it to create a pattern with it as it lands. She thinks of mandalas, the art of forming patterns from coloured powder. How intricate they are, how delicate. The incredible effort involved for something so transient, designed to be swept away as soon as it is completed. She read once that mandalas are a symbol of the universe in its ideal form, transformed from a universe of suffering into one of joy.

She can't imagine such a universe without Felka, but she thinks it could exist, one day. Maybe. It's hard to imagine ever truly being happy again. Who will be her compass now? Michael has so far to go, and Yanni is an uncertainty...

She wipes her hand over the pattern she has created, destroying it, blending it back into the mound from whence it came. As she gets to her feet, dusting off her hands, she looks around. Though time has stood still for her, the rest of the world continues on. How dare the bees buzz happily as they collect nectar? How dare the flowers bloom so beautifully? How dare the people walk by, smiling and laughing, without any regard for the fact that the most important person in her life is now lying six feet under the ground?

The necklace Michael gave her still hangs around her neck. She grasps it, a small comfort.

'Rachel?'

Startled, she looks up. Loretta is standing just a few metres away. She must have waited until the funeral-goers left.

'Loretta,' Rachel says neutrally, as the other woman approaches. In the daylight, the similarity to Shirley is muted, less obvious. A different person entirely.

'I wish you long life,' Loretta says.

'A few of the others said that to me. What does it mean?'

'Jewish people say it as a way of comforting the mourners,' Loretta smiles. 'That they should live long enough to be able to remember their loved one for as long as possible.'

'Huh.' Rachel likes that. The idea of love after death being an ongoing ritual of sorts.

'I came by to offer my condolences,' Loretta says.

'I would have thought you'd be angry with Felka,' Rachel says, surprised.

'Felka did what she thought was best for her family,' Loretta replies. 'Michael, too. I just wish it had turned out differently.'

'Me too.'

'I was hoping we could spend some time together while you're here,' Loretta says. 'If you're interested, I mean. I have at least several birthdays to make up to you.'

Her light tone brings a smile to Rachel's face, and her words make Rachel's chest swell. But she grimaces. 'I'm going to Moscow tomorrow.'

'Moscow?'

'To thank Sugihara,' Rachel explains.

Loretta takes a moment, then rummages in her purse. She takes out a piece of paper and a pen, scribbling on it. 'When you come back, call me. Here's my number and address. I'd love to show you around Tokyo.'

'I will,' Rachel promises, securing the paper in her bag.

Loretta smiles apologetically. 'I should get going. It's a long ride back to Tokyo.'

'I'm glad you came,' Rachel says quickly. 'Thank you for coming to see me. There's so much I want to know.'

Loretta smiles and reaches out, tucking an errant strand of hair behind Rachel's ear.

'You look just like Shirley,' she says. 'I can't wait to tell you all about her.'

***

Rachel stares at the ceiling, unable to sleep. The group had organised for her and her father to sit *shiva* after the funeral, the Jewish mourning ritual which means 'seven' in Hebrew; it usually runs for seven days following the burial, and friends and relatives gather to care for the bereaved and share memories and stories. Despite being the chief mourner, despite the small steps he had taken forward with her, Michael said little. He was also the first to leave, explaining he had arranged drinks with a business associate who offered to facilitate meetings with some key players in the fashion industry. As usual, he had planned an exit strategy.

Rachel was incensed by her father's early departure, but now she wonders if he simply couldn't bear to be there, surrounded by people heaping attention and expectations on him. Regardless, she wishes he had stuck it out. It felt lonely being the only person there related to Felka, people mourning around her. Besides, she had been planning to talk to Michael about Moscow. She hadn't told him, and his early departure meant she still hasn't told him. In the end, she excused herself early too. It was simply too much.

The only bright point in the evening was the survivors handing her their letters to Sugihara. The looks of gratitude had fortified her; they still do now, as Rachel looks at the pile of envelopes on the coffee table. It makes her feel a little less lonely, knowing that she carries so many messages of goodwill, and is part of this unique group who owe him their lives, but it doesn't stop her feeling desperately sad and tired.

She wishes she had company. Her thoughts turn to Yanni, then to Mizumi, who was there to share her grief, and she's overcome with a wave of guilt. Poor Yanni is in Sydney, faithfully waiting for her, and she is here with barely the capacity to give him a thought – even *kissing* someone else. And Mizumi? After everything she'd done for her, Rachel could barely look Mizumi in the eye when they said goodbye. What does she want from these kind people, so willing to lend her their strength? When will she grow up and learn to take care of herself?

She thinks back to how she felt when she held Mizumi, when she was able to bolster her. That's the person she wants to be. Someone giving strength to another instead of the reverse. She wipes her eyes, turning over and trying to get comfortable. When she stirs again, it's almost five. A little sleep is better than none. She'll have to rest on the plane. She has a mission to accomplish.

She adds the last little things to her rucksack: her and Felka's traveller's cheques, all of their cash, her toiletries, and then, as she checks one last time that the suitcases are ready to leave at reception for Mizumi, she sees Felka's fur coat in a corner of the room.

How did she miss it when she packed the suitcase? Then she understands: it almost blends in, resembling part of the soft furnishings in the modern, stylish room. All she knows of the USSR is Communism. And snow. Although, it's actually summer, she thinks. Maybe summer there is cold?

She grabs the coat. It smells of Felka. Even if it's too warm to wear, it will bring her comfort.

Indeed, several hours later, as the plane begins take-off and it hits her – what the hell is she doing, flying to the USSR by herself?! – she looks to where the coat sits in the unoccupied seat next to her. Even unworn, it's thick enough that it almost sits upright, imbued with the personality of its former owner.

Rachel closes her eyes as the plane's wheels leave the tarmac. Her stomach clenches. She imagines Felka is there beside her. It's easy; the coat has her lingering, floral smell.

You are doing so well, pupelle, she would say. *I am so proud of you.* And then she would get distracted. *I hope the food is edible! I didn't like it in 1940. These Russians, they are no match for us Poles...*

And somehow, miraculously, Rachel falls asleep.

MOSCOW, 1964

Moscow in autumn is a sad, muted place. Every year it comes, and every year he thinks of the beautiful trees that must be shedding their leaves in Japan, the festivals and traditions that his family must be carrying on without him. Chiune has lived here now for nearly five years, and he misses his home every day. He counts down the months and wonders how his children will have changed since he saw them last. And then, always, he tries not to think of how Haruki, his precious son, will never change again. Seventeen years on, that grief will not fade.

Sometimes he still feels anger at his dismissal from the diplomatic corps, at the distinct lack of explanation. He knows it must have been over the visas, but as to why they could not simply say that, he can only speculate. Perhaps because they knew that it had been the right thing to do.

Still, Moscow in autumn is better than the Romanian prison camp, especially when he knows his family is safely tucked away at home. His countrymen still mourn Japan's humiliation in the war; Chiune is simply grateful his family experienced minimal suffering. He had thought the Romanians and Soviets would never let them return home.

Coming to Moscow for business was never something he thought would happen after his years of service to Japan. To only return home two weeks every year is punishment, and he dreads the day his alias as Sempo Sugiwara is discovered, that he's exposed as the Russian persona non grata he's been declared. But the pay means his sons will be able to live a good life, with nourishing food and a strong education. It was a simple choice, in the end. And so the time passes.

He lives frugally in Moscow. There is little for him to enjoy in the USSR. Save for the few nostalgic treasures he brought with him from Japan, a collection that slowly grows once a year, his apartment is not really a home. His family are not with him. And though it's in far better condition than many of those in Moscow, it's simple and spare. For him, a treat consists of sausages and potatoes grilled over the small gas stove that he balances on the closed toilet lid.

His work has little regard for schedule, and so when he finds himself with free time, he passes it by walking the streets of Moscow. It's meditative, rarely with any end goal in sight. He watches the people line up for food stamps, sees how they struggle on. The Russians are a proud people, but it still disappoints Chiune that so much suffering persists.

His time in Japan always goes too quickly. Though Yukiko is pleased to see him, he can feel the distance that grows between them a little more with every visit, and his two older adult sons are out living their own lives. Only Nobuki is still home. On the flight back to Moscow, he closes his eyes, pretends that he's still at home, that when he opens them his family will be there with him.

Yukiko never once rebukes him for how things have turned out, a fact that he endlessly appreciates. He thinks of the refugees, sometimes; remembers them crowded outside his door, how his hands were gnarled and cramped for months after he signed that last visa.

And, despite it all, when Chiune lands back in Moscow and returns to his lonely, crude apartment, he never regrets helping them. He doesn't know how many refugees he saved, but even if it was just one person, then it was worth it.

Chapter 18

On approach to Moscow, the morning skies are foreboding. The antiquated aircraft rattles through rumbling, dark grey clouds, causing it to heave and toss about. Rachel grips the armrests. The flight to Tokyo was smooth, easy – nothing like this. The other unsettled passengers clasp their seatbelts tightly with white-knuckled, sweaty hands and stare ahead. *Please, God,* Rachel prays more than once, *Let this plane land safely.* To have nobody she can glance at for reassurance, nobody who can hold her hand, makes it all the more harrowing.

The touchdown is bumpy, unpleasant. At least two people gasp as the plane shakes, and Rachel lets out a trembling breath as the wheels finally make contact with the ground. Through the window, the weather looks heavy, appropriate for landing on Communist soil: misty, gloomy skies and driving rain, the occasional flash of lightning.

Somehow, the airport is even darker than the weather. A massive, squat grey building, it's a daunting-looking place. The other travellers look sombre. Most of the passengers are middle-aged men – there are no happy families returning from memorable holidays in exotic locations. They disembark from the plane down rickety metal stairs onto the tarmac, are ushered, conveyor-belt style, onto an ugly beast of a bus and ferried to a terminal that resembles an oversized shed.

Inside, there are no baggage carousels in sight; instead, all the suitcases and bags are strewn across the floor by careless baggage handlers. Rachel gapes at the rapidly growing pile of bags and the passengers descending upon it – how on earth is she going to find hers? As she approaches, she's horrified to see uniformed men toting Kalashnikovs in every direction. They seem to have replaced the usual array of pleasantly smiling staff Rachel expected; rather than greeting travellers and informing them of the delights the country has to offer, they stand around, scowling at anyone who seems to be loitering.

Between the bag pile and the soldiers' presence, as well as the deafening noise of the aeroplanes arriving and departing, Rachel finds herself approaching a state of controlled panic. She takes a deep breath, exhales slowly. She made this bed, and now she has to lie in it. If Felka were here, she would wade into the crowd, elbowing people out of the way. The image makes Rachel smile. One step at a time, she tells herself, and eases into the mass of people searching for their bags. After a few minutes, she finds hers beneath an enormous suitcase. She drags it out, thankful she packed light and brought nothing fragile, and wanders down the hall to the first information desk she can find. There's several minutes of misunderstanding conducted via hand gestures between Rachel and a less-than-obliging attendant before the man calls over the other attendant, who speaks a little English.

She shows this attendant Joshua's directions and the map with its marked locations. 'Kursky Train Station?'

'Yes,' the attendant says. 'This way. Train. First, immigration.'

He points at the immigration line, which is moving slowly. She sighs, thanks him, and joins the queue. When she finally reaches the security officer, he regards her, stares at her passport photo, then calls over another official. He also looks her up and down and flicks through her passport. A discussion ensues in Russian. They inspect her hotel details, the confirmation that Intourist has been involved and, indeed, that there will be an official guide waiting for her, and details of her return flight out to Tokyo. Finally, with a sense of grudging suspicion, the first security guard decides she is worthy of permission to enter the glorious Soviet Union. He stamps a document, hands it to her, stresses she must go straight to her hotel and ushers her on.

By this point, the panic has simmered down into impatience, and Rachel is glad to be swept along with the sea of travellers into the vast arrivals lounge. There's a smattering of families, sporting dull expressions and colourless, mismatched clothing that suit the setting. Otherwise, she can see the vast majority of people are individual men – many official-looking types in bland, outdated, inexpensive suits.

The surroundings are more sterile and antiquated than her hospital's washrooms, she thinks. Monotonously tiled walls are adorned with the hammer and sickle wherever possible. Even the gargantuan murals – of workers in the fields, army personnel and loyal comrades – are cheerless, despite the smiling and purposeful subjects. All signs are in Russian, and its characters resemble nothing she's seen before.

No baggage trolleys. Rachel is glad again that she's brought her rucksack as she follows the crowd, watching several people struggle with cumbersome suitcases. Everyone seems to be heading for the same destination. She taps a lady on the shoulder and asks, 'Kursky?' The woman curtly nods. It seems following the crowd is the correct procedure – they come to an outdated locomotive to Kursky station. Rachel boards, feeling a little more confident in the company of others. This isn't as bad as Joshua made it out to be, perhaps because she is young and feels a sense of adventure. She spends the trip staring out the window. Though it should be warm and sunny, the landscape looks just as dour as the overcast sky. The few buildings they pass are featureless grey things, not unlike the airport, and the roads are cracked and sad. It's a relief when the train stops at Kursky, because at least there's a little more to look at. She has to ask one of the station employees to direct her to a taxi but he suggests a bus is easier and cheaper, directing her to the embarkation point. She takes the risk, still feeling emboldened, and gets there seconds before it arrives. In a feeble attempt to be understood, she reads the anglicised hotel name to the stone-faced bus driver. He has no clue what she is saying. The anxiety begins to return as she repeats herself, scrambling for her map.

A fellow passenger pipes up. 'Rossiya Hotel?'

A professional-looking woman in her late thirties, the passenger comes to the front.

'You are going to Rossiya Hotel?' she asks Rachel in broadly accented English.

'Yes,' Rachel says gratefully. The woman speaks in Russian to the driver and gestures for Rachel to sit.

'Thank you, thank you so much,' Rachel says. The lady smiles politely, then returns to her seat. Rachel is somewhat dejected; she would have welcomed the chance to speak to someone for a while. As it is, she holds tightly on to Felka's fur coat. Almost there, she tells herself. When Rachel was a child, she had one of those Russian nesting dolls, filled with several smaller versions of itself, stacked in internal layers. The smallest was barely larger than a pea. This is how she feels now, surrounded by drab landscapes and drab buildings. Pea-sized and inconsequential. A babushka doll. That's what Felka had called it.

Like the views from the train trip, the scenery the bus passes is uninspiring – a long ride past monotonous housing estates, uniformly designed and constructed, does not make for an exciting sightseeing experience. So far, Rachel does not think Russia seems very frightening or dangerous, besides the armed airport guards. She thinks that it largely seems a very sad place.

Finally, the bus comes to a stop, and the woman who helped her taps Rachel on the shoulder.

'This is your stop,' she says. Rachel thanks her, gathers her things and realises she has no clue how much to pay the bus driver. She takes out several US dollar bills, offers them to the driver. His face lights up like a Christmas tree, but the woman intervenes and hands several back to Rachel.

'Thank you again,' Rachel says, and the woman nods, offers a smile. Clearly grumpy, the bus driver almost closes the door on Rachel's leg as she steps out onto the ground, then he zooms away.

Rachel takes a moment to observe Moscow. The vehicles all seem to be relics from the 1940s, and monotone fashion over a decade out of style seems to be the norm. Schoolchildren walk past in uniforms resembling 1920s surplus. The colours of the suburb are as dreary as the airport, and most surfaces are chipped, crumbling and rundown. In a supermarket across the road, Rachel sees people inside lining up. It would appear there is a line for each item, which bemuses her. A line for cheese, a line for rice, a line for eggs – each indicated by poster-sized black-and-white illustrations of each item. There are no colourful billboards, no flourishes, nothing to draw the eye. Rachel finds little desire to paint the scenery before her.

But it isn't all that different, once Rachel adjusts to the greyness. Men and women still go about their business, mothers and grandmothers carrying shopping, men walking to and from work. And, as she looks closer, there are hints of a more familiar world: a young woman wearing a dress strikingly similar to one she owns; a man sporting a Hawaiian t-shirt and sunglasses. Perhaps the USSR isn't as out of touch as first glances would suggest.

She pulls the map from her bag and looks up to the closest street sign, carefully comparing the unfamiliar lettering to that which Joshua circled on the map. She's only a couple of blocks away from the hotel. Almost there, almost there. She starts walking, hoisting her rucksack up on her shoulders, trying not to stand out too much. She passes a group of soldiers and relaxes a little when she sees they're unarmed. They eye her, but let her pass, and shortly after she arrives at the hotel without incident.

When she approaches the revolving doors, a man wearing a dark grey suit immediately walks up and stops her before she enters, demanding to see her documents. She shows him her hotel booking.

He reads it and says, 'Rachel Margolin?'

She nods.

'Guide. Intourist. Passport, ticket. Please.'

She quickly removes them from her handbag and shows him. He hands them back and ushers her inside to the reception desk and gives her name to the front desk attendant, who hands her the room key. The bellboy gestures he will show her to her room. She turns around and notices her guide remains, taking a seat in the foyer.

Exhausted, desperately wanting to sleep, she follows the bellboy.

***

Michael is used to getting his way when he wants it, on his terms. He runs a large business, and appreciates efficiency and good conduct. The Russian embassy seems to value anything but, he decides, as the woman across from him checks her paperwork.

'Is there some sort of issue?' he says in fluent Russian, an attempt to exert more pressure. A fellow comrade.

The response is curt and swift. 'One moment, please.'

Another few minutes go by, testing what little patience he has. 'Please, this is quite urgent. My daughter is alone in Moscow.'

The matronly attendant who is serving him seems unperturbed by his predicament. 'Who is your family in Moscow?' she barks. 'What is their address? How are they related to you?'

Michael can feel the muscles in his jaw clench. 'No family, as I explained already.'

She ignores his aggressive tone. 'But you are fluent in Russian. So you are Russian, yes? What is your family's name?'

'No family,' he repeats. 'I am Australian. Please, my daughter travelled to Moscow alone. I am going to meet her there. I learned Russian as a child in Poland.'

She purses her lips, and he endures several more minutes of paperwork until she hands him some documents. 'Three days. Then your visa will be ready.'

Michael is furious. 'Three days?'

She eyes him. 'We can do one, but there will be a significant extra charge.'

'Fine, yes, whatever you need. One day.'

She waves him on to another desk where he begrudgingly surrenders a ludicrous amount of cash for an expedited visa, and he stomps out of the embassy. He only found out about Rachel's plans minutes after her flight had departed; when she hadn't come down for breakfast, he called Joshua Nishri, assuming she was with the Jewish group.

She's just left for Moscow to see Sugihara, Nishri said, confused. *Didn't she tell you?*

Michael's next stop is the Takashimaya Department Store for a meeting with the buyer's agent at one of Japan's largest retail outlets. He puts his annoyance at the USSR embassy and anger at Rachel aside, and the meeting goes well enough; they go from the business room to a lunch that extends on through the afternoon, and when Michael finally meets Joshua Nishri later that evening for a drink, he's full of dumplings and sake.

The bar is quiet, relaxed. When Michael arrives, Joshua waves him over, a warm smile on his face. Michael is ready to tear it off.

'Michael.' Joshua smiles. 'How are you finding Kobe?'

He speaks in Yiddish. Michael replies in English, skipping the pleasantries.

'So she told you she was going, and you couldn't convince her otherwise?'

Joshua blinks, swapping back to English. 'Rachel? You have a very determined, very headstrong daughter, Michael. She was on a mission, and that was that.'

'So you just let her fly off to Moscow?' Michael hisses.

Joshua regards him with a frown. 'Of course not. I gave her advice about staying safe, made sure she organised everything through Intourist. I gave her my phone number so she could call me. I assumed she would be sharing these plans with you.'

'Well, she didn't, obviously,' Michael says, too loudly. He is furious again, all the goodwill of the afternoon bubbling away under Rachel's carelessness and deception. How could she think this was a good plan? Why did she not tell him?

Why would she? A small part of him says. *When have you been there for her?*

'With respect,' Joshua says, a little coolly, 'she seemed devoted to Felka. She wanted to go to Moscow out of love and a sense of duty towards her late grandmother. You know the young. Once they get something in their heads, there's no stopping them. They have no sense of fear, of danger.'

This does not placate Michael, though he can't help but see the similarity to his own return to Kobe for Shirley. The thoughtlessness, the confidence. Still. Kobe and Sydney are far from the likes of Moscow.

'Mr Nishri,' he says. 'We're talking about Communist Russia. Need I say more?'

Joshua has no comeback to that, clearly. 'The Intourist guide won't let her out of his sight, have no fear. When do you leave?' he asks instead, pouring himself a glass of wine.

'Tomorrow. Hopefully she can hold off from getting into trouble in the meantime.'

'Indeed,' Joshua says. He pauses. 'I am sorry for your loss, Michael. It is difficult, for a son to lose his mother.'

Michael doesn't know what to say to that. It doesn't feel real, still – he keeps expecting Felka to pop up, annoyingly loud, brash. The factory will certainly be quieter, he thinks, but it's a hollow sentiment.

He's saved from answering by Loretta's arrival. She's aged since he saw her last, of course, but she still looks enough like Shirley that his heart contracts painfully. He meets her gaze, and Joshua sees this as his cue to exit, bidding Michael goodnight. Michael, distracted, nods without saying a word.

'May I?' Loretta says, gesturing at the seat Joshua recently vacated.

'Please,' Michael says automatically.

He had been surprised when she called him at the hotel. News of his return must have filtered through the Jewish community here quickly. He hadn't thought about her in a very long time, mainly relieved that she had stopped calling, relieved that Rachel would be able to move on, unencumbered by the past. He almost rebuffed her invitation, but something in him was moved to agree.

She orders them both a glass of wine, which Michael hesitantly thanks her for, still a little shaken by how much she resembles Shirley. The thick, dark hair, the bright brown eyes, the thin lips. Michael all but drains his glass seconds after it arrives.

He has no idea why she has called him here. No idea what to say. Fortunately, Loretta takes the reins.

'I'm so sorry about Felka,' she says gently.

He nods mechanically. 'Thank you. How is your family?'

'My mother passed quite a few years back, not too long after Shirley ... but my father is well.'

'I'm sorry,' he says automatically.

She shrugs. 'It's a part of life.'

'Yes.' He takes a sip of wine, steels himself. 'I must admit, I was surprised when you contacted me.'

'Rachel was very upset when she found out about me,' Loretta says matter-of-factly. 'More so when she realised you had lied about me and the rest of Shirley's family.'

Michael stares at her. 'She knows?'

'Yes.'

Rachel knows. And yet, she seemed ... calm, when they spoke before the funeral. He's not sure what to make of it, but it does make sense now that she didn't tell him about Moscow. Something in his gut tightens. A lie for a lie.

'Why did you call me?' he asks. He isn't stupid; Loretta must have been furious with him back then. She very well may still be furious.

'Rachel is my niece,' Loretta says, swirling the wine in her glass. 'Our families will always be connected, whether you like it or not.'

She looks at him, clearly gauging his reaction. He says nothing.

'Before Shirley died, she begged me to keep in contact with Rachel,' Loretta continues. 'Did she say that to you?'

Michael opens his mouth to reply, but nothing comes out. He can barely remember that whole terrible period of his life, when he was spending hours at work, trying to keep the family fed and supported while Shirley was dying before his eyes. She was keeping in touch with Loretta towards the end, he knows. He remembers fighting with her about it, arguing that she was dragging the past along with her.

'She was so scared,' Loretta continues. 'She didn't know what the afterlife held for her, after leaving her faith behind. Did you know she started praying again, towards the end?'

He shakes his head dumbly.

'She was so worried for Rachel. She told me how you were working so late, every day of the week. Felka was doing her best, but she was getting older and couldn't do all the work of raising Rachel herself. So she told me to try and call, to speak to Rachel, to let her know she still had family. That she would try to convince you. She didn't, clearly. And you intercepted calls.'

'I was trying to protect Rachel,' Michael says. The words are empty, meaningless, when faced with Shirley's likeness.

'You failed,' Loretta replies. 'And we have all suffered because of it. But I did not call you here to argue. I called you because I wanted our families to move forward. Together.'

Michael frowns. 'Rachel is an adult. If she wants to speak to you, she will.'

'You are my family too,' Loretta reminds him. 'My brother-in-law. Shirley loved you. We loved you too, until you convinced her to leave us. To abandon your faith.'

And they did, he knows. Before he left Kobe the first time, there were many family dinners, full of cheer and sake. He remembers finding the joy incomprehensible even as he was warmed by it. He doesn't know what to say.

'I've invited Rachel to visit me in Tokyo when she returns from Moscow,' Loretta continues. Michael winces – did everyone except him know of his daughter's plans? 'If she does, I have no doubt she will ask me many questions. I plan to answer all of them. Truthfully.'

'I see.'

'Felka told me that your relationship with Rachel is strained,' Loretta adds.

'You spoke with Felka?'

'Briefly. She told me that she blamed herself for your behaviour. That she was dying. And that Rachel desperately needed someone Jewish who could teach her about her culture.'

'Why?' Michael bursts out. 'It's never done anything good for us!'

'Not all of us can cut parts of ourselves away so easily,' Loretta says. 'I love my culture, my people. I could never give them up. Neither could Shirley. She may have agreed to go with you, but she could never really leave us behind.'

Michael sighs. She's right.

'Your daughter is about to start a whole new part of her life,' Loretta continues. 'One that will take her even further away from you, if you aren't walking alongside her. Do you understand?'

'I...'

'Think about it,' Loretta says. 'For Shirley.'

She finishes her glass, bids him goodnight, and leaves.

He thinks about it, alright. He can barely sleep for thinking about it, and even as he boards the flight to Moscow and leaves Kobe behind, her words play on a loop.

You failed.

***

When Rachel opens her eyes to the dark hotel room, her lips are parched, her mouth devoid of saliva. She swallows hard, staring up at the darkness, before reaching for the bedside light. The completely foreign surroundings confuse her for a moment – the repetitive, geometric patterns on the wallpaper, the blocky wooden bedside table and dresser – and then she remembers where she is. Moscow. She made it.

She clambers for the telephone and dials reception. She asks the concierge what day it is. August 31. It has taken her two full days to recover. She feels well rested in a way she hasn't since all of this started, but when she gets up and goes to the bathroom, clumsily swallowing water from her hands, she can see she looks like a mess. She rummages through her purse for some crackers she stowed away. They quiet her stomach long enough for her to shower, dress, realign herself with reality. When she's confident she no longer looks like a corpse, she heads down to the lobby, planning to get an updated map of Moscow. She's surprised to see that Yuri, her official 'tour guide' – aka KGB agent – is ready, waiting for her.

What did he do, sleep there? Joshua warned her that her guide would not permit her to wander the streets or sightsee alone, but seeing it in effect is another matter. Yuri sees her, rises. She asks him where she can grab something, anything, to ease the rumbling in her empty stomach. He walks her to a simple store a few doors down where she buys a bread roll and then lines up for a small wedge of cheese. Satisfied, she then tells him where she wants to go and shows him the address.

It's time, finally, to see Sugihara.

***

Sugihara's apartment building was once a hotel. Joshua described it to her, but seeing it – 'The Minsk Hotel' spelled out in erratically flickering neon – still seems strange. The letter 'S' has lost its power supply, but 'Mink' remains intact. It's cool outside, and Rachel is glad for Felka's coat, clutching it around her, wearing a mink to the Mink, she muses.

Rachel and her guide stand outside. Yuri waits, face neutral, as Rachel stares up at the building. The determination that brought her here has been replaced by a knot in her stomach.

It has all come to this. This moment.

'Ms Margolin?' Yuri says after a moment. 'Shall we go inside?'

He has said very little on the way here, sticking to simple 'yes' and 'no' answers to any of her questions.

'Sorry,' she says. 'Yes. Let's.'

The lobby is far smaller than her own hotel's, a little shabby. Yuri takes a seat on a nearby bench, nodding to her. She takes the elevator to the fifth floor by herself, chest tight.

The elevator moves terribly slowly, clunkily. Rachel could not have imagined a month ago that she would be here, now, doing this. The gravity of this meeting has her trembling, checking the letters she stashed in her purse. All of them are there, of course. It's like she's taking everyone with her – a buoying thought. Without them, how could she possibly convey to Sugihara the gratitude so many have? How else to impress upon him that one act of kindness and the vagaries of chance tumbled into a chain of events, saving hundreds, even thousands? That without him, she would never have been born?

It's an awesome task. One that Felka would have been perfect for, with her storytelling and generous heart. But it has fallen to Rachel. She will simply have to do her best.

The elevator doors creak open. The Minsk Hotel was elegant once, but its decor has faded. A stained, threadbare carpet covers the floor, poorly lit by a weak, dusty lightbulb dangling from the ceiling. She checks the door number once again, and makes her way down the hall until she reaches his and knocks.

The sound of someone approaching the door, a wait that feels like an eternity, and then the world falls away as the door opens just enough that Rachel can see a Japanese man in his late sixties standing behind it.

In a feeble, shaky voice, Rachel enquires, 'Chiune Sugihara?'

MOSCOW, 1968

The young woman standing at Chiune's door looks out of place to him: wrapped in lush fur, with big, dark eyes. When she asks his name, he can only nod, bemused. He had been in the middle of preparing some food when she knocked.

'My name is Rachel Margolin,' she continues in English. The name is familiar, but he can't quite place it. 'I'm from Australia. You ... you saved my family in Lithuania, in 1940. With a transit visa to Japan.'

His heart skips a beat. She takes a deep breath, reaching into her purse, and withdraws a bundle of letters. 'These are from some of the people you saved. As thanks.'

Though she is a stranger, unannounced, he can do nothing else but open his door, as he did all those years ago at the consulate, and beckon for her to come inside. She clutches the coat about herself, examining his home. She seems particularly intrigued by a kintsugi-repaired vase on the mantle before turning to him. She offers the letters wordlessly; he takes them and is surprised by the weight. There must be at least a dozen letters in here – thick, multi-paged ones. He swallows, sliding out the first envelope from the bundle, and opens it. He takes care to peel the flap without tearing the paper.

'My grandmother wrote that,' Rachel says. 'She wanted to deliver it herself, in person. But she passed away last week. In Kobe. Many survivors gathered there to meet you, to thank you for your incredible, selfless deed. It's all there, in their letters.'

Chiune scans the contents here – a thorough reading of each will have to wait, but he can't help but take a look. That this woman was so moved to write to him, all these years later ... The words are written in loopy, clear cursive.

> My name is Felka Margolin. You saved me and my son. My late husband too but he didn't make it to Japan. May his memory be a blessing! We can never thank you enough. You gave us life, you gave me a granddaughter, a diamond! You give her life now and her children one day, please God. You are an angel. God bless you and your family.

'My grandmother so wanted to thank you,' Rachel continues. 'She should have been here with me. It shouldn't be like this. So ... unceremonious.'

Chiune gently places the letters on the mantle, feeling guilt tighten his chest. 'You came here on your own? That is very brave of you. I am sorry I couldn't meet you in Japan. My work here is—' He cuts himself off. How to describe the Russian government in English? Where to begin? 'It is not more important, but it is something over which I have little control.'

Rachel nods, and then asks timidly, 'Do you remember my family?'

'I remember many of the people from that time,' he says slowly. 'But there were so many faces.'

'My father, Michael, was fourteen,' Rachel tries. 'He and his father got their visas from you at the embassy. His father died not long after, I think. Oh, I should have brought a picture—'

A boy, dark hair falling into his face, running alongside the train.

The gunshot.

'Michael,' Chiune repeats. 'Yes. Some scenes one cannot forget.'

She looks astonished.

'Yes,' he nods. 'I remember him. He was running alongside the train, waving goodbye to me. His father called out for him to stop. He did not.' He pauses, scolding himself. It is not his sorrow to share, especially when she has travelled all this way to share her and her community's gratitude. He deeply wishes he could have stayed even a few more days in Japan. That he could have met these people. That he could have spent more time with his precious sons.

'I wish I could have accepted your grandmother's thanks personally,' Sugihara says after a moment. 'I wish I could have met all of them. Another time, I hope. Though there was never need for any thanks,'

he adds. 'I would have simply been delighted to meet them and hear their stories.'

Rachel looks teary. He offers her a warm smile as she draws her coat closer to herself.

'To them, it would have been so much more than sharing their stories, Mr Sugihara,' she says. 'You saved their lives. So, I travelled to Moscow to thank you. For my grandmother, for all of them.'

'I only did what was right. That is all.'

She shakes her head. 'That's everything, Mr Sugihara.'

'It's what anyone would have done.'

'But they didn't,' she says. 'They didn't. So thank you.'

He doesn't know what to say, and instead nods reluctantly. He wishes he had some biscuits or pastries he could offer her. All he has is his tea. 'I would love to hear about your life,' he says after a moment. 'About your family, your grandmother. I was just about to make some tea. Would you like some?'

'That would be lovely,' Rachel says. He's pleased he can do that much for her, and so the next few hours pass. He listens attentively as she shares her life with him, in turns saddened and relieved as she tells him about her family's lies and how she came to the truth of them. Chiune wonders if Michael knows how much he has hurt his daughter. She does not say it, not *clearly, but it's obvious in the omissions, the careful neutrality in her voice when she speaks of him.*

When she is done, Chiune reaches out. 'You have endured tremendous pain in your life, so far. I am truly sorry, Rachel.'

She blinks away tears, but before she can answer, there is a knock at the door.

'Excuse me,' he says, and answers the door. A middle-aged man is waiting there, a gentleman Chiune recognises from the floor above his office. His heart falls. The USSR waits for no man, of course; the mantells him the papers from his meeting on Friday need to be signed right here, right now. When Chiune politely asks if it can wait until tomorrow, the man's blank stare makes it clear this is unacceptable.

Chiune closes the door and returns to where Rachel sits at his dining table. 'I am terribly sorry. I know it's a Sunday, but my associate needs to come in and sign some documents with me.'

'Of course,' Rachel says. 'Thank you so much for meeting with me.'

Chiune bows. 'It was my pleasure. Please, pass on my gratitude to everyone for their letters, and my apologies for not being able to meet them.'

'Thank you,' she says again.

'No, Rachel,' he says. 'Thank you.'

Chapter 19

Michael is just stepping out of the hotel-cum-apartment building's elevator when he looks up to see Rachel, who appears shocked.

'Dad?'

'Rachel,' he says, pleased he's caught her before she can be abducted by the KGB or something similarly sinister. 'I – are you alright?'

'I'm fine.'

Indeed, she looks well. And with that confirmed, he can finally give her the scolding she deserves.

'Do you realise how dangerous it is, coming here?' he tells her. 'You know nothing about the world, how stupid it is to come to the USSR alone, as a woman!'

Rachel's nostrils flare, but again, there's that calm that is as admirable as it is frustrating. 'I know it was risky,' she says evenly. 'But I'm here, aren't I?'

'You should have told me,' he snaps.

'I was going to,' she replies. 'And then you left your own mother's memorial service early.'

He refuses to react to this.

'Besides,' she continues. 'You wouldn't have wanted to come with me. You would have tried to talk me out of it. And I can't live the way you do, Dad. Hiding from your emotions, from the truth. It's not right.'

'I am your father. You will not talk to me like this,' he says, a little desperately.

She sighs. 'Why are you here? It's not to see Sugihara, I take it.'

He glances at the doors lining the hall. 'I came to make sure you didn't get into any trouble.'

'Why?' she asks. 'Why?'

He shifts uncomfortably. 'I'm your father.'

He doesn't know what she wants from him. A father's duty is to protect, to intervene, to attack. Is that not what he's done for her?

'So because you had to. Out of a sense of duty.'

'That's what a parent does, Rachel,' he says, frustrated.

'A parent should care about more than just duty, Dad.'

Her face is set in a cool, neutral expression.

You failed.

'I came after you because – because I care about you,' he says roughly. 'Of course I do.' How can she not know? The proof of it hangs around her neck. 'I know how much you and Felka loved each other.'

She blinks. 'Then you should know I haven't done anything Grandma wouldn't have wanted.'

He can't believe this. 'Yes, you have! You put yourself in danger! You have risked your very life coming here! My mother would never have wanted—'

'Felka wanted me to come with her,' Rachel protests.

'Because she adored you!' he all but shouts without a moment's hesitation. 'Far more than she ever loved me! She cherished you. Her everything. But she would never have expected you to come here by yourself. Felka was fluent in Russian, she had been to Moscow before. She could have protected you here. But she would not have wanted you to do this alone! *I* did not want you to do this alone!'

'I just wanted to thank Sugihara,' Rachel says in a small voice, and suddenly she's his little girl again, five or six, not understanding why Daddy's upset that she's playing with the knife Shirley left on the kitchen counter. 'For Grandma, because she couldn't. And for you, because I knew you wouldn't—'

'Hello, Michael.'

Michael and Rachel both turn to face Sugihara. He stands before them, another man standing awkwardly behind him. Michael's breath catches in his chest.

'Rachel, why don't you give your father and me a minute?' Sugihara says with a soft smile. The man behind him slips between them all and takes the elevator downstairs. 'You can wait in my apartment.'

Rachel nods and walks up the hallway, disappearing into one of the doors. Once the door closes, Sugihara turns to him.

'I was very sad to hear of your mother's passing,' Sugihara says. 'Rachel delivered a letter from her. I understand she led a vibrant life. She was very proud of you.'

He pauses, waiting for Michael to respond, but he can't. He's back running along those train tracks, ignoring the angry shouts of the Russians, his father's desperate calls...

'Your mother's letter was not the only one. Your daughter delivered many others from those who gathered in Kobe, hoping to meet me. Mr Nishri explained, when he first made contact with me, how many people made it out of Lithuania. I can't remember every face. There were so many. It was a frantic time. But I remember you, Michael. You looked bright and curious. And I remember seeing your father. It is good to see you again.'

He offers his hand. Michael, a businessman through and through, automatically shakes it. His palm is clammy, his hand is trembling, but Sugihara seems unbothered. He offers Michael a warm smile, and gently guides him to sit on the first step of the staircase leading down to the fourth floor – an impromptu bench.

He sits first. Michael follows, jerky.

'Rachel came here on her own, just to see me,' Sugihara comments. 'Very brave.'

Michael nods, finds his voice. 'I came to take her home. She left right after my mother's funeral. I think our family has had enough adventure for the time being.'

Sugihara hums an agreement. 'When we're young we have a tendency to ... abscond.'

'Not all of us,' Michael says, thinking of Shirley and how she had wept, stepping out into the Australian sun for the very first time.

'You must have had difficulties transitioning to a new life in Australia—'

'Yes. No. I ... I had to grow up fast.'

'My children have had challenges themselves, I am certain, simply because I have been absent so often.' Sugihara looks down the dark, dingy stairwell, clearly somewhere else. 'No, I'm not sure if "challenges" is the right word. It is sad, to be apart from your father. And yet, I remain in this line of work...'

'I'm sure you made the best choice for your family.' Michael drags his gaze to meet Sugihara's. The man's eyes are just as kind as he remembers. 'That's what men do. Fathers provide.'

Sugihara sighs. 'I often find myself wondering what it is I provide to my family besides money. I feel more like a benefactor. I hope they don't feel that. I didn't leave just to provide. I left to pursue something I'm good at. I could provide for my family by staying in Japan. But it would be just a job.'

Michael knows what that feels like. He loves his business, far beyond what it affords Rachel.

'I feel frustrated that perhaps my children didn't need my attention, and yet I feel guilty that I can't be there every moment. Can they see that?'

'No,' Michael murmurs. Rachel certainly doesn't seem able to. But it would be a lie to pretend it's all for her. When he's in his office or at a meeting, he feels safe, untouchable.

'No.' Sugihara nods. 'I forget to think like a child. They feel everything. Maybe my children think it's their fault I'm not around. If they hadn't wished for that toy, or to learn piano, then maybe I wouldn't have needed to work so hard, so far away. But sacrifices need to be made, priorities need to be determined. And I had boys to put through university! Have I sacrificed their emotional needs for pragmatic, material ones? Have I deprived my family by absenting myself? Have I made errors? I think I have. But these things are essential for life.'

Michael's lungs are struggling to expand. 'Children can learn,' he says weakly. 'Whatever the situation, they can adapt. They must.'

Sugihara returns his gaze to the staircase. 'Still, I hope I haven't deprived my children of their childhood.' He looks to Michael, a kind expression on his face. 'I saw them shoot your father, Michael. I'm so sorry.'

And now Michael is back in 1940, Sugihara's train speeding away from him, turning back to see who is shouting, seeing the Russian soldier shoot his father, who is chasing after them as they catch up with Michael. Michael is seeing the bullet hit his father in the chest, in the heart. Michael is searching for Sugihara's face as the train disappears around the bend.

Michael is looking for his mother, nowhere in sight, and even though he'll later learn that she was trying to help someone with their luggage, that she had no idea what had happened, he will always remember she wasn't there when he needed her. That she wasn't there to tell him it wasn't his fault. That she never discouraged his emotions, the excitement, the curiosity, the joy and the sorrow – the things that led him to chase after Sugihara's train in the first place. The things she boasted were a part of her faith.

***

Rachel gasps at the words. The door is open just a crack, enough that she can hear their soft voices.

'You weren't responsible for your father's death, Michael,' she hears Sugihara say. 'Neither was your mother. You know how awful the war was, how casual the terror. So many children grew up with a hole in their heart, just like yours.'

She can hear her father is gasping for breath; she dares to open the door, just a bit, to peek out. It can't possibly be her father making that noise, but it is, she sees; his shoulders are trembling with the sound. Sugihara's hand rests on his back. Sugihara glances up, clearly seeing her, but his expression holds no disapproval.

He turns back to Michael. 'You must find forgiveness. For yourself. For your mother. And then you must allow your daughter to help you heal.'

Rachel is crying silently, tears streaming down her cheeks. She wishes Felka were here. But not for her – for Michael. Because now, finally, she sees her father, *really* sees him, and he makes sense.

And she forgives him. Not for everything. That will take time and effort on both their parts. But she forgives him for not being there for her, for not being able to be there for her. For the hurt he's been carrying his entire life and passed on to her. It feels strange, almost too easy, but simply knowing that his pain is the reason for his distance, that it's not personal, eases her own.

She wants to run out and comfort him, but she stays still. Her way of loving is not her father's way. Instead, she holds there behind the door. Waiting. Listening.

After a few minutes, Michael's breath becomes more even, and Sugihara speaks again.

'It's always easier to stay in the present, to stay in the moment,' he says. 'Why bring up the past? But when we do, sometimes we find the answers that will help us move forward. Let's do that now, shall we? Let's go and join your daughter.' He stands and helps Michael to his feet.

Rachel darts away from the door, sitting down on one of the chairs in the corner of the room. When they enter, Sugihara gives her a small, knowing smile.

'A vodka is in order, I think,' he says, ushering Michael to take a seat.

'An apology, too,' Michael says roughly, looking at Rachel. 'Long overdue.'

And for the first time in a long time, he smiles at her.

Chapter 20

When Rachel returns to Kobe, the sky is clear, blue, warm. She feels wrung out in a good way for once, ready to soak up life.

Michael is back in Sydney, Felka's belongings in tow; he has a business to run, and Felka's affairs to get in order. He hugged her, before he left.

I'll call you when I get back, he told her. And he does. It's perfunctory, a check-in. Sugihara bridged the distance between them, but crossing it is another matter – one that takes effort, time.

'Are you going to visit Loretta?' he asks down the line. She's still groggy, recovering from the jet lag.

'Yes,' she says, instinctively preparing for disapproval.

'Good' is all he says. 'I have to go now. Be safe. Please.'

'I will,' she says. It's no *I love you.* But it's getting there.

The next phone call – to Yanni – is one she makes herself after she's eaten and showered. Between the distance, the experience, and the resurfacing of trauma, she finds she is ready to give him an answer. His family was right, in a way: her relationship with Yanni was always going to be caught in the crossfire. She misses him still, but she doesn't think it's enough, yet. There are things she still needs to understand, things she still needs to learn. It's surreal how much has changed in the space of only a few weeks.

When he picks up, she closes her eyes at the sound of his voice. He chastises her for not calling while she was in Moscow, but he's more relieved than angry. They talk for a while. It's a little awkward at first, the result of time and distance apart. Thomas has been fired, he tells her, and she's not ashamed to admit it's a satisfying thing to hear. Finally, though, she has to address the elephant in the room.

'We need to postpone the engagement,' she says, and is glad that the words bring tears to her eyes. 'I'm sorry, I'm just not ready to commit. Not to anyone. There's so much I still need to learn about myself, my family...'

'Rachel, darling,' he says gently. 'Are you sure you don't just want to call it off altogether? You don't need to protect my feelings.'

The words startle her. Does she? And should she mention Mizumi? No, she thinks. She doesn't even begin to know how to categorise the experience, doesn't know what she wants from Mizumi. But she will call her – not today, but soon. She owes it to herself and to her future with Yanni to explore this side of herself that Mizumi has drawn out. She wants Yanni's security, his reliability, his earnestness and, she thinks, his love, but there is a part of her that wants something Mizumi can give, and to give it back

356

in return. A kinship and comfort, for both of them, even if nothing else ensues.

'I don't know,' she says to Yanni. 'I think I need more time.'

'I'll wait,' he promises. 'But don't take forever, okay? If I'm going to have to bring someone else home to my grandmother, I'm going to need a lot of time to prepare myself.'

Rachel laughs, and they bid each other a loving farewell. She does love him still, she's pleased to realise, but the question is whether it is enough.

The third and final call of the day is to Loretta.

'It's me, Rachel,' she says down the line.

'Rachel!' Loretta says, sounding so pleased that Rachel finds herself warmed by it.

'I'm back in Japan, and I wanted to take you up on your offer to show me around Tokyo.'

'Yes, of course,' her aunt replies. 'I'd love that.'

Loretta offers to come pick her up, but Rachel wants to do it herself. The time on the train will be nice, will give her a chance to think. They plan to meet the next day, at Loretta's house, for lunch.

***

Rachel meets Judit in the hotel restaurant that afternoon, eager to share her impressions of Sugihara.

She's barely sat down when Judit begins firing off questions.

'What was he like? Was he surprised? How does he look? Is he happy, do you think? Does he live well? I want to know that life has been good to him, to such a worthy person.'

Is he happy? He lives alone in such a drab, harsh country. But then she thinks of his warm presence, his patience and insight with her father, the conversation so cleverly engineered to draw her father out from his shell. He takes pride in what he does, she thinks. That is happiness enough for him. And three grown-up sons of whom he is so proud.

'I was nervous about meeting him,' Rachel tells Judit. 'But he is just an ordinary man. A kind, quiet, caring person. Very humble, very moved by our gratitude, but not wanting attention or accolades at all. I think he truly doesn't know what all our fuss over him is about. He says he only did what anyone else in his situation would have done. An ordinary, extraordinary man.'

'But does he have a good life?' Judit asks.

'I think so,' she says. 'But after really seeing how the Russians live, I'd say he has made sacrifices on behalf of his family. It seems like a hard place to be happy.'

'Perhaps we can all help him. Financially, I mean,' Judit says. 'We owe him so much. We could reach out to Yukiko, to the family.'

'I'd love to help with that,' Rachel says, and then she pauses. 'Judit, I wanted to thank you so much for everything you've done. When Grandma died, I couldn't have managed without you and the others.'

Judit takes Rachel's hands in her own. 'You have been through so much already for such a young girl. But don't ever doubt your strength. You have Felka's blood after all! Such a strong and capable woman. A survivor, too. You are just like her in all the ways that count.'

Rachel nods, tearing up. They hug each other tightly.

'Now remember, don't be a stranger,' Judit tells her. 'Stay in touch. You always have a bed in my house!'

'Be careful,' Rachel laughs. 'Now that I have a taste for adventure, you may find me on your doorstep one day!'

Judit hands her the address of the local stonemason. It's time to choose the design and words for Felka's tombstone. Michael has taken care of the expense, Judit tells her.

They say goodbye, and Rachel walks away with a mission to accomplish.

The stonemason's factory is tiny. He is a Japanese local, but explains he has been servicing the small Jewish community for decades. He advises on the font and the style, lets her choose from some stone samples and gives her a character count to adhere to. She sits nearby at a table and drafts some words, crossing them out, not happy, and redoing them. Finally, she has something that she thinks encapsulates her grandmother.

Here lies Felka Margolin 1908–1968.
Loving mother of Michael and Rachel Adele
Loving wife of Myetek
Adoring grandmother of Rachel
Cherished daughter of Shmerl and Ruchli Szput,
 murdered by Hitler
Afforded the gift of a long life by Chiune Sugihara
 and Jan Zwartendijk, brave men
She died living
'Finita la commedia!'
May her dear soul rest in peace.

***

As Rachel disembarks from the train in Tokyo, the sight of so many bodies, neatly pushed into carriages by white-gloved attendants wearing crisp navy suits and caps, makes her smile rather than feel overwhelmed. She notices how the commuters don't seem to mind being crammed in, sees how they carefully make room for the other passengers stepping out onto the platform. How do they do that – maintain politeness, respectfulness, manners, with such ease – when a million people are aiming for the same vehicle at the same time? And how do the attendants calculate, with such precision, the exact number that will squish in? She marvels at the lack of fuss. No drama, no complaints. Just logic, and patience, and consideration for others. She thinks she can understand a little better Sugihara's view on his actions in the war. There were desperate people in need of help, and he was able to offer it. A logical decision. A simple, pragmatic act.

This is the first time Rachel's been in Tokyo without being under pressure. Because Rachel and Felka only transited through Tokyo, Rachel never properly saw it or walked through the streets. When she visited the embassy, there was no time for meandering, and her heart was heavy with grief.

It is very different to Kobe, she observes. A jungle of haphazard neon has grown over the traditional temples and trees carefully placed over centuries. Giggling teenaged schoolgirls slip past the throngs of serious-looking adults. At this time of the day, scruffily dressed youths dominate the streets, but, very occasionally, tiny, traditionally dressed elderly ladies and gentlemen from a bygone era can be spotted, delicate bonsais struggling to stay alive in a forest of progress.

Loretta's directions are clear, easy to follow: a bus to here, turn at this street, follow the path. Loretta lives on the edge of Tokyo, in the suburbs. Her house is a traditional one, lovingly tended. When Rachel arrives, she knocks on the door, but no one answers. Strains of big band music drift up a small path leading down the side of the house, and Rachel follows it to the backyard. It's coming from a small shed.

'Hello?' Rachel calls out. She definitely has the right house – or so she hopes.

Loretta opens the door, beaming. She's covered in white splatters. 'You made it! Come in, come in. I was just cleaning up.'

Rachel steps into the shed and gasps. It's an art studio, filled with landscape paintings and ceramics. It's a mess, following a system that only Loretta must know. She loves it.

'You're an artist?'

'Yes,' Loretta says. 'It's not the highest-paying job, I suppose. But I'm proud of it. My vases are probably my favourite thing to make.' She gestures at one of the shelves, filled with elegant, beautifully shaped vases. Several are veined with gold, and Rachel gasps again, fumbling with her bag. There is one more thing to repair.

'I was hoping you could help me find someone,' she says, taking out the little bag. 'But maybe – perhaps you could...'

She shows Loretta the shards of black porcelain. Her aunt turns a couple over in her hands.

'How about we fix it together?' Loretta asks with a smile. She takes out two little containers and sets up a space for them at the studio's table, explaining the process: the specially treated tree-sap lacquer that will bind the pieces, the gold she'll dust over the cracks. As they organise the shards, they talk. It's easy, as if they've known each other their whole lives. Rachel tells her about Kate and Susan and Yanni and Thomas – 'And then I called him an arrogant wanker. To his face!' – and then about Moscow, the harshness of it, the kindness of Sugihara.

'My dad saw his father get shot by Russian guards, and thought it was his fault,' Rachel confides in Loretta, carefully daubing the edge of a small shard with lacquer. 'It all makes so much more sense. He even apologised to me.'

'I'm so glad,' she says, and Rachel can tell she means it.

'You must hate him,' Rachel says. 'For keeping us apart. For taking Mum away.'

'I did at first,' Loretta says, slotting one piece into the vase that's slowly being rebuilt. 'But Shirley wasn't some passive object. She was an adult. She made the decision to leave with him.'

'I think I heard them arguing about you once,' Rachel says.

'Michael was so upset when he found out we were still talking. I think he must have felt like he wasn't enough for her. But she loved him so, so much.' Loretta sighs. 'The war was so terrible, Rachel. I think our families will bear its scars for a long time yet.'

Rachel thinks of Mizumi's wound; the softness of it. 'Scars aren't always bad,' she ventures.

Loretta gives an approving smile. 'That's true. Your grandfather likes to boast about his.'

'What's he like?'

'You can meet him tonight, if you'd like. He's quite loud, used to getting his way. He was a doctor in the war, and it got him a lot of respect. I don't think he ever recovered.'

Rachel laughs.

'And stubborn, so stubborn,' Loretta continues, and Rachel offers her the shard. She slots it into place too. 'I think he regretted cutting Shirley off the moment he did it. But he couldn't say he was wrong.'

'Does he still regret it?' Rachel asks, forgetting to pick up a shard until Loretta looks at her expectantly.

'Yes,' her aunt replies. 'I think it's the biggest regret of his life.'

***

When the vase is reassembled, the gold dusted onto the cracks, Loretta tells Rachel it needs time to set. They look at it admiringly, how it gleams in the sunlight coming through the studio windows, and then Loretta makes them lunch.

'Do you think you'll go back to nursing?' Loretta asks her over the bowls of matzo ball soup – apparently it's far easier to get a hold of wheat flour in the country's capital.

'Maybe,' Rachel says. 'I haven't had time to think about it. If I do, I think it would be part-time, so I can go to art school.'

Loretta's brows rise. 'You're an artist, too?'

'Yeah – nowhere near as good as you, though.'

'Nonsense,' Loretta says sternly. 'That type of talk will get you nowhere. After lunch, we should paint together. It's a good day for plein air.'

'Plein air?'

'Outside,' Loretta explains. 'In the sun, in nature. It's one of my favourite ways to paint. Your mother's, too. Did you know your mother was an accomplished painter?'

Rachel shakes her head, food forgotten.

'Excellent with a brush. She was better at portraits than I ever was. She stopped when she moved to Australia, I think,' Loretta says, mouth twisting. 'Homesickness is a terrible thing.'

Rachel shouldn't be surprised that she gets her love for painting from Shirley's side of the family; God knows that Felka or Michael never expressed an interest.

'But yes, plein air. Unless you have somewhere to be,' Loretta says hastily. 'No pressure. I imagine you're wanting to unwind.'

'Painting is how I unwind,' Rachel says. 'I've missed it, actually. Not being able to take out my feelings on a canvas over here.'

'Well, you're welcome to stay the night,' Loretta offers. 'It's a long ride back to Kobe. We could paint, I could take you to your grandfather's for dinner – he'd love to meet you.'

Rachel's heart is full to bursting. 'I'd love that. Yes.'

***

Their styles are very different, as it turns out. Loretta's is free flowing, abstract, employing broad brushstrokes. Rachel, meanwhile, favours detail and careful planning. She must get that from Felka, she thinks.

As the afternoon passes, they drink tea and comment on each other's work. Rachel loves how Loretta manages to capture so much with so little, and Loretta is impressed by Rachel's technical skill. Occasionally, Loretta interjects to offer Rachel a suggestion, or introduce her to a new technique or philosophy. It's gentle and encouraging, not at all overbearing or arrogant. The sun is beginning to set when they finish, and Loretta regards Rachel's work, hands on hips.

'You have a lot of talent. Do you know that?'

Rachel flushes. 'You really think so?'

'I do,' Loretta nods, still looking at it. 'You could sell a painting like that, easily work up to an exhibition. Art school would open your horizons even further, with this sort of skill.'

It's one thing hearing it from Yanni or friends, another hearing it from an actual artist who sells her pieces. She's never seriously entertained the notion; it was never an option. Nursing was the ideal career for a young woman, according to her family. Art was only ever permitted to be a hobby.

'Let's get these inside, and then check the vase,' Loretta says cheerfully. They bring the easels, paints and canvases back into the studio, stacking them carefully – Loretta does have a system, as it turns out – and then Loretta carefully picks up the vase, turning it in the setting sun. The gold veins glow in the light, so perfectly that Rachel can't imagine the vase without them.

'Perfect,' Loretta says, gently passing it to her. 'Let me get a box and some packing materials so you can take it back on the train with you tomorrow.'

As her aunt bustles around the studio, Rachel stares at the vase, taking it in, how the dark porcelain gleams against the gold. Her chest feels lighter, buoyant. She can't replace what was lost. But she can fix what was broken, with time and patience.

Perhaps, like the art of kintsugi, it can become a more beautiful version of the original.

She doesn't know what's next for her; whether she will return to Yanni in Sydney, stay a while in Kobe, or even take a different path entirely. But whatever she chooses, she knows now that she has somewhere to belong, a richness that she will take wherever she goes. She can finally do what Michael never could: draw on the past to move forward into the future.

'Here we go,' Loretta says, bringing over a postage box and a roll of bubble wrap. 'Oh, look at you – you've got paint all over your face. You'll need to wash up before we go see Dad...' Loretta stops, looking at Rachel. 'Is everything okay?'

Rachel tears up and, on an instinct that she cannot fight, she throws her arms around Loretta.

'Rachel?'

'I'm fine,' Rachel sobs. 'I'm really fine, I am...'

'Oh, darling,' Loretta says kindly. She strokes Rachel's back, but doesn't let go.

And, closing her eyes, Rachel is lost in her mother's embrace.

Author's Note

My father, Michael Margolin, and my grandparents, Felka and Myetek Margolin, fled Nazi-occupied Poland in December 1939. They left behind their four parents, who eventually were interned in the Warsaw Ghetto; one was murdered there, and three were murdered in Treblinka extermination camp. Save for the rape scene in the hut and my grandfather being murdered in Kaunas, what I have written is true: Felka luring the officer in fluent German to organise a German staff car to pick her and my young father up in the dead of night, and the journey to Lithuania. In 1940, they met Chiune Sugihara in his embassy in Kaunas, where he wrote them two visas: one for my grandfather, the other covering my grandmother and father. My father, who was twelve at the time, remembered his 'kind' eyes. They were saved, along with six thousand other Jewish refugees in Lithuania, by an entry permit to the Dutch colony of Curacao – issued by the Netherlands Honorary Consul Jan Zwartendijk – and transit visas – numbers 745 and 746 on Sugihara's list of visa recipients – illegally issued by this courageous Japanese diplomat.

Sugihara did so at great personal risk, defying his government – which, on three separate occasions, gave him express orders not to issue visas to these people. Despite this, Sugihara persisted, saving thousands of Jews from certain death. Zwartendijk, meanwhile, was not a diplomat but a businessman who was a director of the Kaunas-based Lithuanian branch of the Philips corporation. In May 1940, Dutch envoy De Decker asked him if he would agree to become honorary consul. He was appointed on June 14, and the Soviets invaded the next day. He found himself in a very precarious position. To do what he did was also extraordinary.

In June and July 1941, detachments of German Einsatzgruppen together with Lithuanian auxiliaries began murdering Jews across the country. At least 90 per cent of the Jews in Lithuania were murdered – the largest death toll for any European country during World War II. Had Zwartendijk and Sugihara not intervened, the fate of these visa recipients would have been sealed.

My mother passed away during the writing of this novel. She would have been so thankful I was able to tell this story. She was born in London, where her father had moved in 1919. The vast majority of his family who remained in Poland were murdered in Auschwitz. Soon after World War II ended, when my mother was twelve, my grandfather travelled to Europe and scoured the refugee camps for family members. Out of hundreds of relatives, he located only three surviving nieces, whom he took back to live in London. He brought one, Mina, to live in his own home with his wife and children.

My mother, young and impressionable, never forgot the harrowing stories Mina told her about the concentration camp. How she longed for a sliver of soap to wash away the dirt, or for a crust of bread. My mother could never throw away uneaten toast and kept every remnant of soap, washing with them until they were completely gone. She was a dedicated volunteer at the Sydney Jewish Museum, working for nearly twenty years as a tour guide into her mid-eighties, educating on the Holocaust.

In 1985, Israel honoured Sugihara as one of the Righteous Among the Nations for his actions. He is the only Japanese national who has been given this award. Decades later, Lithuania declared 2020 the Year of Chiune Sugihara, to mark the eightieth anniversary of the Japanese consulate in Kaunas, where he issued the life-saving visas, and to celebrate what would have been his 120th birthday.

On 14 September 2023, as this book was in its final stages of editing, Jan Zwartendijk (who died in 1976 believing he only saved one person, and was honoured as Righteous Among the Nations in 1997 by Yad Vashem) was posthumously awarded the Medal for Acts of Humanity in Gold on 14 September 2023 by the Dutch Prime Minister, Mark Rutte.

Despite Chiune Sugihara's and Jan Zwartendijk's actions, few have heard of these brave, selfless individuals. I feel, given I owe my life to them, that they deserve the same recognition as Oskar Schindler.

As a writer, I felt it my duty to perpetuate their memory through story in the form of a book and, hopefully, a film. As such, this book is inspired by this story and the role they played in my family's salvation.

This story also deals with the impact of trauma on survivors, and how it is passed on to subsequent generations, as well as the plight of refugees starting afresh in new homelands. It also sheds a light on anti-Semitism and how easily individuals can be swayed to participate in racist behaviour; or alternatively, to go against the crowd and think for themselves when they see wrongdoing, and the significant impact such bravery can have.

My relationship with my late father was, unfortunately, strained. He was a damaged individual. Had I understood the impact his traumatic and disjointed childhood experience and swift relocation to a foreign environment had on him, and how it shaped his character, it may have helped me be more compassionate and understanding towards him. Although this story is a work of fiction, this book is also peppered with the true story of his and my grandmother's escape. It is therefore dedicated to perpetuating his memory and that of my grandmother, with whom I was exceptionally close, and who remained upbeat, positive and hilarious throughout her life, never revealing an inkling of the trauma she was carrying, and doing everything purely for the love of her grandchildren; and my courageous grandfather, who got his wife and son safely to Australia but who died before I was born. It is also dedicated to all the victims of intergenerational trauma, who must deal with the consequences of their parents' experiences.

To break down the myth and misinformation surrounding Sugihara, I interviewed Nobuki Sugihara, Chiune's only surviving son. I wanted to understand what makes one individual act in a manner that most would not and did not dare to. I hoped to gain a clear understanding of the man behind the hero – a loving family man who left his children for long periods of time to make ends meet and provide for them. Nobuki told me that his father had a long history of defying orders, thinking for himself and following a strong moral code, which led him to fight for justice on many other occasions in his life. For the sake of authenticity and depth, an account of some of the events of Sugihara's life is woven through in a parallel narrative.

While I have drawn on Nobuki's memories and the established facts we have available, Chiune Sugihara never met my father again after issuing my family their visas. I invented this scenario to demonstrate his impeccable character, a saviour in every sense of the word who, if given the opportunity, would no doubt have tried to help those in need if he saw that he could. Similarly, Rachel is a fictional character who represents me and the thousands of other children of Holocaust survivors, as well as descendants of Sugihara visa recipients who would have dearly loved to meet and thank him. Joshua Nishri, while a real person who did in fact locate Sugihara, never met my family and, to my knowledge, never organised a reunion of survivors in Japan. However, the survivors were very close, and the Australian contingent remained so throughout their lives. I can only speak on behalf of them.

The overriding thread that bonds, however, is that survivors carry lifelong trauma, which impacts their relationships with those closest to them.

May the memories of all those murdered by Hitler's regime be an eternal blessing.

Acknowledgements

As a professional writer, I always wanted to eventually pen something significant. In 2008, my late father told me a story about our family, about me, that changed the trajectory of my life. I started work on turning my family's incredible escape from the Holocaust into a movie. This then segued into a book. It's a venture that would not have been possible without invaluable input from some very special people.

Needless to say, first and foremost, the ongoing support from my family: my husband and three beautiful children, whom I have doubtless, on numerous occasions, pushed to their limits with the highs and lows of the creative process. There have been endless waves of self-doubt and tears, and finally the elation that comes with gaining credibility and validation for all the tireless work. We've shared the joy of knowing it has all ultimately amounted to something, and my dream is slowly becoming a reality.

To Nicholas Lathouris, a very accomplished writer and dramaturg currently working on the first draft of the movie script. Nicholas needn't have given me the time of day, and yet he gave weeks, months and years, continuously and selflessly, to being my mentor and now wonderful friend. He believed in this project from the moment I approached him with a written story based on my family's escape and rescue, hoping to collaborate on the script. I pelted him relentlessly with a barrage of emails and texts as thoughts flowed from my subconscious, and he has responded with unwavering support. He even encouraged me wholeheartedly when I suggested I might also diverge and write a novel, assuring me despite my utter reticence that I had the ability.

To Joshua Lundberg, a highly intelligent and talented young man with such a keen eye for the nuances in cinema, whom I brought in from the get-go. He contributed so meaningfully to our long brainstorming sessions, helping to get this story to a point where it was worthy of being told in cinema. His input was invaluable for both the novel and film versions.

And then, when I finally had a book manuscript, I was so fortunate to find my talented and intuitive literary editor Alison Fraser, who patiently taught me the craft of novel writing. She helped me get my work to a state worthy of attracting the right publisher, and I would still be floundering without her vital input.

Next, to my lovely confidante and now close friend Catriona Hughes, whose knowledge, intuition, business acumen, contacts, resources and incredible mind have been offered to me with gay abandon and sincerity.

To the Sugihara community, starting at the top with Nobuki Sugihara, only surviving son of Chiune Sugihara. He has become a lovely friend and has been there all the way with insightful answers to my relentless questions about his late father, ensuring I portray the most authentic possible version of the real man behind the hero.

Thanks also to the Sugihara/Zwartendijk family of survivors and descendants worldwide, who all know we owe our lives to these incredible individuals, and who have been most supportive and encouraging. To the many contacts and supporters who have closely followed my progress on social media and constantly offer words of encouragement and praise. To contacts I interviewed within the community who all gave me real life, detailed accounts of conditions in the USSR in the 1960s and an image of how Kobe and Japan were back then as well. To psychologist friends and professionals with whom I shared storylines to ensure the generational trauma about which I was writing was authentically portrayed to be respectful and supportive of those who experience it. Also to those with whom I have a close affiliation in Australian Jewish community organisations, who helped me immensely to get word out about my venture and educate on this topic by way of speaking events, some together with Nobuki Sugihara. To my wonderful friends who have been there with words of support and encouragement through my years of slog, the many lows and the recent highs, I thank you all. I can finally stop driving you nuts!

Last but by no means least, to Martin Hughes and the wonderfully supportive team at Affirm Press – my publishers, who had the courage to believe in me, and invest valuable time and money in me, a first-time novelist. They took me under their wings and guided me through uncharted waters towards a wonderful outcome: pushing me towards a completed novel so much richer than anything I could have hoped for, thanks to expert guidance from my talented editors Ruby Ashby-Orr and Laura Franks.

I can never thank any of you enough.

Book Club Questions

1. Why do you think the Margolins chose to leave behind their Jewish identity? What were the consequences of that decision?

2. How do you think Rachel changes over the course of the novel?

3. Chiune Sugihara always maintained that he was not particularly heroic, and had only done what most people would in the circumstances. Do you think he's right, or was he exceptional?

4. 'Rachel, dear, there are many differences between your family and ours. If we all agree to this union, you would need to entirely embrace our way of life for it to work. Is that what you want?' Sophia and Dimitri's advice is hurtful to Rachel, but are they ultimately right?

5. What do you think is the significance of the scene where the Sugihara survivors meet the Hiroshima survivors?

6. 'But how can you do it – revisiting the past? Why do you want to put yourself through that?' What, if anything, is the value of going over painful experiences in personal and cultural histories?

7. What do you think of Rachel and Mizumi's relationship? What has brought them together, and where is it going?

8. The revelation of Michael's trauma explains his treatment of Rachel, but does it justify it?

9. 'No. She can't go back to Sydney in the way Yanni wants her to. She can't give up what she's found here, this past and future of her own.' What do you think Rachel's new future holds?

10. Why do you think the author chose to celebrate Sugihara through Rachel's story, rather than through a novel centred on Sugihara himself?

Made in the USA
Las Vegas, NV
30 June 2025

24243543R00214